A Bitter Harvest

A Bitter Harvest

Charles Ellingworth

QUARTET BOOKS

First published in 2019 by Quartet Books Limited
A member of the Namara Group
27 Goodge Street, London, W1T 2LD

A catalogue record for this book is available from the British Library

ISBN 9780704374591

Typeset by Tetragon, London
Printed and bound in Great Britain by
TJ International Ltd, Padstow, Cornwall

To the memory of Edna, Frieda and Mary Voss,
the sisters, whose decent, hard and poignant lives
provided the inspiration for this story.

1

Cambridge. Girton College, 1917

The last chair scraped the floor as a hundred young women settled.
A cough, then silence. The Mistress of the college looked over
them, spectacles on the end of her nose. She mouthed to speak
then stopped, visibly rearranging her words. She pursed her lips
and began again.

'Girls... I have something important... no... something terrible
to tell you today. It is not a surmise, I'm afraid; it's a certainty; a
mathematical certainty.'

She hesitated; then continued.

'Only one in ten of you... only one in ten of you, is going to
be married and have children. This war... this terrible war... has
killed your future husbands.' She paused, visibly moved. 'I wish it
wasn't true, but I'm afraid it is.'

The silence below her was crushing. Isobel Richmond, seated
just under and to the right of the speaker, glanced sideways. The girl
next to her was blinking rapidly and another was shaking her head.

The Mistress continued, 'It is my... it is going to be our task
here at Girton to help you prepare for life on your own. You will
have to support yourselves and make the best of what you have and
what we can give you. I cannot tell you how much it grieves me to
tell you this – but it is the truth and we must face it no matter how
hard that may be.'

She looked down. Isobel saw a single tear roll down her cheek.

'So... we must pray; pray to God for the strength to lead our
lives...' she swallowed... 'lead our lives in the way that he has
chosen for us. It is our cross, and we must bear it as best we can.
God bless you all.'

2

Dorset. Eighteen months later, early spring 1919

The impact hammered the wind out of him. Fireflies criss-crossed his vision as he dry retched, groaning the air back into his lungs. Either side of him he could hear the grunting strain as horses kicked off the top of the bank and the squeak of leather alongside shouts of warning. On all fours, he could not move as he fought for breath, his backbone feeling as if it had been battered by a club. The sky was circling him and the fireflies refused to land. He rose to his knees. His chest felt sore and his breastbone tender where his horn's mouthpiece had done the damage. He saw two horses coming towards him; one his own, with an empty saddle, led by a woman wearing a bowler hat and veil. He tried to smile while inwardly cursing. The shadow of the veil obscured her expression.

'Come on. Get on. He's gone left-handed. The lead hounds are casting the other way. Probably another fox.'

She shook the bridle impatiently.

'Where's Ralph?' he asked through gritted teeth.

'With them. Come on!'

He swung his leg towards the stirrup and missed. He still hadn't caught his breath and his chest hurt. Please not a rib. He swung again – successfully – and hauled himself into the saddle, grunting with pain as the pommel caught his chest. He gathered together his reins in a practised motion and teased his other boot into its stirrup.

'All there?'

He nodded, and she galloped towards the gate. He followed her, pulling round a garter strap where the buckle was digging into his knee, gathering together his limbs and thoughts to concentrate on the task at hand. Crossing the road, he saw the hounds were clustered by the stream on the valley floor. The whipper-in was dismounted.

'Damn him,' he thought as he anticipated the polite scorn of the professional huntsman towards the amateur to which he would be subjected. She would be no better. He pulled back to a walk and attempted to compose himself. The hounds were milling around a hole as he approached. Ralph, the whipper-in, turned away, calling individual hounds towards him, their names, Thruster, Thunder, Bowlman, snarled out.

He saw a couple of hounds casting along the line of the brook and pulled out his horn, grateful not to have to say anything to either of them. The fieldmaster detached himself from the melee of horses in the gateway and trotted towards him, laughing as he approached. Julian knew there would be neither humour nor sympathy from that quarter. He knew of what the man was capable. Too well.

'I could see you were going to mess that one up, Belmore. This isn't Ireland. If you want to clear those oxer-rails you have to kick. You alright?'

Julian Belmore nodded and, without replying, sounded his horn, using it as an excuse to turn away. Out of the corner of his eye he could see the fieldmaster undoing a leather pouch containing a flask that was held out to him as he finished with his horn. Still not speaking, he took it and tugged gratefully at the mixture of port and brandy, feeling it radiating from his throat to the extremities of his stomach.

'Cigarette?' He took one, again without comment, and accepted the proffered light.

'No harm done. He was set on that hole the moment he left covert. It should have been stopped. Have a word about it.' He nodded towards Ralph who looked after the hounds but deferred to Julian as the amateur huntsman and master. 'When you've got all the hounds together, I'll get the terriers.'

Julian shook his head. 'She's a vixen, and heavy. We'll leave her.'

'Are you sure?'

'I saw her, didn't I?'

Robert Granville, the younger brother of Lord Milborne, on whose land they were riding and whose hounds they were following, was the fieldmaster in charge of the mounted riders but not the business of hunting. He considered the huntsman coolly.

'Fair enough. Where now then?'

'Everlanes. I know that was properly stopped even if they missed this one.'

'Where do you want the field?' The field was the bulk of the riders not involved in the business of hunting the hounds.

'Down the bottom. We don't want a fox ending up in the village.'

Granville touched the brim of his cap in an ironic salute, reined his horse round and cantered back to his charges standing in the next field in a self-contained fog of horse sweat, steaming breath and tobacco smoke. Buzz of conversation and shared flasks floated on the still air, chilled by a near-frost. The woman riding side-saddle turned from the melee of hounds towards him. She rode with the ease of someone for whom two or four legs were interchangeable. Her coat displayed the evidence of multiple soakings and mud splatterings; what had once been black was now a streaked grey. Her boots, modelled on army field boots, were laced and practical – for utility rather than elegance. Through the veil could be seen a thin Roman nose and a corresponding mouth – handsome rather than beautiful. Her name, Ariadne, suited her. She was the only daughter of Lord Milborne and spoke in sentences short and to the point.

'Your horse looks unsound.'

Julian looked down. Four hooves were flat on the ground. 'Trot him up.' He did as he was told while she considered. 'Off front. Must have knocked it on the rail you made such a mess of. I'll send for your second horse.' She looked back at him. 'Are you alright?'

'I think so. Ribs are a bit sore.'

'You can strap them up. It's only a week to the end of the season and you'll have the whole summer to recover. Papa always swore by neat brandy to get him through. She laughed bitterly. 'Now it's every day.'

Julian looked at her in surprise. She never normally made any reference to the stupor into which her father descended from lunchtime onwards. His grief for his son was visceral.

'Good decision on the vixen,' she added, 'Uncle Robert couldn't give a damn.'

'No. He doesn't.'

They looked at each other, surprised at the thread of sympathy that arced between them. Almost as if to break it before more weight was applied, she turned back towards the stream where Ralph was wading through a surf of hounds. She counted in twos.

'Fifteen couple. All there, Ralph.'

The whipper-in nodded an acknowledgement but said nothing as he led his horse towards a tree-stump mounting block. He was the professional, the kennelman in charge of the kennels and the hounds. For the purposes of hunting he handed over the hounds to Julian who was an amateur. He was out of earshot when Julian spoke again.

'Did he ever make small talk?'

'Used to. But he had a bad time at Passchendaele. He was buried by a land mine and only survived because his helmet was blown in front of his face giving him enough air to survive until they dug him out. The rest of his platoon died.'

'I knew he'd been through things.'

'You all have.'

'Not me. Not really. The navy was nothing in comparison – just the sunlit joys of Scapa Flow.'

She looked at him sideways, considering what he had said.

'It wasn't France.'

'They're all here now,' he nodded at the hounds who jostled each other in contained energy, 'let's go.'

They trotted towards the gate as the mist of conversation still settled, the hounds following in his wake with no bidding. As the riders made way for him there were greetings of sympathy that he dismissed with a smile, patting his chest with a theatrical wince to avoid answering specific questions. Ariadne said nothing until they were back on the road and the battering of metal shoes on the hard surface gave them privacy.

'Ralph resents you. You know that don't you?'

'I would if I were him. He's the professional who's hunted these hounds for nearly ten seasons and now he's got to play second fiddle to an amateur. That's tough.'

'You're lucky to be here.'

'I am – and you don't need to rub it in. Your father's very generous and I'm lucky to have the chance.'

'Papa was given the same chance by his father when he was your age, give or take a year or two. I asked him if I could do it, but you know how traditional he is: he's not convinced that women should be hunting at all, let alone hunting hounds.'

'You'd have been good at it. You have an affinity for hounds. I've watched you.'

She accepted the compliment without reply, but he sensed she was pleased. They halted while a hound defecated in the middle of the road. They both waved to a motorist who had pulled over awaiting the passing of the cavalcade.

'Can you join us for dinner on Thursday?' she asked. 'We have the new vicar and his daughters coming. He's a second cousin and hasn't been well: his wife died last year and his son was killed at Gallipoli. Papa has given him the living at St Mary's. I don't know anything about the daughters – but I think one's not all there; perfectly sweet by all accounts – but simple.'

'I'd like that. Thank you.'

'Good. I'll tell Mummy.'

They were opposite a gate into a wood. The hounds spilt through it with their noses to the ground. She rode on, speaking over her shoulder.

'I'll wait on the other side. And ask Uncle Robert if he could send half a dozen on to line the railway: there's a train due in fifteen minutes.'

6

3

Julian arrived for dinner slightly earlier than the designated eight o'clock. He had walked from his small house by the kennels to the castle. Lord Milborne was a stickler for punctuality and the navy had left its own imprint. Wyatt's castellated facade reared into the darkness above him as he waited. He heard the bell echo inside.

'Good evening, sir.'

The voice came from behind the door as it opened.

'Evening Goodrich. I'm early. Shall I wait?'

'No sir. Lady Milborne is down already. She likes to mix the cocktails herself – as I think you know, sir.'

Was there a note of disapproval in his voice? Julian followed the butler through the triangular hall that rose the full height of the house, the cold barely delineated from the outside by two fires and the gloom mitigated by two sconces that left only puddles of light. The door into the drawing room was ajar. The clink of a spoon in a glass came from within.

'Mr Belmore, your ladyship.'

'Julian! Perfect timing. Taste this.'

She held out a stemmed glass with a clear liquid and thin slice of lemon. He took it and sipped, feeling the coursing of spirit down his throat. Intravenous alcohol. He coughed.

'Delicious.'

'Good. I was told by an American I met in London that Vermouth isn't the done thing.'

'You've certainly taken that to heart, Lady Milborne. It tastes like pure gin to me.'

'Excellent. As it should be. Come, sit by the fire.'

She led the way and sat on the sofa, crossing her legs as she did so. She considered him in her own distinctive way, with her head held back through half-closed eyes. Still beautiful, Violet Milborne hid her life of excess with powder, the hairline cracks of cobweb veins barely visible. A slight plumpness added to her allure along with the accentuated pout, wrapping her lips around her cigarette holder and holding the smoke in her mouth, allowing tendrils to play and escape before she inhaled. This, and the way she worked the Martini around her tongue before swallowing...

'How is the house? We felt terrible that you moved in before the men had painted it. No one around to do the work. All off at the war. But you know that.'

'It's fine, thank you. After a cruiser in the North Sea, everything is luxury. And it's only for a few more weeks.'

'Indeed. What will you do then? Will you go back to Ireland when the season's over?'

'I haven't got anything there. The house was torched before the war and my mother hasn't the money to rebuild it. There's a farm – but it's rented.'

'But your family are Catholics?'

'Yes – well, my mother is.'

'Difficult.'

'I'm afraid so; especially in the west. I've just done one war. That's enough for now.'

'Running away then?'

He had been looking at his shoes but his eyes snapped back to judge the tenor of the question. She was smiling.

'Yes. If you like. It's a difficult war to win when you don't know which side you're on.'

'Meaning?'

'I'm not a unionist.'

'Better not tell my brother-in-law that.'

'I won't.'

She watched him carefully. 'You don't like him do you?'

He paused before replying. Was it that obvious? He had heard talk that Robert Granville, her brother-in-law, was also her lover. 'I'm not sure he likes me.'

'I don't think he likes anyone. It's not how he thinks.'

8

He felt uncomfortable with this intimacy. It was not why he had arrived early. Despite his best efforts, he found her disturbingly attractive. She was stroking an earlobe as she spoke and the diamond earring diffused a rainbow light on to her neck and breasts.

'I'm not really in a position to have any opinion on him. I'm sure you can understand why.'

'As a retainer?'

'If you want to put it like that.'

'How would you put it?'

Though he had the status of a master of the hunt, described as an amateur huntsman, the reality was that, like the vicar of the church, he was dependent on the Granville family who owned the kennels, the hounds and the house in which he lived. He was their social equal but their economic dependent. They both knew this – but it was unstated. She had crossed a line with her last remark and he didn't know why. Before he could reply, the sound of footsteps in the hall saved him. It was exactly eight o'clock and the chimes of the clock outside the door heralded the entrance of Lord Milborne and his daughter.

He was fifteen years older than his wife but it looked like a generation. He had the whiskers of the 1890s, grey and straggling, and his hair was thin. Though tall, a premature stoop made him appear almost shrunken. His tailcoat seemed a size too big, though the white tie was symmetrical and the press and studs of his waistcoat immaculate. His daughter held his arm as he studied the room.

'Evening, Belmore.'

The slur was only just noticeable. Julian bowed slightly.

'Good evening, sir. Good evening, Ariadne.'

She smiled back but made eyes at her mother who sat smoking and toying with her glass, refusing to acknowledge her daughter's signals.

'Darling, Julian and I were talking about his house. I really do think we need to do something about the state of it, don't you?'

Julian hesitated before interjecting. The house needed a great deal of work but he did not want to appear to have been complaining. He sensed that this was a shell-scarred battlefield that had been fought over many times.

'If we had the men to do it, we would. You know that, dear. Things are different.'

'And I'll be gone for a couple of months at the end of the season, sir,' interjected Julian. 'I'm still in the reserve and I'll have to go up to Scapa Flow for a couple of months in the summer.'

'Why?'

'Guard duty, sir. As you know, the whole German fleet is there and we have to make sure it doesn't head for Wilhelmshaven if the negotiations break down in Paris.'

'You're not deserting us, I hope.'

'Not at all. Ralph is the man the hounds need over the summer. I'll be back before cub hunting in August.'

'Good, good. My dear, where are our other guests?' There was irritation in his voice.

'It's only just gone eight, dear. Julian here is even worse than you are. He was ill-mannered enough to turn up early. That way you surprise your hostess in the bath; or maybe that's what he intended.'

She laughed at Julian's obvious discomfort.

'Mama, in this house you're damned whatever you do,' said Ariadne.

'Not if you turn up on time. Anyway, here they come.' She waved her glass towards the hall where the doorbell was audible. 'I'll only talk about theology from now on. How is your knowledge of the Mystery of the Trinity, Julian? I'll test you once I have sucked all the answers out of Dr Richmond. Do you think he knows anything about bridge?'

They were all standing when Goodrich showed in, not the Richmonds, but Lord Milborne's brother, the Hon. Robert Granville and his wife, Daphne. They were an ill-matched couple. His hair was thin, almost albino blond and combed back. He had the same thin face as his niece but where her eyes were brown, his were blue – probing, questioning and alert. In contrast, his wife had almost no distinctive features. Middle age had left her face like worked putty where traces of former prettiness were discernible but overwhelmed. Her hair was thin to the point of alopecia and her evening dress only emphasised the squareness of her figure. His dominance over her was palpable.

The Richmond family arrived a minute behind them, and five minutes after the appointed hour, with Lord Milborne looking at his watch. Dr Richmond, Lord Milborne's second cousin, wearing a dog collar and a black frock coat, led the way. He moved slowly, with the uncertainty of a convalescent, leaning on a walking stick. His hair was silver and his complexion matched. He had a kindly countenance but the marks of too many emotional blows were imprinted on his face.

'Charles, how good to see you.' Lord Milborne grasped his free hand and gripped his shoulder. It was a sincere and affectionate welcome from a fellow sufferer – and the vicar was visibly moved.

'And you, James. It is good to be here. Very good. And Violet, it's been too long.' He kissed Lady Milborne on both cheeks before turning to his daughters, one of whom hid behind him holding a button on the back of his coat. Her large head marked her out. The others smiled nervously and waited to be introduced.

Isobel was first. Her auburn hair was down to her waist and her finest feature, shining in the candlelight. She was tall, pale and striking rather than beautiful, though that description would be apt in a certain light and from a complimentary angle. She was wearing a sash that mimicked in silk the patterns of a peacock tail and gave her a bohemian aura. In her nervousness she called her hostess Lord Milborne – which was ignored as if it hadn't happened – but which made her blush. Her elder sister, Rose, a head smaller, had the fair skin and dark hair so much admired in Ireland. She entwined her arm around that of her other sister, Davina, stroking her hand in what was obviously an habitual comfort. She bowed and smiled to everyone as she was introduced but stayed next to her father. Davina dropped a curtsey before retreating once more behind her father's back. Violet Milborne filled the silence that followed the formal introductions.

'Isobel, I hear you were at Cambridge. How very clever you must be.' She said this in a way that made it clear that she did not rate cleverness in women. 'Wasn't it rather dreary there with all the young men away in the army?'

'Thank you, Lady Milborne,' Isobel ignored the irony – or failed to perceive it. 'I suppose it's what you're used to. I was there during the war so I don't remember what it was like before. And at Girton we weren't allowed to spend much time with men. The Mistress didn't see the point.'

'Of men?' Robert Granville smiled – but not with humour.

'Yes. Well not men in general, but men mixing with women socially; even at lectures. We didn't take much notice of that though.'

'So you went to lectures?'

'Of course.'

'But you weren't allowed to mix with male undergraduates?'

'It wasn't forbidden; just not encouraged.'

'There were no women at all when I was there. I don't think they are up to men intellectually.'

The colour in Isobel's face rose again, this time in anger rather than embarrassment. 'Women at Girton get the same, if not better, results. As there weren't any women for you to compete against, I think it may be a presumption to assume that you were better.' She looked him in the eye, her jaw clenched in anger. 'I wonder what degree you got, Mr Granville.'

'A second.'

'I got a first.'

'In a proper subject?'

'French and German.'

'Blue stockings obviously work harder.'

'Robert, please,' Violet Milborne intervened, 'you're being rude. Poor Isobel can't answer back.'

There was a brittle silence in the room.

'I think she's well able to look after herself, Violet,' said Granville.

'Thank you, Lady Milborne, I can look after myself. I'm used to being patronised by men. I deal with it by doing better than them.'

'Touché! And I apologise, Isobel. I was rude.' Granville held up his glass. 'My wife is always telling me to behave better, aren't you, dear.'

The object of his question looked up like a startled fawn. Her eyes darted round the room. 'No, I don't think so.'

Julian waited for the awkwardness to subside before crossing the room to where the vicar and his other two daughters were standing with Lord Milborne. He hovered while the two older men's interchange reached its natural conclusion. He pointedly bowed towards Davina – who hid behind her father, smiling shyly – and towards Rose who held out her hand which he shook.

'It's good to have you all here at Milborne. Have you been to Dorset before?'

'Once. As a child – so that really doesn't count. But Papa tells me it's very beautiful. Better than where we were in Kent.'

'The garden of England?'

'Not where we were; pretty well in London.'

'Did you like it, Davina?'

Davina nodded but said nothing. Rose answered for her. 'She liked our house, didn't you, Dav? She loved the attic where she made herself a den. I hated the mice up there but she made pets of them. We drew the line at rats though.'

'Rats?' Lord Milborne swung round.

'No rats, Lord Milborne,' said Rose, 'only mice – and small tame ones. They're in a cage and they must all be females – or males – as there are still only three of them.'

'Good, good. But make sure the cage is properly secure will you? Don't want another infestation.'

'We could get Julian to hunt them with his hounds, Papa,' said Ariadne, 'even he might be able to catch one...'

'Are you a huntsman?' The question was from Davina. Her voice was unexpectedly deep.

'I am. I hunted a pack in Ireland before the war.'

'Will they eat me?'

'The hounds? Lord, no; they're dogs – and rather sweet ones at that. They all live with local people and farmers when they're puppies to get to know humans and farm animals before they join the pack.'

'Will I be scared of them?'

'Do you like dogs?'

'Oh yes! I have a dog. He's called Bracken and he's a terrier.'

'Then you'll like hounds. Will you come and see them with me? Tomorrow perhaps?'

She hesitated.

'We'd love to, wouldn't we, Dav?' This was from Rose. Davina smiled and nodded.

'Good.' Julian continued, 'So why don't you come to the kennels after breakfast? They'll be fed and cleaned out by then. Thirty hounds can produce quite a smell. There would have been over a hundred before the war.'

'Thank you Mr Belmore, we would like that.'

'Have you ever hunted?'

'No. I can ride though.'

'Would you like to?'

'I'll lend you a horse,' said Ariadne.

'Thank you, but I won't know what to do.'

'Kitchener is sixteen and knows everything. He'll look after you. You'll need to ride him first though.'

'And you'll have to ride sidesaddle,' interjected Violet Milborne. 'My husband doesn't approve of women wearing trousers, let alone riding astride. He's very old fashioned, aren't you dear?'

Lord Milborne banged his glass down on the piano and a second awkward silence descended on the room.

'Not old fashioned, Violet; just trying to keep to the standards that I hold to be important – even if you don't. I pay for these hounds and they live in my kennels – so I think I am allowed to say how I would like them used and how those that follow them behave.'

'Things do move on though, don't they, darling?' She drew on her cigarette. 'And even hunting might have to change a bit, don't you think? There has been a war after all, and many women have done jobs that men would normally do.'

'You take no interest in the hounds at the best of times – so why now? What do you think, Charles? Do you let your girls wear trousers?'

The vicar made to reply but Isobel answered for him. 'Not at dinner, Lord Milborne, or anywhere that would cause offence, but it would have been difficult to work on the land or do many of the physical jobs we've had to undertake during the war in a long dress.'

'There you are, dear,' said the hostess, 'it's just practical.'

'If we were being just practical then we wouldn't house and feed over a hundred hounds and employ six men to look after them. There are cheaper and more practical ways to keep foxes under control and more practical ways to keep warm than wearing diamonds and...' but he was stopped in mid-flow by the boom of the dinner gong.

'And that means that we can carry on with this over dinner...' interjected his wife, standing to emphasise that the conversation was over.

*　　*　　*

Rose found herself between Julian and Robert Granville: the placing of alternate men and women was a prewar luxury that now rarely occurred. She used the hiatus, while Violet Milborne decided which direction she would turn to start the conversation, to take in the scene. Her family's domestic situation was far from grand; they lived in other peoples' houses in genteel poverty – but they had aristocratic cousins on both sides and were used to formal dinners – as guests. Two footmen were passing around a tureen of soup and the candles gave an effulgence to the silver that shimmered the view of the diners on her opposite side. She stole a glance at Julian in profile.

He was under thirty she guessed but his thinning hair, combed back leaving a widow's peak, made him appear slightly older. His face was unlined – but marked by a scar that ran jagged from the bow of his lip to just below his eye. He had one tooth that slightly overlapped the other which, along with the scar, gave his face an unevenness that viewed from straight on was disconcerting on first impression. He had a mannerism of touching the side of his nose as he spoke that gave the impression of attention and concentration. She saw him glance to see the hostess turn to her right and followed suit.

'Forgive me, Rose; I know nothing about you. Isobel told us something about herself before dinner' – they both smiled – 'but you… well, will you tell me?'

'Not much to tell. I look after my father; and Davina. My mother died last year. One of the first to get the flu.'

'I'm sorry.'

'It was a quite a blow; but nothing compared with when we heard that my brother had been killed at Gallipoli. I didn't think Papa would survive it.' She felt herself welling up. 'I'm sorry… you would think four years would be enough to get over it.'

He touched her arm. 'It's fine. We all have someone.'

'Thank you.' She could see it was genuinely meant. 'And you? Do you have someone?'

'Not close. I've been lucky. Luck of the Irish. A cousin was killed four months ago; two days before the Armistice. I only have a sister and a mother to worry about.'

'Maybe some would be luckier if they were dead; the ones that are badly wounded. I have a cousin, not as close as my brother, but of whom I'm very fond. He won't let me see him. His face was burned away. He has a mask.' She stopped. 'Why are we talking about this? There must be something more cheerful?'

They both looked awkwardly across the table. Lord Milborne was talking to Davina, his head close to hers as if imparting a confidence.

'We could ignore it; of course we could,' Julian continued to look across the table as he spoke, 'but doesn't small talk seem… I don't know… frivolous, after what's happened? I've been here since Christmas but haven't spoken about the war… properly… about what it meant… since I've been here. It's as if everyone is trying to turn the clock back and pretend all the sadness and horror never happened.'

Rose nodded as she considered what he was saying. 'It's the same with us. I can talk to Isobel, and Davina even, about my brother – but not to Papa, even though I know it's all he thinks about. He's trying to protect us. From what?'

They both paused again, surprised at the direction and the depth of their first conversation.

She retreated. 'Do you read, Mr Belmore?'

'Yes. A good deal. And Julian, please. What about you?'

'All the time. Maybe it's an escape. Not that I really need it; I mean compared with so many.'

'You think reading's an escape? I don't. Do you have a favourite?'

'Author or book?'

'Either. Both.'

'Thomas Hardy. *Tess of the D'Urbervilles.*'

'Me too.'

Her smile was like a curtain drawn on a spring morning.

'And we are here, aren't we? In Hardy's country?'

'Yes. Well not quite. He lives just outside Dorchester but wrote one of his books, *The Return of the Native*, I think, in Sturminster Newton which isn't far. Mrs Granville loves his writing too.'

Daphne Granville, who had been struggling in a three-way conversation caused by uneven numbers, heard her name as an invitation to join in. She leant across.

'Mrs Granville, we were talking about Thomas Hardy. I believe you are fond of his novels.'

'Yes, very much so. His poetry even more. He is the greatest poet writing today... I think anyway.' Her retreat from her earlier certainty was mirrored in her body language. 'But I love his novels. And I like him too. He has a face of so much wisdom and thought; and he's kindly with it.'

'You know him?'

'Not well. His wife, Florence, is a friend; no, that's too strong, a good acquaintance of mine. I've been lucky enough to visit them a number of times.'

'She's much younger than him, is that not right, Mrs Granville?' said Rose.

'Yes. Mr Hardy must be nearly eighty now and Mrs Hardy around forty, I would guess. His first wife died before the war. I don't know much about her other than that she was known locally to be rather strange and they weren't happy – though I have read some of his

poetry about her and his regret and sadness are very poignant...
I think.' The verbal tic again.

'You are so lucky. I would love to meet him,' said Rose.

'If you would like that, I'm sure it could be arranged. He likes
pretty girls.'

Rose acknowledged the compliment by smiling and looking
down as she replied. 'I would like that very much. Could Mr
Belmore – Julian, I mean – come as well? He loves Hardy too.'

'I don't see why not. Max Gate, the Hardy's house, isn't that big,
so the three of us should be fine; any more would be something of
a crowd. Robert won't come. He doesn't read novels – or poetry;
doesn't see the point.' This window on to the void in their marriage
created an awkward silence that Julian filled.

'How did you meet Mrs Hardy?'

'It was in Aldeburgh, on the Suffolk coast. I used to go and stay
there with my aunt in the summer. Mrs Hardy, or Miss Dugdale as
she was then, was with him as a secretary. I hasten to add that there
was no scandal as there was always a chaperone of some sort and he
was an old man even then... this was eight or nine years ago. Though
she is around him all the time, I sense that she's lonely. He lives an
internal life, full of his own thoughts and memories with not enough
space for another. Strange for a man who writes so much about love.'

'But it always seems to be cursed love,' said Julian.

'Complicated certainly. But there are happy endings.
Domesticated anyway.'

'The country that Mr Hardy describes is so wonderful,' said
Rose, 'I can smell the cut hay and the wildflowers as I read. So few
writers are able to do that.'

'But he doesn't let you smell the cottage with two rooms, a dirt
floor and a family of eight children living in it. Or hear the old
mother at the back of the parlour coughing her lungs out with
consumption,' Julian replied. 'I see all this when I visit farmers
before hunting. Being poor in the countryside is every bit as grim
as in a city, believe me. And in Ireland it's even worse.'

'But at least you can go outside for a walk in the summer and
you're surrounded by beauty. Surely that counts for something?'

'You're right. And, to be fair to Hardy, the lives he describes are hardly easy ones: poor Jude Fawley, for instance. I suppose I tend to see the physical conditions more than I hear the personal stories. Anyway, Mrs Granville, I would love to accompany you to Max Gate, if you would allow me. It's funny to think of Hardy as still alive. He seems to belong to another century, another world.'

The older woman considered this for moment. 'If you're talking about his novels, then yes, you're right. *Jude the Obscure* was his last novel and it was published a generation ago; but it feels like an aeon with all that has happened. Funnily enough, the countryside doesn't feel so foreign. As you say, ordinary lives still go on much as usual.'

He hesitated. 'Is that true? Not many men – and women working the land. And this awful sadness everywhere.'

They all contemplated again their own variant of grief. Julian knew that Daphne Granville had lost a brother and a nephew. 'But if you read Hardy's poetry,' she continued, 'I don't think he is old-fashioned; quite the opposite. It's still lyrical; and no one observes the minutiae of the natural world so beautifully. But the way he explores the human heart – his heart – is truly moving. And modern. He is a man of nearly eighty – but you hear the voice of someone half that age; old enough to know regrets but young enough to be still exploring. It's writing of great beauty.'

Both her companions saw the dampening of her eyes and both were moved themselves. Neither had suspected this cultivated passion in such a plain package.

*   *   *

At the other end of the table Ariadne turned towards Isobel.

'I'm sorry. About my family.'

'Why?'

'Because my father is drunk, my mother impossible and Uncle Robert... well he's just rude.' Isobel looked disconcerted. 'And you've only been in the house for half an hour.'

'But I like your father,' replied Isobel, 'He seems sweet to me. Look at the way he's talking to Davina; not many men would do that. And your mother is perfectly friendly. Believe me, I've met worse than your uncle…'

'That's the point: you've met worse. Not exactly a ringing endorsement of his charm or kindness, is it? Actually he can be charming when it suits him – but I see through it. I've known him too long to be taken in.'

'Please; I feel uncomfortable with this.'

'Well don't. He's my uncle and I'm allowed to dislike him.'

'Even so.'

'Even so, what?'

'Can we speak about something else?'

She arched an eyebrow. 'If you insist. What have you got in mind?'

'Hunting?'

'It's all I talk about every day.'

'Then you must love it.'

'How else do you get through these interminable winters?' She softened and smiled. 'Actually I do love it – but I'd still like to talk about something more interesting.'

'Like?'

'How about God?'

'That's a big one.'

'Rather relevant given how much my father speaks about him. And writes to your father about him. The two of them have been corresponding for some time now – especially after my brother was killed. Your father's letters meant a lot to him. He would reread them throughout the day that he received them. I don't know what he said, but it helped poor Papa as he struggled… with his faith. It's difficult to believe in a caring God after all that's happened.'

'And you?'

Ariadne looked at her, chewing her lip in consideration. Her long face had a freshness of complexion that comes with physical exercise and no make-up. Her hair was worn tied back, which emphasised the sharp planes of her features. Isobel sensed a shrewd intelligence under a carapace of flippancy.

'If he did exist I would have to hate him, wouldn't I? Wouldn't you?'

Isobel blinked in shock. Doubt was one thing; such a brutal rejection another. 'No. No, I do believe. I suppose I have to.'

'Why?'

'Because God can... maybe because I need to... to make sense of it all.'

'I don't see the sense. It looks like a mess to me. A rather cruel mess.' Ariadne stabbed at her food for emphasis. 'I didn't go to Cambridge, so I'll have to bow to your greater knowledge.'

'It's nothing to do with education. Or intelligence. Just faith – if you have it.'

'I don't.'

'What about your mother?'

'"Tiresome" is what she'd say.' Ariadne leant back in her chair and beckoned Isobel to follow her gaze. 'Look at her. She's listening to what your father's saying but not hearing anything.' At the head of the table Violet Milborne was looking intently at Isobel's father as he gesticulated to make a point. 'Watch her eyes.' They did and Isobel could see that far from bestowing intimate attention, she was looking at a point just over his shoulder. 'She does it beautifully doesn't she? It's fine until she's doing it to you when you're trying to talk to her about anything important – and you know she's not listening.' Ariadne shifted her gaze back to Isobel. 'What was your mother like? I have a tendency to think that all mothers are like mine. Do you mind talking about her? If it's too painful, don't worry.'

Though Isobel found Ariadne's abruptness unsettling, she had begun to get the measure of her.

'No. I like to talk about her. But I don't get much opportunity – with Papa anyway. It's almost as if her death has been drowned out by the war. Papa finds it very difficult to speak of her. We all loved her very much. She always saw what she wanted to see and ignored what might be upsetting. I found that irritating... and used to argue with her about it. She wouldn't be drawn. She hated arguments but would never take no for an answer when she believed something strongly. It was her that insisted that I went to Cambridge when Papa was against it.'

Ariadne looked at her, for the first time, with a softening of her eyes. 'Somewhat different to my mother: she's only interested in herself – or anyone who can give her pleasure. Occasionally that's me; but not often. But I'm used to it. I think she misses my brother, but she doesn't show it – unlike poor Papa. And she drinks too much...' They watched as her cocktail glass was refilled by a footman. '... and takes drugs that a friend gets for her in London. I can always tell when she's had some: she goes too far and Papa gets furious. Like tonight. I wish they were happier – but that's the way things are; with me in the middle most of the time.'

'I'm sorry.'

'Don't be. Many families are much worse. Dead, for instance. There's a family near here where the father and son were killed in France and the mother and two daughters by the flu.'

'It's one of the reasons Papa decided to leave his last parish. We thought there would be less infection down here. Obviously not.'

'Seizing the day?'

'Not really – but perhaps that's what we should all be doing. It feels as if someone's drawn a curtain over life? There's daylight out there and some light coming in but just no sunshine. I know it's winter and the grey days seem interminable but... I'm sorry this is too gloomy. I just can't shake it off.'

'It's why I hunt. Not quite true – but mainly because it gets me out of this house and away from my parents. I'm dreading the spring. Mummy will want me to go up to London for the Season, even though she knows I'll loathe it. It's all backed up because of the war: four years' worth of girls shovelled on to the marriage market – with no buyers in sight. I don't mind Ascot or Henley – but the thought of those awful balls with only two men for every ten girls is not a thrilling prospect. Apparently they're drafting in fathers and uncles to fill the gaps.' She made a face. 'What about you? What will you do?'

'Not the London Season. Not my thing.' There was defiance in the way Isobel said this: they both knew that a Season was neither a social nor a financial possibility. 'I have to look after Papa and Davina.'

'All the time?'

'No. Rose is doing it too. I'm a sculptor; and I am going to try and make a career out of it.'

'You didn't say anything about that before.'

'You didn't ask. No reason why you should; it's not exactly a normal occupation – even as a hobby.'

'You must be good.'

'I think so. Good enough, I hope. Whether that is good enough to make a living is another matter. It's expensive. I want to cast bronzes and for that you have to have access to a foundry and the materials. Papa has paid so far – but I know I can't expect him to do that forever. Painting would be much cheaper and easier.'

'So why not paint?'

'Why not write? It's just different. It's shape and texture, not colour that I do well.'

'I'm sorry – that was stupid.'

'Not at all. I ask myself the same thing. I could just work in clay – or stone. But there's something about casting. And you can reproduce – which makes it more commercial. Well I hope so anyway.' She looked at her food as if deciding what to eat. 'I wanted to ask you something.' Ariadne raised an eyebrow in anticipation of the question. 'How much is Mrs Pankhurst followed down here? I don't want to upset your father. He has been very kind in giving Papa the living here.'

'Why does that matter?'

Isobel looked at her coolly. 'Of course it matters. Without your father, we wouldn't have our house and my father wouldn't have his income.'

Ariadne lost her sangfroid for a moment. 'That was insensitive of me.'

'It's fine. You're right, of course. But being a suffragette seems to upset everyone – including other women; I suspect your mother wouldn't approve. So it's bound to annoy your father – if he finds out, of course. If it's in Bournemouth I don't think he's going to notice, do you? I doubt he reads the local paper too carefully, even here, and as long as I don't chain myself to his railings or get arrested, he'll probably never know. And if I get bored of throwing stones at policemen I can always take up hunting, can't I?'

Ariadne raised her glass with a smile that changed her again. 'That would nice.'

* * *

With the clearing of the main course, Rose turned towards Robert Granville with trepidation. He waved away the proffered pudding and leant back fingering his wineglass with two fingers and massaging a signet ring with his thumb. She was still angry with him over his earlier rudeness.

'I heard you plotting with my wife,' he said. Rose's alarm must have shown. 'Don't worry, I'm only teasing. I think a visit to the Hardys would be a perfect way for you to see this part of Dorset – God's own country I say – but then I'm biased. Tell me, have you had any chance to explore it?'

'We've only been here a few weeks and the weather has been dreadful.'

'Wait until spring. It's lovely. Never more than when the early blackthorn is in blossom and the vale looks as if it has been splashed with whitewash and the first flush of new grass is emerald green. If we have some sun over the next week or two, it will burst into life. We could take the hood off my motor car and take in the sun and spring if you would like.'

'We would like that very much.'

'And you, Rose; were you at Cambridge too?'

'No. Isobel is the brains in our family.'

'So it seems. And Davina? Has she always been… ?'

'Very lovable and affectionate. Yes.' There was steel in her voice.

'Of course.'

Rose felt the anger rising. 'People think she's stupid. She's not. She just sees things simply.'

'How charming.'

'It is actually.'

24

'She certainly seems so to me – but I've only had a few words with her.'

'You'll learn a lot from her if you persist.'

'I'll make it my business to do so.' He looked at his glass rather than at Rose. 'But tell me how you occupy your day.'

'I don't think it's very interesting compared to your life.'

'Why so?'

'I care for my father and Davina: fulfilling – but not very interesting. I understand you have a job in the government – something to do with the intelligence services. I don't think there's a contest in the interesting stakes?'

'I'm very lucky.'

'And are you ambitious?'

Granville looked at her in surprise. He had clearly not anticipated the tenor of the question. He pursed his lips and squinted which reminded her of a goshawk that she had once seen on a falconer's fist. 'Yes. You're right. You don't do what I do unless you're ambitious.'

'For what? I mean what are you ambitious for? Do you want to do something – or be somebody? I'm sorry: that's a rude question.' She hesitated.

'Rude? Not at all. An interesting question that I'm not sure how to answer.' He was now sitting forward, his flippancy gone. 'I'm the one normally asking the questions – so I know a good one when I hear it. I stop things happening – bad things – so it's difficult to be ambitious for that as it's a negative. So I suppose I want to be something: the top of what I do? Does that answer your question?'

She considered this. Her anxiety was evaporating as she got the measure of the man. He was no longer patronising her. 'In some ways. But isn't what you are describing just power?'

'Is there anything wrong with that?'

'It depends. If it's just for the sake of it, isn't it just vanity?'

He laughed. 'I admit it. I do like power. And I am vain. Aren't all men?'

'Not my father.'

They glanced across the table where the vicar was nodding to a story being waved hard at him by his hostess. He looked beaten by life.

'You don't become a vicar if you like power. Unless it's on a small scale that is. But there must be vanity in anyone that likes dressing up in those clothes. Or who feels they can talk at you without interruption for half an hour from a pulpit.'

'That's different.'

'Is it?'

'Yes. I was talking about power: proper power – the sort that kills people or changes their lives. That's not my father. But it is you – isn't it?' Rose was astonished at her own assertiveness.

'Yes. I admit it.' He leant forward, elbow on the table, and stroked his moustache as he observed her. 'It's also about being at the centre of things, knowing what is really going on and making things, important things, happen. I don't say this to my brother, and I wouldn't say it to your father, but I don't believe in God or the sort of power that might interest them. As I don't say that to many people, I'm not sure why I'm saying it to you.'

'Your secret's safe.'

'It's not that big a secret. I've never sought to be loved.'

'What about feared?'

'It goes with the turf.'

'And it doesn't worry you?'

'It doesn't seem to be affecting you.'

To her surprise she realised that it wasn't. Her father had always said that bullies couldn't bully those who weren't afraid of them. She disliked his arrogance and could sense his cruelty – but found his openness to her direct questions intriguing.

'It is – because I don't think you take women seriously.'

'After what I said to Isobel?'

'Yes. And the way you talk to me.'

'Now? I thought we were having a rather interesting conversation.'

'We are. But I suspect that you wouldn't have time for a suffragette.'

'Not much.'

26

'Then I rest my case.'

He laughed again. 'Rose, you are an interesting woman. I will admit that I prefer the company of men because, for the most part, they are educated and have more interesting things to say. Most dinner conversation is insufferably dull; a mixture of gossip and family detail that, I'm afraid, interests me not one jot.'

'If women aren't educated and are excluded from public life, what do you expect? And when they are educated and have things to say for themselves you treat them as you treated Isobel.'

'Guilty as charged. I'll try and do better.'

'Will you?'

He was about to reply when they saw Lord Milborne rise to his feet. The conversation ebbed to a silence. When he spoke, his voice was thick and his speech peppered by pauses.

'Family… and friends,' he looked towards Julian, 'it is a real pleasure for Violet and me to welcome you all to Milborne, to what I hope you will all consider now to be your home. We have all taken some terrible blows over the last four years, losses that are almost too much to bear. Our boys,' he shifted his gaze to his cousin, 'are gone and so many of the certainties of the past have gone with them.' He ruminated on this for some seconds. 'But families go on and we take comfort from our other children and each other; from my brother who is now my heir and, of course, from our wives, for those of us that are fortunate enough to still enjoy that blessing.' Violet Milborne blew an insouciant mushroom of smoke over the table. 'We are fortunate in many ways and I thank God for all that he has given us which is some compensation for what he has taken away. If you could now all rise, please. Ladies and Gentlemen, the King!'

4

Julian walked back to his house in cold rain flecked with sleet. It was entirely dark and he sensed, rather than saw, the edge of the lane, waving his stick in front of him like a blind man and navigating the last quarter of a mile by a light in a downstairs window. He was looking forward to the kitchen stove's antidote to the chill as he let himself in through his unlocked front door. He picked up the oil lamp and took it through into the kitchen, the only room – apart from a spartan bedroom – that he used. He placed the lamp on the table and began to trim the wick.

'Evening lad.' The lamp nearly went on the floor as he wheeled round to the source of the voice behind the door. Julian's shadow obscured the seated figure. 'You are looking smart; a fine figure of an English gentleman.' Julian knew those Cork cadences. 'And a nice spot too. Sorry to give you a fright.'

He moved the lamp between himself and the seated figure. The visitor's hat was on the arm of the chair. He was dressed in a tweed suit and holding out a packet of cigarettes. 'I've been bustin' to have one of these for a couple of hours now. You must have had a good evening.' Though the man was smiling, the edges of his mouth turned down. He had a thick head of hair that parted at the side and swept across his forehead and his height was apparent even when sitting down.

Julian took a cigarette and the proffered light. His hand was shaking as he did so. He sat at the table and pushed an ashtray in reach of the visitor.

'You don't seem pleased to see me.'

Julian shrugged. 'Just surprised.'

'The way things are, it didn't seem to be a good idea to arrive in a shamrock-covered landau. And a letter giving you a couple of weeks' notice didn't seem wise either.'

'Would you like a drink?'

'Never turned one down.' Again the curious smile with the turned down mouth. Julian gathered together two glasses and a bottle of whisky in silence. The visitor swallowed a whole mouthful, swirling it round in lustful appreciation.

'Scotch. Irish whiskey not good enough?'

'It's from the Orkneys. I spent the last two years there.'

'Indeed. Serving the Emperor.'

'Fighting the Germans.'

'A neat distinction.'

'It's the way I see it.'

'It's a big point. Men have been shot for less.'

'Are you threatening me?'

'Lord no! Why would the minister of finance be doing such a thing?'

'I'd heard. But you're better with a gun than a double entry aren't you?'

'I'm a quick learner. My da would have been proud. He'd have preferred General Collins to Minister Collins though. The way things are going, I may save him from disappointment yet.' He stood up, ground his cigarette into the ashtray and poured himself another drink. He swallowed a mouthful and contemplated Julian. He was an intimidating presence, tall and broad. He tapped his teeth together as he pondered.

'Why are you here?' asked Julian.

'Business.'

'Money or people?'

'A person. A real bastard.'

Julian felt a familiar dread: violence was this man's twin. 'I think I know who.'

'You wouldn't need to be Sherlock Holmes to figure that one out.'

'Why now?'

Collins shrugged. 'As good a time as any. With that one I'd be happy to wait a lifetime to get him.'

'A bit below you now to be doing this sort of thing, isn't it?'

'Oh, it won't be me. I'm out of practice. I'm here to make sure that our man has a bit of local knowledge.'

'I'm a civilian now.'

'I thought you were in the Naval Reserve.'

'I am.'

'Well look at it like this then: you're in the Irish Army Reserve as well.'

'Except I never joined up.'

'Didn't you now? My memory's a bit different.' There was a menace in his voice that had been jocular until then. Julian, still seated, felt the full gamma burst of power. 'You may not have been pulling a trigger – but you were one of the boys, weren't you? Won't wash lad.' He returned to his seat and looked at Julian over the lip of his glass. 'So?'

'So? So I'm a civilian.'

'No one is. Certainly not you.'

'And if I don't?'

Collins stared at him. 'Lad, who am I?'

Julian hesitated. 'Michael Collins.'

'Don't be fuckin' stupid now. I'm the man whose going to drive this whole thing through. You know that. De Vallera and the others are talkers; good men – but they don't have the balls for it. Or they think that sacrificing themselves is going to get the bastards out of Ireland. Look at Pearce during the Easter Rising; lovely man, but what does he do? Gets himself into St Stephen's Green with no way out for retreat or way in to get supplies. They say it was murder. It wasn't. More like suicide. So when the Brits finally got their act together and brought in the grown-ups, the whole lot got stuffed – including me. They were about to tie me to a post and shoot me when I got reprieved. I'm not going back there again; the ladies of Ireland need me too much.' He was smiling again. 'So no more Custer's Last Stand for me: it's carrot and stick: politics – and the occasional bullet to make sure that no one who has messed around with us ever feels safe: *pour encourager les autres*, as the man said. You're getting my drift?'

Julian nodded. 'So it's Granville.'

'I knew you weren't stupid. But don't tell me he's a friend of yours?'

'I loathe the man. But it's close to home.'

'Always is.'

'Why him?'

'You know he was in Dublin after the Rising, don't you? He was the man in charge of finding out who they hadn't got; who were the boys who'd escaped. Your friend is a man of imagination. Not for him some rough stuff and a few bruises. No. He was a man of refinement. Upside down for a few hours, hanging by the feet, and then the bastinado. You know what that means? It means beating the soles of a man's feet until he passes out; then lowering his head into a bucket when he comes to. Then doing the whole thing again. Lovely man, your friend. Never missed a moment I'm told. "Leading from the front," is what he said.'

Julian could believe it; he knew of what he was capable. 'When?'

Collins shrugged. 'Next couple of months. Maybe sooner. Depends. Might have to be refined around the politics. Applying a bit of pressure when its needed – you know the sort of thing.'

'And what do you want me to do?'

'Not much. Maybe give our man a roof for a couple of days and show him the lay of the land. Wouldn't want him shooting the wrong man, would we? That's it. Then back to whatever you're up to – until the next time we need something.'

'And if I refuse?'

'Not very patriotic.'

'And?'

Collins stood up and slowly paced the room. Though first appearances were bluff, the way he moved reminded Julian of a panther he had seen in London Zoo – menace contained.

'Well, I'd have to think a bit about that, wouldn't I? Maybe a letter to your friend with the bastinado? He doesn't take too kindly to Fenian renegades, I'm told. Then there is a little rumour that I heard in a pub in Cork about a police raid on a certain house. I'm sure there's an innocent explanation…' Julian felt his chest constrict and his heart hammering in his temple. He started to frame an answer but thought the better of it. He was aware of Collins staring at him even though his own gaze was focused on the lamp.

'No problem as far as I'm concerned. Couldn't care less what a fella gets up to behind closed doors. We're not all made the same. But I suspect some of your new fancy friends here might not take the same view about you if they knew what you got up to in the bedroom.'

'That's blackmail.'

'You're a perceptive lad.'

'Is that how you get things done these days?'

'When I have to. I find it's more humane than beating a man's feet or shooting him.'

'And that makes me feel better?'

'I didn't come here to spread sunshine.'

'I don't have a choice, do I?'

'You do; but it's not much of one, I'll grant you that.'

Julian stood up and faced the Irishman. 'When are you going?'

'Tomorrow. I'll leave after dawn when you've gone to the kennels. I took the liberty of making myself at home in one of your bedrooms. The mattress is a touch damp, but it's better than some of the ditches I've slept in over the years. Someone will pick me up after you've gone and I'll be wearing this…' he reached into his pocket and pulled out a false beard, 'which I think should be enough to stop you suffering any embarrassment. What do you think?'

He held it against his face laughing as he did so. 'Come on lad. Cheer up. Anyone would think that it was you I'd come to shuffle off this mortal coil. It's not too bad. All you're doing is making sure our fella' hits the right man. And that bastard is not exactly going to be sitting at the right hand of the Almighty is he? Let's see what we can do with the rest of that bottle shall we? For whisky that didn't originate in the Emerald Isle it's slipping down a tickle.'

Julian hesitated, as if about to say something, shook his head and held up his glass in a toast.

'The Emerald Isle.'

5

The Irishman was still asleep when Julian left, just as the sun was slanting down the valley after dawn. The kennels were out of sight, but not sound, of the cottage and, as he set off through the dusting of snow, the baying of the hungry pack echoed mournfully off the sides of the valley. He had slept little, woken intermittently by the snoring coming from the second bedroom. He thought he had left that part of his life behind: a clean start was what he had hoped for with the distance of the war years to quarantine him from his past. But now this. It brought back a tide of memories – some sunlit, others as overcast as the skies under which they had been formed. He had dreamt in between – but where the memories stopped and the dreams began he could not recall.

He remembered the house of his childhood, a Georgian creation in the grey stone of his native Galway, standing within a mesh of stone walls and small fields that bled into the bog. In the distance, seen in his dreams, as the last slash of sun touched the sea, were the waters of Galway Bay. Thatched whitewashed cottages peppered the patchwork of fields and the smoke from peat fires, flattened to the breeze, carried within it the scent of his youth. As dreams came, the skies darkened. He was standing on the lawn watching flames lick the painting of a horse on the wall of his bedroom, while below a furnace bellowed yellow in the dining room, shattering windows with its heat. Bats, smoked out of their eyrie in the roof, raced around the swirl of sparks that fought the steady rain. He heard the howling of his dog as he burned alive and the whinnying of horses as they pounded the doors of their stables in terror; the crash of a collapsing staircase and the rumble of the fire as it disembowelled his home. He saw his mother, hair plastered to her head by the rain, orange in the fire's light under a blanket, eyes staring at the cremation of her life – her past and future rising with the smoke and sparks into the void of the night sky.

He had woken and cursed the injustice of it. His father had been a Protestant, but hardly a man of his caste: he had wanted Home Rule and married a Catholic. His tenants had had nothing to complain of: when crops failed he had forborne his rents.

His only son, Julian had been educated by the Christian Brothers in Galway and then in Yorkshire by the Benedictines. When his father died from an aneurysm caused by a hunting fall over a Galway wall, his widow had continued with no change. Julian's boyhood friends had crossed the fissure in Irish life. His cousin, and best friend, divided his time between an estate on the Shannon and a London house of some grandeur. His local friends were Irish boys, sons of doctors, teachers and farmers, one a relative of the poet Yeats. Fenian myths were in his blood and he had grown up in the local pubs, singing songs that rang with Celtic echoes. He had run errands for some of the local chiefs but noticed that he was passed over for anything too close to the hub. He was tainted by the Ascendency – but he had accepted that he straddled some invisible line that gave him access, but not intimacy, with either side.

He was now an Englishman – and he looked the part in his thick tweed coat, trench boots and flat cap pulled over the tops of his ears to almost touch the collar of his coat. Spring, the season only in name, seemed a long way off with every arctic eddy of wind. Trees that only days ago had their first tincture of green were returned to winter's skeleton shapes. The kennels, a handsome stone quadrangle, built fifty years previously to match Wyatt's castellated efforts on the main house, stood on their own, flanked by two cottages. The smell was not for the faint of heart: canine, offal in the early stages of decomposition, urine and dog excrement. As he walked under the arch, he met Ralph coming the other way with a barrow of the latter. The kennel huntsman nodded a taciturn greeting. The welcome of his hounds was altogether more joyful as they surged towards him, dogs and bitches in different cages but joined in their delight at his presence, howling their joy, their tails – sterns in hunting parlance – waving like a squall in a maize field. He rubbed the noses pushed through the bars calling their names as he did so, feeding each a biscuit. He did this surreptitiously as he knew that Ralph disapproved. They were canine perfection and Julian loved them for it.

Ralph returned with a different barrow loaded with haunches of meat, crudely butchered with pieces of hide or fur still attached. These were the detritus of farming; cows that had died of disease or ewes during lambing; old horses or deer that the gamekeepers had felled to keep their numbers in control. During the starvation years of the war, when German submarines had choked off food supplies, the numbers of hounds had been cut by nearly two-thirds and fed on meat not fit for humans even in the prevailing hunger. Dead badgers, ground-up acorns and any rough protein had been added to the mix. Without ceremony the hunks of meat were thrown into the snarling melee to be set upon and torn apart in seconds. The quicker this was done, the less the competition – and within seconds each hound had its own to gnaw and gulp in its own space. For a short time the baying leitmotif of the kennels was reduced to the odd snarl of possession or yelp of pain. Without speaking, both men lit cigarettes and watched their charges with the pleasure of parents watching their children, observing each hound individually for any sign of sickness or injury. One bitch listlessly pulled at the shoulder of a cow without enthusiasm. Ralph raised an eyebrow. They would separate her out later: to do so during feeding could be dangerous.

Both men then moved on to the whelping shed where the season's puppies were being suckled by their mothers. Two bitches were lying heavy with pup. Half a dozen others lay with swollen teats as their blind offspring mewed and chewed as they fed. Julian lent over each in turn, stroking the mother's head as he made sure her teats weren't inflamed and that each puppy was getting its share. One was smaller than the others. He summoned Ralph whose experienced eye knew the losers. He shook his head. Sometimes a runt could be pulled out and saved like an orphaned lamb by individual feeding – but in the world of a hunt kennel there was no room for sentimentality and a physically weakened hound had no place. As in a beehive, the good of the whole was paramount.

The flesh house was next, where the cadavers of horses, cows and sheep awaited evisceration. Ralph had already disembowelled a horse and in the corner was a purple and grey mound of intestines awaiting burial. The offal – hearts, liver, kidney and lungs – lay on a separate pile. The head of a horse, hoisted on a butcher's hook, lay alongside a bucket. The smell was enough to make the uninitiated retch and Julian, inured though he was, felt his need for breakfast evaporating. Ralph shovelled the intestines into the bucket with nothing to suggest that this was anything other than prosaic. Julian had heard that for veterans of the trenches the smell was unendurable. Both men worked hard for half an hour until the floor was clear and scrubbed with only two carcasses swinging on hooks. Neither man spoke during their labours – but Julian expected no more. With only a wave, he left the kennels for his breakfast.

It was with some trepidation that he opened the front door. There was the smell of Sweet Afton cigarettes but no sign of his midnight visitor. He glanced into the second bedroom and the bed was made. In the kitchen a loaf of bread had been broken and there were gouge marks in the tub of dripping next to the sink. The Irishman had trodden lightly. Julian made a pot of tea but his mind was back in Cork before the war.

He remembered Collins on his return from America, visiting his family and holding court in pubs, surrounded by acolytes. Only in his early twenties, authority seemed to have devolved on him as a divine right: men recognised it and all but kissed his hand. He mixed the authority of a cardinal and the charm of a porpoise, already the man of the future. It was in Cork that Julian had fallen under his spell. He had listened to him talking of how Irishmen would wrest their destiny back by force if the talking failed. This was no romantic, but a practical politician for whom violence was a necessary tool. And yet he would wave his wand when filled with 'whiskey' and take his audience with him into a dim Celtic past or to the blood-spattered predations of Cromwell. With tears flowing down his face, he would lead songs of the Famine and have all in the room wiping their eyes. As they finished the bottle of 'whiskey' in the early hours, Julian had been drawn back into the folds of the wizard's cloak, emotionally reconnected to the cause of his youth.

The war had been a saviour of sorts. The crusade against German aggression had trumped his nationalism. As he had spent his childhood summers fishing and sailing in Galway Bay, he had volunteered for the Royal Navy and been accepted as an officer, sent to Dartmouth and commissioned into a cruiser as third lieutenant attached to the Grand Fleet, initially at Rossyth in the Firth of Forth and then with the bulk of the fleet in Scapa Flow in the Orkney Islands. His principal memory had been of tedium: endless watches from an open bridge either in the shelter of the Flow or outside in the North Sea with its grey, steep seas and the constant danger from submarines or mines; hours spent as the radio officer deciphering the chatter of morse code carried in the ether; or off-watch, pacing the main deck between rain bursts from a pregnant Orkney sky. Though his independent cast of mind had initially kicked against the rigid hierarchy of the Navy, with time the unrelenting discipline became a security of its own, focusing everything on the task at hand with no need for complexity or ambiguity. The Navy had given him a rest from the contradictions of his prewar life – and he missed it now. He had assumed that living in England and the four years of war, with its separation from the cause, would leave him free to build his life. But now this ghost had appeared demanding his pound of flesh and he cursed him for it.

The Irishman had pride of place in his cluster of thoughts – but the dinner had left plenty to consider. He had walked home under the cloud of yet another altercation between the Milbornes. The cause had been the insistence by Violet Milborne that the women did not leave the dinner table when the port arrived. She then drank too much of it herself and by the time they were once again in the drawing room, its effects were manifesting itself in a flirtation with Julian that had him reddening with embarrassment. Ariadne had come to his rescue but the hostess's slurred inanities hung like a pall over the rest of the evening and the polite conversation that continued in huddles was strained by the anticipation of the earthquake to come once they were the other side of the front door. On leave during the war, and in its immediate aftermath, Julian had enjoyed the attention that he had received as a survivor of a decimated generation of men. Only now was he beginning to understand the complications.

It was his custom to eat breakfast and then read, smoke or doze in front of the fire before returning to the kennels at ten o'clock – unless it was a hunting day, in which case he would be struggling with studs, ties and boots. With the end of the season, everything relaxed – including the horses that were kept in their stables overnight but turned out into the first shoots of spring grass as soon as their growing coats and frost allowed. He would inspect the grooms' work on his return – anticipating that by then the stables would be mucked out and the horses shining and smelling of hoof oil, their monogrammed stable rugs as clean as the horses they covered. Despite only two postwar grooms in charge of a dozen horses, there had been no slipping of standards. Today he smoked – but as a nervous tic with the night's events replaying in his mind.

As arranged, the Richmond sisters arrived on foot at the kennels accompanied by Ariadne. They were clutching their hats and taming their coats and hemlines against the wind that ricocheted off the valley wall in freezing gusts. Ariadne was all business. During the war she had been the unofficial kennel huntsman who had supervised the hounds and rolled up her sleeves to do every job – including the butchery in the flesh house. She knew every hound better than either Ralph or Julian, and their chorus of welcome for her was ecstatic. The bitches were released and they fanned out around the yard, noses twitching, each responding to their name when called out by Ariadne. Davina cowered in alarm behind Isobel as one jumped up with her paws on the front of her coat. Ariadne called her off but summoned another who stood meekly as her head was stroked. She coaxed Davina towards the hound who licked her outstretched hand. They saw the puppies and patted the horses, all of which took enough time for the cold to seep into their bones.

'Where do you live, Mr Belmore?' asked Isobel.

'Close by, and there's a fire. I'm afraid it's a bachelor's house with not much in the way of creature comforts – but it's warm and I can make tea.'

'It's a slum,' interjected Ariadne, 'but it's not Julian's fault. Papa hasn't spent a penny on it in years – his idea of contributing to the war effort – but if the range is stoked up then let's make the best of it. I'll go and tell Ralph what we're doing. You go ahead and I'll join you there.'

Julian watched her making her way towards Ralph's room in the corner of the yard. Her walk had a femininity that belied the masculinity of her direct manner. She dealt with Ralph with a mixture of businesslike questions or requests, mixed with an intuitive, wordless understanding that often consisted of only a nod, a gesture or raised eyebrow that both seemed to understand. They had known each other since her early adolescence and had developed a mutual sympathy that was almost telepathic, linked by a shared passion – but held in a certain place by the formality of their respective positions. Julian often found himself communicating with the taciturn Ralph through her. He was still uncertain as to what either of them thought of him.

Julian purposely walked alongside Isobel on the way to his cottage. They had only exchanged handshakes the previous evening.

'That was a tricky start,' he broached, 'but you handled it well. Were you warned?'

'About Cousin Robert? No.'

'If it's any consolation, that's not the worst I've seen.'

'He's always like that?'

'Pretty well.'

She considered this.

'I'm surprised Papa didn't say anything. But they were brought up together so maybe he sees a different side. Rose said that Cousin Daphne was delightful. How did they get together you have to wonder.' She looked at him sideways as they walked along the narrow lane. 'Rose also said she had a nice time sitting next to you. You both like Hardy, I gather. That's a bit unusual for a master of the hunt.'

He glanced at her to catch the tenor of her question. She was smiling.

'It's not as grand as it sounds. I'm what they call an amateur huntsman – which basically means that I work seven days a week for nothing except a cottage to live in and some pocket money. I'm supposed to have a private income – which I do – just that it's not very big. Rather small in fact. But I rub along. And you?'

'Income? None. I still have an allowance from Papa – but I'm trying to start a career as a sculptor. I love bronzes.'

'You have a studio?'

'In the stables of the rectory. Freezing cold, but I can work there and make a mess. There's a foundry near Sherborne that I've found; cheaper then where we were in Kent – but it still costs a fortune so I need to sell some pieces soon if I'm going to make it work.'

'I've never seen a casting.'

'Then you're in luck. I'm at the foundry on Thursday – if you're interested.'

'I'd like that. I have my kennel duties, but I can be finished by ten.'

'I'll be there earlier to prepare – but join me there when you can. It's about fifteen minutes by bicycle. It's hot but that's an advantage in winter – especially when it's this miserable.'

The sisters pretended that his house was a palace and fussed around his bare kitchen. They were seated by the fire when Ariadne joined them. Julian offered round a packet of cigarettes, declined by all except Rose.

'May I try one?'

'But you don't smoke,' said Isobel tartly.

'Well I'm going to try.'

'Papa hates smoking.'

'Well he's not here, is he?'

40

'That's not the point.'

'It jolly well is. Please, Mr Belmore... Julian... will you show me?'

Julian hesitantly shook out a cigarette and gave it to Rose under the disapproving gaze of Isobel.

'And me too,' said Ariadne. 'Why should Mummy have all the fun? Should Rose inhale?'

'Probably not to start off with as it'll make her sick. Just suck it and hold it in your mouth.'

'You'll be sick,' stated Isobel with satisfaction.

'Maybe. Like this?' Rose pouted around the cigarette and then smiled up at Julian. Only he could see her face. There was something sweet but also something lascivious in that look, invisible to the others, that caught Julian by surprise – so much so that he forgot to rasp the flint of the lighter. He recovered himself. Rose puffed and coughed slightly – but mastered it: 'There. That was fine. Come on Ariadne, your turn.' Julian lit Ariadne's cigarette on which she drew, held in her mouth and then inhaled with the aplomb of a past master. 'You've done this before!' said Rose, 'here we go again.' This time she inhaled and bent over in a paroxysm of coughing from which she emerged laughing and spluttering. 'Not very sophisticated. I need tutoring on this. Can I appoint you as my smoking mentor, Julian?'

'You shouldn't smoke.' This came, unexpectedly, from Davina whose face betrayed a confusion between concern and laughter.

'Don't you start too, Dav,' said Rose. 'Look, I haven't made up my mind if I want to make a career out of it yet. I'm only learning and I haven't been sick.'

'Not yet,' said Isobel. 'Don't expect any sympathy from us.'

'Everyone's sick to start with.' Ariadne took another deeply held drag. 'Ralph taught me during cub hunting when I was nineteen. Having your first cigarette with brandy at seven o'clock in the morning was interesting.'

'Brandy in the morning?' Isobel looked shocked.

'Delicious. On an empty stomach it certainly wakes you up. And a cigarette at the same time... Mummy's been doing it for years. Come on Isobel, have a go. If you are going to be a proper suffragette you're going to have to learn to smoke like a man.' It was Davina's turn to look on with disapproval as Isobel reached out to the proffered cigarette.

'I'll help you make the tea,' said Rose to Julian, setting off towards the kitchen. She put the kettle on the range and turned to him, holding the cigarette with the casualness of a sophisticate. Tendrils of dark hair were loose and framed the oval of her face that glowed from the massage of the bitter wind. Her waisted coat accentuated the curve of her breasts and hips.

'You didn't tell me last night why you're living here rather than in Ireland.'

'It's complicated. Ireland's not an easy place to live – at the moment, anyway.'

'The Troubles?'

'And somewhere to work.'

'There's hunting in Ireland.'

'But not where I can survive as an amateur.'

'Why's it different here?'

'Lord Milborne. He pays me. Well it's not exactly a salary that will make me rich – but somewhere to live, pretty well all my expenses paid and enough to supplement the rent I get from the farm in Galway.'

'Is that in the west?'

'The wild west. Stone walls and burning houses. Including ours.'

'I'm sorry.'

'It was grim at the time – but oddly I now think it may have been for the best. It got me away from the problems. Over there they see it as a war to get the British out, but we experienced it as a civil war. My family may have been of English decent but we think of ourselves as Irish – and got our house burned down for our pains. You can't win because you're on both sides. A world war was easier: you knew who you were fighting – and why.'

Rose held up the last inch of her cigarette. He took it from her and tossed it into the open door of the range.

'Did you enjoy it?' he asked.

'No. I can't say I did. But I'm still learning.'

'It looks as if Isobel might be joining you.' Julian nodded towards the open door through which Isobel could be seen fighting back the urge to cough on Ariadne's cigarette. 'But she doesn't look as if she's enjoying it much.'

'Typical! Miss Prim – and then this.'

'Not a woman of many vices?'

'Unless you count tea with sugar.'

'She does drink.'

'Sips it. Better than Lady M, I suppose.'

'Indeed.'

'That was pretty hideous last night, wasn't it? Poor you. And poor Ariadne having to apologise for her. Lord M is a sweetie – but I think he has a lot to put up with. I was wondering whether it's better to have no mother than one like that. What do you think?'

She had one hand on the handle of the kettle and the other in the pocket of her coat. It was a question that was above small talk, delivered quietly so as not to be overheard. Julian pulled out another cigarette and lit it before replying.

'The embarrassing bit? My mother's a bit "touched" as they say in Ireland – batty over here. And embarrassing sometimes – but not in a way for which I've ever had to apologise. Never. But I get the feeling that Ariadne's mother has never been maternal. And probably never loved anyone other than herself. Is that unfair?'

'Not unfair at all; from what I saw last night anyway. And from what Ariadne told Isobel at dinner. It's sad don't you think? What a waste.' She hesitated. The kettle rushed steam from its spout. 'I need a teapot.'

They looked at each other. Once again their small talk had segued into an intimacy that was unexpected, made more intense by the grasped moment. They could hear Isobel coughing, the concern of Davina and the encouragement of Ariadne.

'We're very glad you're here,' said Rose, 'all of us. We've led a rather peripatetic life moving from parish to parish and, though Isobel and I love Dav and Papa very much, it's not exactly been lonely – but a bit dull. Isobel and I get on each other's nerves when we're together too much. I think Isobel and Ariadne have hit it off.'

She took the proffered teapot and busied herself while Julian watched her. She was too round-faced to be considered classically beautiful but there was an intrinsic sensuality in her trim figure and mouth that pursed in smiles.

'What are you going to do here?' asked Julian.

'Find a husband, I suppose. Except that there aren't any – present company excepted of course.' She looked at him with her challenging smile. 'So if one doesn't hove into view, I suppose I'll have to be my father's companion and a spinster sister for Dav. Why do you ask me that? Cousin Robert did the same last night in his rather patronising way.' She hesitated. 'The truth is that I simply have no idea what I'm going to do. I have no qualifications or skills that might be valuable. I worked in a hospital for the last two years of the war, helping with the paperwork and the administration – and I wasn't very good at that. God, it was boring. I wish I could say that I was some sort of Florence Nightingale but I feel sick even thinking about wounds or even very ordinary illnesses. Isobel will be fine with her education – but me? I suppose it is a good thing that Papa and Dav need so much care. There you are. The story of my little life in a couple of sentences. Not much to put on the tombstone if the flu gets me, is there? Maybe something will turn up.' She looked at Julian directly as she spoke, pouring boiling water into the teapot. 'Maybe.'

'Rather pessimistic?'

'Is it? A one-in-ten chance of getting married? That's all. Unless, I suppose, I go for someone with no arms – or no face. It's shallow, I know, but I can't do that. I'm not a saint. I want a full marriage; to give myself to a man that I love and desire. Is that such a terrible thing to ask?' Julian glanced towards the room where Isobel was persevering with her cigarette. 'It probably is, I know. And now you'll think of me as someone irrevocably frivolous. But I can't pretend. I couldn't go to bed every night for the rest of my life with someone I found physically revolting. I'd rather be on my own. Or with Papa and Davina. There you are. You know me now.' She laughed without humour. 'I don't want sympathy or comforting words. It's just a fact of life – or death actually. And there's no

44

answer to it. I could emigrate – but to where? It's the same the world over – except America, perhaps. I have thought about it but I did the weighing up and I think I would, on balance, rather be here in England on my own than living in some Mid-Western town with nothing to remind me of home. Is that unadventurous? It is, isn't it? How pathetic that I'm too scared to bid for my own happiness. Maybe I wouldn't know what to do with it if I found it.' She picked up the teapot and nodded towards the next-door room. 'I've told you all about me. All you need to know. The deal is that I need to know more about you in return. I'm not very experienced with men: the way they think: the inner sadnesses and the insecurities. Will you tell me? Believe it or not I'm a good listener – and the soul of discretion.'

'I'd like that.'

'Would you really? Most men I know aren't too keen on it. They think that it's a weakness. Maybe that's the difference between us. Women think that a sharing of an insecurity is a strength. I don't think men do.'

There was a defensive tone to his reply. 'You're right. But men is a general term. I'm a man – but I think that I can think for myself in my own way.'

She laughed. 'That's why we're having this conversation – because I don't think you are like most of the men I've met. It's a limited repertoire, I grant you – but I've known a few: nice ones, funny ones, gentle ones – some cruel, some sad. But not many who really want to talk to you. Not many who really like women.' She held his eye as she spoke.

Julian held out a cup. She poured but left the silence unfilled in anticipation of a reply. The sound of coughing and encouragement filtered through from the sitting room.

'We just suffer from our upbringing,' he said, 'nanny, mummy – then no women to practice normal life with until we are into our twenties. It's not surprising that we aren't experts in women with that sort of handicap.'

'Women manage. Or maybe they don't. Maybe that's what Cousin Robert was telling me last night. Does he give you the creeps? Maybe if we raised our game he would take us more seriously?'

'I doubt it. There are things you can change…'

'… and he's not one of them. But I wasn't expecting to change him – or anyone for that matter. I'll just keep looking for ones that do get it – and maybe then I'll be happy and marry and live happily ever afterwards. Sounds simple doesn't it?'

'Simple. But difficult. Let's keep trying.'

'Yes. Please. Will you bring the cups?'

With that she carried the teapot through the door.

6

Spring came abruptly. Banks of dead grass and brambles were transformed by shoots of cow parsley, wild garlic and bluebells. Elms sprayed themselves with a fur of green. Only the ashes held back, their stark outlines in contrast to the budding of the hedges in which they stood.

Stirred by the sunshine, the expedition to visit Thomas and Florence Hardy came to fruition. Daphne Granville offered her car and driver and the small party consisted of Julian, Rose and Daphne. The roof came down to enjoy the sun and, without the overbearing presence of her husband, Daphne was transfigured. The mousey self-abasement and darting eyes were left behind and laughter and repartee replaced them as they drove through the vale towards Dorchester. The country was familiar to Julian from hunting. He knew the farms and the families who worked them and he told his companions of their eccentricities and tragedies. They were held up repeatedly by herds of cows being moved to take advantage of the first flush of spring grass. Farmers, drifting their animals along the road, halted to Julian's greeting and, as their stock grazed the verges, leant over the door of the car, having doffed a cap to the ladies, and passed the time of day with no hint of urgency. Some worried away at a misdemeanour by the hunt – a broken fence or a gate left open. Others talked about their families and the predations of the war that had taken their sons. One, with tears running down his weather-scoured face, told of a formerly clear-eyed child unable to leave his bedroom for terror.

They stopped in Cerne Abbas and admired the giant etched out of the chalk of the hillside, club in hand and outsize erection paraded for the world to see. Julian's anxiety as to how this would be taken by the ladies was allayed by their ribald laughter. As they drove, Daphne told them of local legends and histories, pointing out the hill forts and landmarks of Dorset.

Max Gate lay behind a garden wall on the outskirts of Dorchester. Its dark brick and heavy eaves gave it a forbidding mien that the gloom of the hall did nothing to alleviate. They were shown to the drawing room where they waited for their hosts. Florence Hardy appeared first, a handsome woman treated badly by age; her hair, worn in a tight bun flecked grey; her face the victim of dark bags under her eyes that gave it a lugubrious cast, accentuated by a mouth that rarely smiled. The awkward silence after the introductions was broken by Julian.

'Mrs Hardy, I understand that your husband designed Max Gate. It's a fine house,' he lied.

'I'm glad you like it, Mr Belmore, because I don't. Too many ghosts.' She let this hang in the air. 'Cold in winter and gloomy in summer – but my husband loves it, so I have to tolerate it.'

'I hadn't realised that he was an architect,' said Rose.

'Regrettably he's not, Miss Richmond. He trained as one – but it doesn't follow, I'm afraid, that because you are a genius in one art form, your genius will follow you into another. I don't think anyone would have gone to Rembrandt for a symphony or Mozart for a palace and expected too much. But the countryside is beautiful and Tom and I both love it... don't we dear?'

Silently, Hardy had entered the room, as startling as an apparition. He seemed ephemeral, bird-like and insubstantial. An outsize moustache dominated his face, challenged by a pair of glittering eyes that took in the entirety of the party with quick sweeps.

'I do apologise for not being down to greet you, but I've had a good morning and when the muse is speaking, I have to listen. My dear Mrs Granville, how good to see you... and you must be the famous beauty, Miss Richmond.' His voice was reedy and his Adam's apple quivered over the compliment. The burr of a Dorset accent was discernible. 'And Mr Belmore – if Mrs Granville's letter is to be believed. Welcome to Max Gate – which I am aware my wife doesn't like,' Florence Hardy pursed her lips in irritation, 'but of which I am very fond. It is really only here that I can work. Selfish, I know, but there it is.' His wife looked away, her jaw hardening, but he carried on serenely. 'If you are a writer, being in a familiar place is very important. It allows your mind to travel…'

'To concentrate?' interjected his wife. 'I find that as long as I have somewhere quiet, I can work anywhere. I love the sound of the sea.'

Hardy looked at the table. 'Not exactly, my dear. Creativity is more than concentration, as poetry is more than writing. Difficult to understand if you aren't an artist.' Though he delivered the last sentence with a smile, its intent was clear – and the wound visible. Julian and Rose exchanged glances as they both remembered Daphne Granville telling them of Florence Hardy's own literary ambitions.

'Are you going to write another novel, Mr Hardy?' asked Rose, attempting to steer the conversation off the rocks of marital discord.

'No, Miss Richmond; no more novels. I finished with them many years ago: something I had to do to give me the means to write poetry. Novels are marching, poetry is dancing – and I'm lucky enough now to be able to dance all day. Perhaps my marching boots have just worn out. Have you read my poetry? I do hope so – but I will give you a folio to take away with you anyway. Ah, I believe lunch is ready.' He was standing again as quickly as he had perched on the edge of the chaise longue. The bobbing of a blackbird was what came to Rose's mind as he nodded towards the door and the servant that was standing there. He indicated that Rose should take his arm, and with overworked gallantry, escorted her across the hall and into the dining room, another room where the light of the spring day was leeched away by heavy damask curtains and the chocolate browns of the woodwork. He drew her chair out and did the same for Daphne. He was a gentleman and Max Gate was his castle. They waited in silence while the tureen circulated. Julian ventured an opening gambit.

'It is very kind indeed of you both to invite us to luncheon, Mrs Hardy. You and Mr Hardy must have many readers beating a path to your door? I do hope this has not inconvenienced you.'

'Not at all. Autograph hunters are tiresome, I admit, but not friends. As neither of us have children, the company of young people is refreshing – for me in particular.' It was Hardy's turn to experience a sting in the tail of an inconsequential remark. The age difference between them was cavernous. 'We don't go away, particularly to London, as much as I would like; so if we cannot go to our friends because of Tom's need to be here at Max Gate, then our friends, like Mrs Granville, have to come to us.'

'You make it sound as if we are hermits, my dear,' said Hardy.

'If that means going for weeks without seeing anyone other than servants, then that is well described.'

'You exaggerate, I think.'

'Do I? We used to go to London regularly, now hardly at all. Not that I am complaining. When we married I accepted that your work comes first and I am not changing my mind. I was only letting our guests know how much we enjoy a bit of variation in our daily routine – especially now that spring is here.'

'Mrs Hardy is right,' said Hardy, 'I am ashamed to admit. She looks after me and helps me more than I can say. Let us drink to women and all that they do for us.' He held up his glass with the most charming of smiles and no hint of irony before turning to Rose with enjoyment. 'Now Miss Richmond, Mrs Granville has told me something about you. Perhaps you can now tell me. And if there is anything in my long life and experience that may be of help to you, I would be delighted to put it at your disposal.'

He encouraged her to ask him about his novels – about which she was initially shy, given his earlier reluctance. Gradually she succumbed to his charm and found herself in an intimacy that had both Florence Hardy and Julian glancing down the table with a worm's turn of jealously. Finally she asked, 'Mr Hardy, there is so much tragedy in your writing. Everyone is battered by life. It is so pessimistic. And yet you don't seem to me to be a pessimist. You look as if you enjoy life. I'm sorry, that is very direct. I hope you don't mind.'

He put his hand on her arm. 'Don't apologise, please, Miss Richmond. My critics have said many worse things and my bones aren't broken yet. I have thought much about this charge of pessimism and I do reject it – not because bad things don't happen to people – they clearly do – but because I actually believe that things, human things, are moving forward. I have an expression for it. I consider myself an evolutionary meliorist.' Rose looked puzzled. 'That word; meliorist – I'm sorry – it means an optimism of sorts; that the world can be improved by human endeavours. We aren't just flies crawling across the glass destined only to be squashed by a random agent. We all struggle – but it's not in vain. Each bit of the struggle moves us forward – though we do get swatted occasionally – but the important point is that each small inch we achieve is added to the last as far as the sum total of the human attainment is concerned. Each generation is a brick on which the next is laid as that structure goes upwards and the next has slightly less of a mountain to climb. No, that is a bad metaphor, because the struggle stays the same. In each generation the view gets better and we can aim higher because of the previous struggle. Does that make sense?'

The conversation had petered out at the other end of the table and all were listening to the seer as he spoke. Julian answered, hesitantly.

'Mr Hardy, I would have agreed with you five years ago. Wouldn't we all? But now? A meliorist? After what has happened?'

Hardy looked at him as if to reply, then shrugged with a sigh. 'Yes. Yes, of course you are right. I can't argue with that – who could? But you could also say that progress is never without a check and in a straight line. There are terrible things that happen along the way. Galileo worked out how the heavens work and then was threatened with the stake. We cast off the superstitions of the past and then had to confront the French Revolution. Now it is a war so terrible that all progress is called into question. But if it is the war to end all wars then it may be, perversely I grant you, the biggest building block of all.'

'You are an optimist after all, Mr Hardy,' said Daphne.

Hardy laughed. 'I told you so. But I'm not Panglossian. All is not, clearly, for the best in the best of all possible worlds. There are plenty of wrong turnings and holes in the road. But I still think the concept of ideas not being able to be unlearnt makes the building block analogy a sound one. The French Revolution tested the Enlightenment view of progress – but didn't send us back to a world of superstition. There was an attempt to do so but it failed: the genie couldn't be pushed back into the lamp. But this makes me out to be a philosopher – which I am not. I'm a poet and I look at life as I find it, not as it ought to be – which will, I'm sad to say, make me a disappointment to you, Miss Richmond... and probably to you all. Ah, Wessie, there you are... come and meet our guests.'

A large and ebullient terrier bowled into the room barking as he circumnavigated the table. He jumped up with his front feet on the old man's knees and licked his ears before doing another turn of the table. Julian held out his hand to pat him and received a snap for his pains that produced instant blood. Neither host seemed too surprised as Julian applied a napkin to his hand as a tourniquet.

'I am sorry, Mr Belmore,' said Florence with little real apology, 'Wessex does get very excited and sometimes his affection gets the better of him.' Julian saw the servants' reaction to the dog. He knew a biter when he saw one. Florence watched her husband as he gathered Daphne into his conversation. 'Are you married, Mr Belmore?' Julian wasn't sure whether this was small talk or the prelude to something else.

'No. Not yet.'

'Do you wish it?'

'Yes. I think I do. Wouldn't that be normal?'

'Normal? Probably. Right? I don't know.'

'Are you counselling me, Mrs Hardy?'

'No. That would be arrogance from someone like me, wouldn't it? But I am curious as to what men want from marriage, apart from the obvious things, of course.' She was looking down the table rather than at him as she spoke – more to avoid looking directly at him he felt. He was conscious of a sadness at her core but also of a carapace with which she defended herself. Against what?

Julian answered. 'Companionship. Children. Love. Someone to whom one can let slip one's insecurities while knowing that they are safe. Is that enough?'

She turned her grave gaze on him. 'Enough? Yes, indeed they would be enough. Any one of them.'

'And care?'

'Yes. Care. But of whom, by whom? It should be mutual, shouldn't it? But then if one marries someone so much older, the care is necessarily one way – so I shouldn't complain.' There seemed no answer to this. 'Is it better than being alone?' This seemed to be a rhetorical question. 'I'm not sure. I'm really not, but then I am a woman.'

'It should be mutual,' tendered Julian.

'Should? But that is not much to do with it in reality, is it?'

'I don't know. I'm too young. But not to my mind anyway.'

'That's good to know. Your wife will be a lucky person.'

'So is Mr Hardy.'

She smiled – for the first time with warmth. She lowered her voice and leant towards him. 'Thank you. I wish he could say that.'

'He did. Five minutes ago.'

'But not to me. Not really to me. To women in general – idealised, admired and desired – but not to me.'

'Maybe he has difficulty expressing himself about such things.'

'Thomas Hardy? The poet? You would have thought not... but...' The bitterness had gone but not the sadness. Julian did not know what to say to this. She continued, 'Maybe it isn't possible to live a deep internal life and run a more prosaic life in parallel. Perhaps the one excludes the other – in which case I have no cause for complaint. Not for complaint – but perhaps for regret. The problem with living with a man who examines the world so intensely is that he overlooks you; a sort of wilful blind spot. Everything feeds the observation. You are looked through – like a living pair of spectacles – rather than looked at as someone with whom one can share the experience. When I first knew Tom, I thought that it would be a shared life. I now know it is a shared house. I would counsel you to share your life, Mr Belmore. That is what I have learned.'

Julian was silent as she tidied the table around her, the laughter at the opposite end a poignant counterpoint. He found himself putting a hand on her arm to stop her. She looked at him in surprise. 'Thank you, Mrs Hardy. I did not expect such... I am flattered that you should treat me with such intimacy. I will take what you say to heart.'

Florence looked at him with a faint smile and then towards her husband who was in the flow of an anecdote. 'Miss Richmond is an interesting young woman. In a number of ways. Are you and she...'

'No. We only met last month.'

'And?'

'Nothing.'

'I think not.'

'Well nothing yet.'

'That's more like it. She will be lucky to have you I think.'

'I can't think why.'

'Don't be too flattered. An object's rarity makes its value rise. A decent, sensitive man is the exception, rather than the rule, at the best of times. At these worst of times there are no men at all for these poor girls. They know that. We all know that. You could take advantage of it – but I don't think you will. At least I hope you won't. It happened to me when I was younger.'

'We're friends.'

'Good. That's better than love. It lasts.'

He intuited a truth in this but found its expression shocking.

'Really? So there is no difference between the love of a man and woman and that of two friends?'

'I didn't say that. I just said that lovers become enemies as many times as they end up as friends. Better a friend whom you love than a lover that you... I was going to say hate – but that is too warm a word. Indifference is more frightening. Despise is a terrible word.'

'The worst.'

'My experience is that friendship is real gold; love is the gold that sits at the bottom of a rainbow – sparkling – but a mirage that disappears as you get too close. Is that very disappointing for you, Mr Belmore? It was for me.' Julian did not answer. 'I'm not cynical, I promise, just sceptical. I don't believe promises any more – because promises are too difficult to keep. How can they not be when we become different people as we get older? And yet we still make them – and encourage others to make them too when we know better. A meliorist? Not me I'm afraid. How ironic is it that the great pessimist should think otherwise.'

'Maybe I don't have enough experience,' said Julian carefully. 'I've never been in love. Well, not that I'd recognise anyway. I've cared for some – a good deal – but "in love"? Not yet.'

'Nor have I, Mr Belmore. I don't really understand it. Tom thinks that he was in love with Emma, his first wife. If he was, it was very curious. She lived in the attic for the last ten years of her life. When she came downstairs for meals, she argued with him and belittled his work. I know this because I was here; living with them both for weeks at a time. She would say that he only wrote anything great under her influence. She made out that she was his muse when that was ridiculous. She was religious, proselytisingly so, when Tom has no time for anything like that – other than the ceremonies, of which he is fond. And yet when she died it was as if everything she had said, all the nonsense she spouted, all the hurt she caused, was transformed into the whispers of a lover and the comforts of a confident. This foolish woman was transformed into the muse that she always claimed to be. How do you explain that, Mr Belmore? I cannot.' There was anger in her voice. Julian looked anxiously down the table where Hardy was imparting a confidence to his companions who leant over the better to hear him. Julian sensed that what Florence was describing was the grit in the oyster of their marriage around which no pearl was nurtured.

'Maybe what you see gets changed as it's forced through a prism of sorts,' he postulated. 'Maybe that prism is what is called love, or being in love anyway.'

'Maybe. It all seems foolish to me. I am mocked by it every day; every day when he raises another poem about that woman which has no bearing on any reality – and despite what it does to me; to my feelings and self-esteem.' She paused and fondled the dog's ear. 'I'm sorry, Mr Belmore, I should not be burdening you with this nonsense. We have only just met and I am telling you the intimate details of our life. I should thank you for having such broad shoulders. To tell the truth, it's easier to say these things to a stranger – someone with no stake in our… relationship. Almost everyone we see has: maybe it's money, or Tom's literary legacy. Most of the friends of his middle age are dead. What's left are the vultures – and vultures don't like the mate who is still alive. It stops them being able to feast in the now. I do hope that we see more of you – and Miss Richmond.' She glanced down the table again, where Hardy was gesticulating with enthusiasm. 'Certainly Tom will wish to see Miss Richmond. It isn't our custom to drink coffee, so would you like to see round the rest of Max Gate? It's a small house so it shouldn't take long.'

She rose while at the same time indicating to Hardy and his companions that they should remain seated. Florence had not exaggerated. They climbed the narrow stairs on to a narrower landing off which was Hardy's study, a sepulchral cell with a high window from which only the sky could be seen from his desk – which was bare other than for a pen and a single sheet of vellum. Two sepia photographs of an indeterminate landscape were the only pictures. They climbed to the attic where the ceiling bore down on them as a spiritual crush. Florence indicated into a small bedroom with a cot bed and tiny coal fire. 'Emma's room,' was all she said as she descended the stairs.

It was with some relief that Julian saw her walk out of the hall and into the garden that was still dappled with spring sunshine, daffodils dipping in the breeze; out of the house with its sun-sucking gloom and its burden of disappointment. He could hear laughter in the dining room but felt a foreigner to its pleasures and a loyalty to Florence's unhappiness.

'Would you care to walk round the garden with me, Mr Belmore. It is such a beautiful spring day and Wessie will come with us.' The dog raced out of the front door in no doubt that he ruled the outside as clearly as he did the inside. Julian eyed him warily. She pointed up at the pine trees that surrounded the house. 'I would have loved to have cut some of these down, but Tom won't hear of it. Emma loved them apparently. I hate them; tombstones to bad memories that shade the house. They don't protect you from the wind but prevent the light getting in. Is that a fair distinction, Mr Belmore?'

'It is quite difficult to make a day like today gloomy – but they certainly make a good attempt. It takes a lot to make me downcast now, though. I'm alive. Many of my friends and contemporaries aren't. I feel I have a duty to enjoy every moment of every day. So many street corners have a man without a leg, sanity or sight – and I'm not one of them.'

Florence stopped with her hand to her mouth looking down at the moss at the base of a tree. She shook her head. 'Mr Belmore, you are right. So right. How could I be so self-pitying? That's the problem with living such an isolated existence. Everything becomes self-absorbed: too much time to dwell on slights and sadness. Thank you for making me see that. I may not have all that I want – but I did choose this; not as a naïve girl, but as a woman who knew the man she was marrying and how my life with him would be. Of course I can find fault with it: you have seen how we live. But I am married to a poet and novelist of greatness and I should appreciate that more. I think it was Napoleon who said that no man is great to his valet. Maybe that's it. I'm too close to the picture. I see the paint strokes but not the painting. Maybe it's about stepping back and allowing the whole to be enjoyed in its entirety. Thank you for making me see that.'

'If only good advice was always that easy.'

'Mostly it is that simple. But we often don't want to hear it and stay in the familiarity of our unhappiness, a sort of wallow that can be strangely comforting. We humans make our lives so difficult. Not like Wessie.' The dog was stalking a starling. 'His life is straightforward.'

'Biting people?'

Florence laughed. Her face was transformed and Julian saw what had attracted Hardy. 'Yes. He is defensive of us both and you were on the wrong side of him.' Julian bit his tongue. 'But I am sorry about your hand. Is it still bleeding?' She reached out for it

57

and gently removed the napkin that was its temporary bandage. The blood had coagulated around the marks of three teeth. She shook her head. 'We have tried to stop him doing this. You deal with dogs all the time. What would you recommend?'

Julian fought the instinct to tell her that sociopathic dogs normally had only one fate. 'You could keep him locked up while you have guests. Or keep him on a lead and warn your guests to mind him. If he is sound with you and Mr Hardy then it will only be the servants who have to watch themselves.'

'The servants adore him.'

'I'm sure they do,' he lied smoothly, 'but I rather think he bites them too – at least I suspect he does from the way that they were watching out for him. Perhaps a pen outside could be the answer.'

'Out of the question. He is too much of a friend to cast into prison.'

'Then I have no answers, I'm afraid. He is what he is – and unlikely to became a lapdog any time soon. The only problem is that you might find your friends become a bit more circumspect about visiting you if they get bitten every time. And it can't be fun being the postman here.'

She smiled again but this time with her habitual sadness. 'Maybe he is our way of keeping the world at bay. But I do hope that will not include you, Mr Belmore. I have bored you, I'm sure, and Wessie has bitten you, so I do hope it will not be a case of once bitten twice shy.'

'Mrs Hardy, a dog is not going to put me off. You and Mr Hardy have been kindness itself and I would much enjoy another visit.' He said this with a sincerity he did not feel and was relieved to see a satisfaction with his answer in her face. He was flattered by her warmth towards him but wary of further intimacy. He sensed that his own equilibrium and happiness could be sucked down in such an environment. He pondered this as they did a turn of the garden with only comments on the progress of spring and an occasional call to the murderous Wessex to accompany their progress.

They met the others in the hall on their way to the drawing room. Hardy was smiling broadly, clearly intoxicated by the company as well as the wine. His attempts to bring his wife into their jollity was met with a wan smile that changed the atmosphere in an instant. They sat in the drawing room making small talk that indicated that the time to leave had arrived. There were mutual protestations of friendship, but as they turned to wave to the Hardys standing in the shadow of Max Gate, his slight frame in the doorway and that of Florence half turned away from her husband, some of the melancholy of the house and its inhabitants enveloped the car. The *joie de vivre* of the outward journey had gone but with every mile from Max Gate some of the house's oppression lifted. Daphne broached the subject first.

'I did warn you. It's not a happy house.'

'But Mr Hardy was charming, Mrs Granville, wasn't he?' said Rose. 'I am so glad that I met him. Mrs Hardy was perfectly polite – but rather severe. You seemed to be getting on well with her, Julian?'

Julian was sitting opposite the two women, facing backwards with his chin cupped in his hand watching the countryside go by, only half listening. He could not wash Florence Hardy's disillusionment from his mind. Though he was no naïf, he rebelled from the bleakness implicit in her view of the world. What compromises had she made? Was the fact of her femininity an imprisonment? He looked surreptitiously at his two companions and wondered. Daphne Grenville would probably have agreed. Would Rose? Or her sister? Or Ariadne? So was it age – or marriage? Was the very thing that he had described – naively perhaps – to Florence as something liberating and enabling no more than a shackle and chain on the journey of life? Or was it something to do with the natures of both the older women that had allowed themselves to be dominated, subtly in one case and brutally in the other. He examined Rose through half-closed eyes and wondered. Her lustrous hair was contained by her hat and her complexion flushed by wine; the fine lines of her mouth and nose were delineated by a sun that was already low in the sky. Would he end up capturing and containing this spirit so that by the fact of ownership he would kill its essence? Maybe that was it. The women that he pitied had allowed themselves to be owned, to be in the thrall of their husbands. This was in his mind as he woke up from his reverie to Rose's question.

'Yes. Yes, I did get on well with Mrs Hardy. She's a kind person – but sad. You were right Mrs Granville; it's a melancholy house lived in by strangers to each other. Do you think it was always like that between them?'

She hesitated before replying, the facts of her own marriage weighing on her words. 'I don't know. Marriages change – not always for the better, I'm afraid. She was a secretary of sorts to him for many years – which has an intimacy of a different sort. I sense that he still treats her like that, as someone to organise and smooth his life. He is eighty after all; and a marriage of passion would be unusual at that age.'

'Is that what she wanted, do you think?' asked Rose.

'I doubt it. What woman would? But maybe it's better than nothing – better than being a spinster.'

'Is it? I wonder.' Rose looked out of the window at the line of downs framing the valley along which they were travelling. 'I'd rather risk loneliness and be free. I don't envy her life. Not one jot. Mr Hardy was charming – but selfish. He takes from her and gives little in return. Is that too harsh, Mrs Granville? It seems ungrateful speaking about them like this when they have both been so kind to us.'

'Too harsh?' She considered this for a moment. 'No, I don't think so. We can like them as individuals but see that the combination is not a happy one – well, one that suits him but makes her unhappy. It's a sad fact of life.'

'How does that happen?' asked Julian. 'How do two people – good people – combine to make such… emptiness? I don't think they were ever happy, Mrs Granville; not from what Mrs Hardy told me. I think it's a fear of loneliness. That fear trumps all else. It's not something that I really understand.'

'Nor I,' said Rose.

There was a silence filled only by the rattling of the windows against the corrugation of the road.

'I do,' said their companion.

7

The following day Julian received his call-up papers for the naval reserve. He would be required in Wick, the nearest town to John O'Groats, in a week's time. He knew its desolate railway station well: the railhead for the Orkneys and Scapa Flow, the wartime base of the biggest fleet the world had ever known. It now contained the Kaiser's fleet, interned under the terms of the Armistice negotiated five months before. He was to spend four months as a jailer of sorts – part of the squadron of ships enforcing an emasculated idleness on a German fleet that was known to be riven by boredom, hunger and mutiny. He had expected the call and so only shrugged with relief that he would be away out of the hunting season and in summer. He knew about winter in that bleak archipelago. It was where civilisation bled away into the Arctic.

As the news of his departure spread, he was at the receiving end of a flutter of invitations, one of which was from the Richmond family for lunch. He accepted another for cocktails with Lady Milborne, knowing that Ariadne would be there as a chaperone of sorts to blunt any advances from her mother that he suspected would follow a brace of Martinis.

His pleasure in seeing Rose, who opened the door of the rectory to him with a smile that showed the feeling was reciprocated, was blunted by the sight of Robert Granville spied through the drawing room door, leaning against the fireplace, and engaged in earnest conversation with Isobel and her father.

'Papa insisted. I'm sorry,' said Rose, sotto voce, as she took Julian's coat. 'I didn't want him – but Papa only sees him as the young cousin with whom he played as a boy. Isobel seems to be getting on with him though.' They heard laughter coming from within.

'Mrs Granville?'

'She has a cold. It's just us.'

'Right,' he said without enthusiasm, standing aside for Rose to lead the way into the drawing room. Granville looked him over with his customary coolness, raising his glass in salute.

'I hear you are departing northwards, Belmore. I'm glad it's you and not me.'

'Indeed,' replied Julian, 'a summer in Dorset would be preferable to one in the Orkneys.'

'I'm off as well; to Paris. Things are getting interesting at the Conference. President Wilson is back from the States and Lloyd George returns next week. I've been asked to attend by my department – which I have to say I am rather looking forward to. Spending too much time in the presence of that Welsh goat is the bit that I won't like. I'll just have to hold my nose and sup with that particular devil with a long spoon. I've asked Isobel if she would like to join me as one of a team of secretaries that we are taking with us. Someone with her brain and fluent French will be a real asset. Dr Richmond has agreed, I'm pleased to say. You don't look so happy, Rose?'

Rose's surprise was obvious. 'No. No. Quite happy for Isobel, of course. I just wasn't expecting it. Sorry.'

'I should have let your sister tell you. The apology is mine.'

'It'll be fascinating,' interjected Isobel. 'What an opportunity! And Papa, thank you for letting me go.'

Her father reached out and touched her cheek. 'Why are you thanking me, my dear? You are a grown-up and an independent woman who is going to have to make her way in the world.' He hesitated; he had touched a raw nerve. 'Cousin Robert will look after you in Paris. One hopes that the war has made it a slightly less permissive city than it was before.'

'We will be respectably ensconced in a hotel and Isobel will be with the other secretaries – and worked much too hard to be led into temptation. But I will take her to see the sights. Not to do so would be a crime.'

Julian lit a cigarette to hide the effect that the conversation was having on him. Every time he looked at Robert Granville the same scene played in his mind. He heard the screams, the wet slaps of bullets as they churned into human flesh and the drumming echo of multiple ricochets off the hull of the ship. The smell of cordite and blood rose in his throat. He felt the cold press of a pistol barrel rammed into the back of his head and the recoil of his own weapon as he fired.

'Are you alright, dear boy?' inquired his host.

'I'm fine, Dr Richmond, thank you. I've had a cold. Not the flu, don't worry.' He had seen the anxious glances around the room. 'If I could sit for a minute or two I will be my normal self – unfortunately for all of you.'

He sensed Granville looking at him and struggling to make a connection.

'You look like a man with shell shock, Belmore. Would you like me to run you back to your house in my motorcar? It would be no trouble.'

'Thank you, no. It's a head cold and if I sit for a bit it will do the trick. Please. It's nothing.'

The lunch that followed was simple. Wartime rationing was no longer in force but the luxuries taken for granted during the pre-war belle époque had yet to make it back into the shops. Rabbit stew and boiled potatoes with some beer for the men and cordial for the ladies was a feast in comparison to the hunger of only eighteen months before when Germany's unrestricted submarine warfare had nearly strangled the world's predominant naval power. After they had finished, Dr Richmond brought out a decanter of port as a signal for the ladies to leave the room. He followed them to arrange some domestic detail leaving Julian and Robert Granville alone. Granville looked at him carefully.

'I've been meaning to ask you, Belmore, have we met before? Before you took on the hounds after Christmas? You look familiar, very familiar – but I just can't place you. And that annoys me as I have a faculty for remembering faces. Help me. Please.'

'Maybe hunting in Ireland?'

'Never been. Hunting that is.'

'Could have been a chance encounter? A club in London? Could be anywhere.'

'No. No. You remembered me. I sensed it. It's my job to sense these things. It'll come to me in the middle of the night if I don't dwell on it.' He carried on staring at him with his finger stroking the rim of his glass. 'You're hiding something from me, Belmore. I don't know what or why – but you are.'

'Mr Granville, I'm not. Why should I? Why should we have met? And if we have, why should I not tell you?'

'Ireland? Something to do with Ireland?'

'I haven't lived there for nearly five years. The war saw to that.'

'But you're Irish.'

'Anglo-Irish. It's different.'

'As I know.'

'From personal experience?' Julian held Granville's eye.

'Indeed. It goes back some years. Before the war – and during it. I was involved in the Curragh Mutiny and in dealing with the Fenian traitors when they tried to stab us in the back in '16. I'll never forgive them for that.'

Julian sipped some port and was offered a cigarette – which he took while being fixed by the goshawk eye. The Curragh Mutiny had been a moment of near civil war when British army officers in Ireland had resigned en masse rather than suppress the Protestant Ulster Volunteers who were threatening violent opposition to Irish Home Rule. Only the outbreak of the Great War had put these other hostilities on hold.

'We have the greatest empire the world has ever seen,' continued Granville, 'and those pusillanimous scum in Westminster were about to hand its heart to a bunch of terrorists and traitors. How could they do that?' Julian looked up to see if this required an answer but saw it was rhetorical. 'What about you Belmore, were you involved?'

'No. Not me. These things passed us by in the west.'

'Hardly.'

'I was in the Navy.'

'That doesn't answer my question.'

'Politics are not my thing.'

'But patriotism is – I hope.'

64

'It's not that simple.'

'Really?' The colour of anger was rising in his face. 'Very simple I would have thought.'

'In Galway – with a Catholic mother and Protestant father – nothing is simple.'

'Meaning?'

'Blurred lines. Ambivalence. Irish or English is not clear-cut.'

'What about British?'

'I don't think an Irishman sees the nuances of that.'

'Even if it's part of Britain?'

'Geographically. But so is Scotland and they don't say they are British.'

'But they don't kill people in cold blood and claim they're patriots.'

'Yet.'

Granville slammed his palm on the table. A glass fell over. Neither man made a move to right it.

'Are you a bloody Fenian, Belmore? If you are, by God, you will be out of that house before the day is out. I promise you that.'

Julian felt the menace burning across the table. He heard the echo of similar words framed by the sounds of agony and bullets. He swallowed and attempted to compose himself before answering, forcing himself to look his adversary in the eye. He answered coolly with a strength he did not feel.

'Mr Granville, I have spent the last four years in His Majesty's Navy. My ship took a torpedo and a dud shell in the magazine. I nearly died when I was all but swept overboard in a January gale last year. I volunteered. I wasn't conscripted. If that's treasonous then I think the word needs changing.'

Granville visibly softened and nodded. 'I... I apologise, Belmore. I went too far. As you can observe, Ireland is something about which I have strong feelings. One of de Vallera's men nearly killed me in my car in Dublin. My oldest friend will never walk again after taking a bullet in the back in County Meath from a gunman hiding behind a cart as he posted a letter to his wife.'

'I understand. There was no offence taken.'

'But I do find your attitude… difficult. If you, as a man who has benefited so much from the Empire, cannot give it the loyalty it deserves then I am… concerned, I won't deny it.'

'You can see all the sides of an issue and not be a traitor.'

'Maybe.'

'And I'm not sure what the Empire has done for an Irishman like me except ask me to fight in its wars.'

'Ireland would still be a land of bogs and hovels without our input. You know that.'

'We'll have to disagree. My brand of patriotism won't let that one go.'

They were sitting in awkward silence as Dr Richmond returned. He was benevolence personified. 'Gentlemen, some port?' He frowned at the spilt glass that still lay on its side. 'I'll get Susan to clear that up.'

Julian leapt to his feet and reached out for the glass. 'No need, Dr Richmond, I'll take it next door.' He used his napkin to soak up the red stain. 'And thank you for the offer of more port – but any more would not be good for me with my cold… and I think the ladies might start getting annoyed if we leave them for too long. Mr Granville has been telling me how much he loves Ireland and the Irish…'

As he left the room he felt a weight lifting from him – but was conscious of a malign stare following him. He placed the glass on top of a tray and composed himself. There was female laughter from the drawing room. He looked around the hall. It was elegant in architecture but shabby in decoration. Evidence of genteel poverty was everywhere: the print outside the dining room was too small to cover the mark of the previous occupants' painting.

'Survived Cousin Robert?' He turned round to see Rose standing by the study door. 'Papa has some hunting books in here. Would you like to see them?' She was leaning against the doorframe with her arms crossed. Julian knew that if there were hunting books in the study they were not the point of the invitation. He could hear the sound of male voices in the dining room and Isobel and Davina next door. His chest tightened and he could feel his breathing shallow. Rose turned into the room and he followed. Within, and behind the half-opened door, she was leaning back against the empty bookshelf. The room was filled with packing cases. She looked at him and tilted her head slightly to the right.

'Will you kiss me?'

She held his stare with a sidewise one of her own and held out a hand. Julian moved towards her, conscious of his arousal pressing against his trousers. He took her hand, which she grasped with a strength that excited him further, pulling him towards her so that he could feel the outline of her breasts against his chest. She slipped the other hand from behind her back and grasped the back of his head, half lifting herself towards his lips against which she smudged her own. He felt the slither of her tongue lapping along his lips and the press of her hips against him.

'It's in the study, Robert.' The voice of her father was just outside the door.

In an instant she disengaged. When the vicar walked in he saw only his daughter reaching deep into one of the boxes.

'Papa, I'm trying to find *Bleak House* for Julian. I can't believe he hasn't read it – especially when he claims to be so keen on Dickens.'

'The boxes were packed directly from the shelf on which they were sitting. I know the whereabouts of the book I want for Cousin Robert. Would you mind opening that one there for me, dear boy?'

When the vicar finally departed with his mission accomplished and they could hear his voice emanating from the dining room once more, Rose spoke. 'That was close. How dull. I've only been kissed – properly – once before. This is much better.' Her voice sank to a whisper. 'Can we do it again?'

'Yes. But not now.'

'Why not? I can hear the girls in the drawing room and we know where Papa is.'

'What about the maid?'

'Why should she come in here? Come on. It's so difficult to get an opportunity. And don't worry, just because you've kissed me doesn't mean that I'm taking it as a proposal. I just want to kiss you. But maybe you don't want me to?'

'I could think of nothing nicer. But maybe somewhere… more private.'

She stepped closer to him and put her finger on his lips. Her smell, allied with the press on his lips aroused him instantly once again. He cupped her face between his hands and drew it towards him. They kissed again, tentatively at first – and then deeply, tongues tip-to-tip and then circling each other with fierce sensuality.

'That wasn't so bad was it,' she said, with her face still framed by his hands. 'I'd like to do that all afternoon.'

'But we can't. Let's go and join your sisters – and hope they haven't guessed what we've been up to.'

'Such a terrible crime! The shame!' She pulled apart from him laughing. 'You might have to wait a bit though – with that.' She pointed at the protrusion in his trousers. 'Don't worry, I'll keep the hounds at bay while you sort yourself out.' Julian felt himself reddening with embarrassment. 'I'd have been insulted if you weren't as excited as I am. It just shows a bit more with you. We had a French governess who told us – well, she certainly told me – all about these things. I didn't have a mother to do it – but I suspect that Madame Gerard had had a bit more experience than Mummy in that department. It was a lot more interesting than Latin.' She kissed him lightly on the lips. 'To be continued, I hope.'

He could hear Isobel talking about France as he entered the drawing room. Rose was poking the fire and glanced at him with a conspiratorial smile.

'Mr Belmore, have you been to France?' Davina's firm and deep voice caught him by surprise again.

'Only once; to Paris, before the war – in 1910, I think. Yes, it must have been then because they were mourning our king – a rather unusual activity for the French. And please, if I may call you by your Christian names, then I must insist that you call me by mine.'

'It's where Isobel is going to negotiate the peace.'

'Hardly, Dav,' replied Isobel, 'I will be typing letters and doing some translation.' There were certain moments when the light

68

caught her, or she held her head at a particular angle, that she became beautiful. This was one of them, Julian thought. 'I may get to see President Wilson or Monsieur Clemenceau across a room – but that will be it. Better than church on Sunday here anyway. And who knows who I will meet – the world is there at the moment.'

'Even the Germans?' enquired Davina.

'Even the Germans,' replied Isobel, 'though I hope I won't have to meet any. What would I say to them?'

'If anything, you may want to feel sorry for them,' said Julian. 'Being a German diplomat must be the lowest circle of hell. Everyone is allowed to hate them and treat them as pariahs.'

'But they deserve it.'

'Germany maybe; the poor diplomats, not really. They're just trying to play a hand that is worse than awful in a rigged game.'

'Rigged?'

'By the British and the French. President Wilson is, by all accounts, a high-minded man but out of his depth with Lloyd George and Clemenceau; a sheep in a shark tank as someone rather unkindly said. Wilson is trying to set up a new world order where there is no chance of another dreadful war. The other two are just trying to get as much as they can from Germany and to make sure she is so weak that she can't invade anyone for a very long time. Not very high-minded or far-sighted – but that's the reality.'

'How do you know all this, Julian?' Rose addressed this to the fire that she was prodding.

'I have a cousin in the Foreign Office. He's been there from the first and I had dinner with him a couple of weeks ago. It's not been an edifying process from what he told me – but these things probably never are.'

'Isobel will be able to make it alright.' Davina had been listening intently. 'She's very intelligent. Did you know she went to Cambridge? People who go to Cambridge are very important and Mr Lloyd George will have to listen to her. I shall write to him at No 10 Downing Street and tell him about you, Isobel. It's important that he knows you are there to help.' She paused. 'I am so proud of you, Isobel.'

'Thank you Dav, you are sweet. Cousin Robert will introduce me to the important people, I'm sure.' She smiled at her sister before returning to Julian.

'Mr Belmore... Julian, I'm sorry... it can't really be as bad as you say. After everything; after all that terrible suffering. It can't happen ever again – surely? I can't bear to think that Richard died for things to stay the same. How can that happen?'

'All too easily. That is what President Wilson thinks and I'm sure sincerely wants. Probably Lloyd George too – but he also needs to keep Clemenceau sweet. If some long-term, high-minded concept has to be sacrificed on that altar, then it would appear that is what he will do.'

'Are you sure, Julian?' Rose was now focused on him rather than the fire. 'Isn't that just what Papa, Cousin James and Cousin Robert would say? They all hate Mr Lloyd George and have hated him for years. I'm sure a Liberal wouldn't say that.'

'My cousin is a Liberal – and most Liberals distrust him too. He's split their party after all. Lloyd George is a pragmatist, not an idealist. No one actually knows how it will all end as there are still months of negotiations until a treaty is signed. But if Clemenceau has allied himself with Lloyd George then that's a powerful force.'

'But Monsieur Clemenceau is a radical isn't he?' asked Isobel.

'Yes – but a Frenchman first. His view of the world – and this is again what my cousin reports, as I know as much as you do from newspaper reports – is that Clemenceau sees his duty as being to make France as strong as possible and Germany as weak as he can for as long as possible – until the next time.'

'Next time? Surely there can never be a next time?' Isobel spoke for the others.

Julian shrugged. 'I hope so. We all hope so. But human nature being what it is, experience seems to suggest that hope is not the way to bet. You'll be able to report back to us what you find when you're there. I hope my cousin is wrong – but he's a brilliant diplomat and has been involved at the highest level. And, as I said, he is a Liberal – though I am sure that he would not entirely trust Mr Lloyd George. Nobody does.'

'It's too depressing,' said Isobel, 'if that really is the case. I wonder what Cousin Robert thinks.' On cue they heard the dining room door open and the sound of male voices in the hall. A billow of cigar smoke heralded their entrance.

'Ah, there you are, Belmore.' Robert Granville's face was flushed. 'It was a shame you couldn't have heard what Cousin Charles had to say about his time in Ireland. I must warn you, ladies, that we have a Fenian in our midst.'

Julian hesitated before answering. He kept a smile on his face and levity in his voice. 'I fear that Mr Granville thinks that I'm a terrorist who is about to blow you all up; all because I don't believe that every Irish man and woman wants to be ruled by England forever. I had hoped that that wasn't too revolutionary a thought.'

'Come Robert,' said the vicar, 'you can't hold patriotism against anyone, surely? There's a world of difference between that and picking up a gun. Even more difficult when someone like young Belmore here has lived there most of his life. You make it sound as if he had taken part in the Easter Rising.'

'Thank you Dr Richmond,' Julian replied, 'I know that Mr Granville feels strongly about Ireland – understandably in the circumstances as I had heard something about the work that he did in Dublin at that time.' Though he was talking to the vicar, he could see Granville stiffening in his peripheral vision. 'He's known in Ireland for his services to the crown.' He knew this was not prudent, but continued. 'He is a patriot too, and he has quite a name for it over the water. At least that is what I heard; but us country boys out in the west only get the rumours and gossip that percolate down from the big city.'

'Did you meet Mr de Vallera?' asked Davina.

'Now, now,' Dr Richmond held up his hand, 'you are putting Cousin Robert in a difficult position. His work is secret and you shouldn't be asking him things like this.'

Granville shook his head portentously. 'Thank you, Charles. One doesn't want to appear churlish but, as Isobel will discover, when we are in France together we will have to be discreet. We aren't spies or anything that dramatic – but indiscretion can cost lives. Something that doesn't seem important can blow up into something that is – so we just keep quiet and treat everything that we do as potentially dangerous. It sounds melodramatic but I hope you can see that it's just caution.'

'Will Isobel be in danger?' There was concern in Davina's question.

'Goodness no! We will be in Paris, not Dublin. Europe is at peace and every world leader is there with security at the highest level – and France is a civilised country – unlike Ireland.'

There was a brittle silence in the room. Julian could feel the eyes of the sisters on him. He replied with a smile. 'I agree with Mr Granville. France is a civilised country – but a few million people have just died stopping an uncivilised and aggressive country invading it. Some would see certain parallels there... but I don't.'

Granville blinked and gave a snort. 'Touché, Belmore. Touché. I asked for that.' He smiled. 'I'm afraid I do get carried away on the subject of Ireland. We just have a different perspective, don't we?'

'We are both patriots, Mr Granville. Shall we leave it at that?'

The older man waved his cigar in magnanimity.

'When do we leave for Paris, Cousin Robert?' Isobel was pacing up and down by the window.

'I leave tomorrow, I'm afraid. You could come later if you would find that more convenient.'

'No. No, that would be perfect. I must pack. Will I need evening dress? Of course I will. Dav, will you help me? Will you excuse me? Cousin Robert, Julian?'

Both men stood as she left the room.

'If only I made all the women in my life that happy,' Granville nodded at Rose. 'Maybe you could come and join your sister, Rose? A visit anyway?'

Rose was prodding the fire again, away on a train of other thoughts. She started, then focused. 'Yes. Maybe. That could be... very nice. Thank you. But I have to look after Papa and Davina.'

'I'm sure they could spare you for a week or two. Charles?'

'Yes. Of course, Robert. But two girls really might be too much work for you.'

'Work? I hardly think I would describe either of them as work. They would be a pleasure, both of them.' There was something mildly sinister in the way he said the last phrase that had Julian and Rose glancing at each other. 'They will both be very welcome, Charles.' Granville tapped the ash off the end of his cigar into the fire. 'I too need to get myself ready for tomorrow; so if you will excuse me, I'll go home now. Please tell Isobel that my motorcar will pick her up at ten sharp tomorrow morning. Thank you, Charles – and you too Rose. Good day, Belmore. And good luck up north.'

Dr Richmond and Davina showed him out leaving Rose and Julian alone. Rose seemed preoccupied.

'Are you worried?' asked Julian.

'No. Well yes, I am. I'm not sure why, but I am. I know he's a cousin – but I just don't like him and Isobel for all her brains is a trusting soul. And I don't trust him. Do you?'

Julian hesitated. It was the hand that fed. He had a rising urge to tell her – but held it in check. 'He doesn't like me and thinks I'm a Republican gunman. No, I don't like him either. Trust? Look, he's a cousin and he's a gentleman – though I'm not sure gentle is one of his outstanding qualities. He will be protective of her, I'm sure.'

'Should I go out too?'

'Do you want to?'

'Go to Paris? Of course. To go with him; to be beholden to him; no, I don't.'

'Doesn't that answer your question?'

'Partially. I want to go to Paris and I ought to keep an eye on Isobel. But she's well able to look after herself and she'll be ensconced in some girl's school dormitory. No danger there.'

'I'm sure you're right.'

'You don't sound very convinced.'

'I feel that I should be going.'

'You can't. You're off to the far end of Scotland. And anyway I don't think you and Cousin Robert should be in the same room as each other for too long.'

'Is it that obvious?'

'You know it is.'

73

'If I tell you something – something about him; something about the war; would you be able to keep it to yourself?'

'Is it about why he doesn't like you?'

'That's about Ireland. He just doesn't like the Irish.'

'So what is it?'

'We have met before. But he doesn't remember it. It was at Gallipoli.'

'Where my brother Richard died!'

'I know. Which is one of the reasons I haven't told you before. Actually I haven't told anyone. Just one question. Where was your brother killed?'

'Sulva Bay.'

'I'm glad about that; that it wasn't Cape Hellas.' He hesitated. 'Do you remember what happened? At the beginning?'

'The navy tried to attack the Dardanelles by sea?'

'It was after that – a good thing for me as three battleships were sunk in one day in February. This was later, in April, when they'd decided that the way forward was to take the Gallipoli peninsula by land rather than risk more ships in the minefields in the narrows. My cruiser had been sent as reinforcement and I was seconded to a troopship called *The River Clyde*. It had been adapted as a landing craft by cutting two ports either side of the bow so that troops could disembark on to gangways that led on to pontoons – and then on to the beach. I was the acting third officer of the ship and had to organise the troops on the lower deck so they made it out of the ship in some sort of order. There was an Irish regiment on board and I knew one of the officers.'

'Why didn't you tell me you had been at Gallipoli?' asked Rose.

He observed her quietly, weighing up his words. 'You've probably noticed by now that anyone who has actually seen people dying or has killed someone, doesn't want to... talk about it; especially to someone who wasn't there. How can they have any idea of what it's like; how it's so much more horrible than anyone can ever describe? It was my business. For you it could only bring... disgust. Why would I, or anyone, want to inflict that on anyone when it wasn't necessary?'

'So why now?'

'Because of your cousin. About what was said between him and me in the dining room. And Isobel and France. I think he's going to remember our meeting.'

Rose looked at him. 'Will that make a difference.'

'I think so.' He hesitated. 'Shall I continue?'

She nodded.

'It was at Cape Hellas which is the tip of the Gallipoli peninsula, just after dawn. There were a number of landings going on down the peninsula along the Aegean side, particularly at Anzac Cove, though that was some way away, twelve miles or more. We were given a beach called Sedd-el-Bahr which had a small ruined fortress looking over it on the eastern side of Cape Hellas. There was a bombardment first. I can't remember what the battleship was called but it was huge and when all its guns were in action against the beach you simply couldn't believe anything could live through it. It looked like an eruption from where I was – on the bridge at the time. When it stopped, we all scanned the beach and the torn barbed wire through our binoculars. Just smoke and dust. We all had the same thought: they must all be dead. The captain gave slow-ahead and we crept forward. The ship was surrounded by lighters and launches made fast to its sides, all of them packed with soldiers. The idea was to beach the ship and then use the boats to make a pontoon to the shore. Once that was in place, the soldiers in the lighters would get ashore and those in the ship itself would file out of the two holes cut near the bow, make their way along a walkway attached to the side of the ship, on to the pontoon and finally to the beach. There was something about the battleship sitting just offshore that made it seem safe: if anyone let off even a firecracker on the beach all it would take was a broadside. And it was so quiet. There was smoke and dust – but no firing. With about half-a-mile to go, I left the bridge and went down to my action station on the lower deck next to the starboard hole in the bow. I'd left the men sitting around smoking, with some of them playing cards. When I returned they were mostly on their feet and checking their equipment. I spoke quietly to them as the sound echoed within the steel hull. I told them that we had about ten minutes before disembarkation and that it seemed as if any defences had been pounded to bits by the battleship. There was a visible relief and some of them began talking amongst themselves. Poor bastards.'

Julian looked up and towards the window. He reached over to the glass of port on the side table and took a sip – and then poured the rest down his throat. He stared at Rose.

'Are you sure you want to hear this?'

She nodded. He looked out of the window again.

'We felt a lurch as the ship grounded on the beach and the scraping of the lighters against the hull as the momentum took them forward and they were pulled back by the lashings holding them in place. There was an electric light inside the hull, but the daylight through the hole in the side made it difficult to make out individual faces, only the glow of cigarettes. The beach looked a long way off. We could hear, but not see, the sailors casting off their boats in order to create the pontoon. How long that went on, I'm not really sure. Minutes? The leading soldiers were in the open port ready to rush along the gangway on the order. I thought it would be better if they were further along so that there wasn't a crush by the steps on to the lighters, so I indicated to the officer at the front that he should lead the men forward. They filed out, still with no sound from the shore but shouts from the sailors. I found out afterwards that the current was making it difficult to get the lighters swung into position. Then it started. I wasn't sure what it was at first as the noise of bullets from machine guns and rifles when they are being fired at you sound very different from when you are doing the firing. The main noise was the sound of bullets striking the hull. The other, like wet slaps, was of bullets hitting flesh. And screams. I couldn't see down the length of the gangway from where I was; only the bit nearest me, nearest the port, where one man was knocked backwards and propped up by the guardrails with the top of his head missing. Another was staggering like a drunk, swaying, when a bullet punched him in the throat, laying him horizontal on the gangway, bubbling blood from his wound.

Just inside the port, next to me, a bareheaded man was kneeling with his head drooping forward. All this happened so fast. And I didn't know what to do. It seemed as if no one could possibly survive outside that port. Two men fell back into the hull – one with a stump where his hand should have been and the other with an arm hanging by gristle from his shoulder.'

Julian stopped. He squeezed his top lip between his thumb and forefinger while staring at his shoes. He felt pressure on his hand.

'None of us – certainly not me, and none of the soldiers – had ever seen anything like this. It was early on in the war and the Somme and all the other slaughters were in the future. It was beyond shocking. It was the officers' job to lead the men out so I was relatively safe – though it felt anything but with the ricochets hitting the bulkheads and spent bullets spattering around us. One hit me in the face – here.' He pointed to the scar that zigzagged from his lip to just under his eye.

'It felt like being hit in the face by a cricket ball. It shook me, but strangely there was no pain other than a feeling of burning. I must have looked a mess though as a sailor tried to get me to go to the casualty station. The lieutenant leading the second platoon pushed me out of the way and ran out shouting to his men to follow. They disappeared out of sight into that firehose of bullets. I couldn't see what happened to him but another man was hit and fell over the top of the dead soldier kneeling just inside the port. I knew I had to clear the way out but couldn't believe that it was possible to survive if I left the shelter of the hull. But I had to.

'I was blinded by the sudden sun and made to heave the two bodies over the side but their packs and the rope guard-rails made it difficult. I succeeded with one but the other got caught around a stanchion. I left him there as he was no longer blocking the gangway. I looked towards the shore and all I could see were bodies – or wounded – piled up on the lighters. Some had made it nearly as far as the shore but were now pinned down. I ran back inside. The next section of men was waiting. I've never seen such terror. The officer blew his whistle and waved his pistol towards the gangway. Almost the instant he was framed by the port he was hit in the face and we were spattered by blood, bone and teeth. The men remained cowed where they were.

'Another officer came from behind. He shouted at them to follow him and ran on to the gangway and out of sight. Still they didn't move. The noise of firing slackened. The Turks must have killed everyone. From the darkness of the hull appeared another officer – more senior. He stood framed in the port so that I could hardly see his face against the glare. He was carrying a pistol which he pointed at the men crouched on the deck. He shouted at them but they didn't move. His voice dropped but he was still shouting. "If you don't move, I'll shoot you." He aimed his pistol at the soldier at the front of the line. I remember he wasn't wearing a cap; this was before steel helmets were the norm. "You. Get going." The man just stood there, his eyes staring in fear.'

Julian paused. 'The noise of the pistol going off was shocking; deafening in that confined space. The soldier dropped like a poleaxed horse. He waved the pistol at the others. "The rest of you – out! And anyone coming back through there will be shot by me. Do I make myself clear? The enemy are on the beach and they might miss, but I won't. Now go!" He grabbed the new leading man and man-handled him towards the port. The soldier started moving and immediately the others followed, stumbling over the bodies on the gangway. It went quieter. The odd single shot. You could hear the sound of the gangway hitting the side of the hull as it swung with the footfalls. The officer bent down and picked up the pistol of the man who had been shot in the face and came up to me. The soldiers were filing past on to the gangway. He handed me the pistol. "You. If any man comes back through there, you'll shoot him. Understand?" I must have looked shell-shocked. He grabbed me by the shoulder and pushed me towards the port so that I was standing between him and the daylight. I felt the barrel of his pistol against the back of my head.'

'"If you don't," and his mouth was just behind my ear, "I'll shoot you."'

'It was strangely quiet, I remember. There was firing, but only desultory. The noise of boots on the deck and gangway outside was louder. The soldiers were now moving past quite fast. Then it started again. If you were a Turk on the shore it would have been like one of those fairground attractions where you shoot at pop-up figures that appear randomly in windows and doors. Easier really; there were only two doors and the targets just kept coming and were exposed the whole way along the gangway and on to the lighters where they were still without any cover, but they could at least crouch or lie down behind the piles of bodies.

'The file of men hesitated. You could sense that they were completely blocked, held on the gangway by the carnage up ahead, exposed to the firing from the shore. The first man stumbled back in and right next to my ear a pistol went off and the man staggered back into the soldier behind him who was now being pressed by men pushing behind him to get back into the shelter of the ship. I felt the gun in the back of my neck again.

'"Shoot him – or I'll shoot you."

'He meant it. I'd seen what he'd already done. The man on the gangway was about five feet away. He only had one tooth and I could see the sweat on his face. I aimed at him and pulled the trigger. Was I aiming to kill him or wound him? I don't know; but I saw a hole appear above his breastbone and he collapsed. But the press was too much. Even if they had wanted to get on to the gangway, they couldn't. It was a heap of panicked men with only one thought, to get back into the ship and away from the mayhem into which they had been funnelled. Even he could see that it was hopeless. It's one thing to get men to mount a trench when they have their mates around them. This was single file into certain death, on to gangways that were already choked with corpses. Even if you were willing, it would be impossible to make it to the beach. Suddenly, again, the firing died down to single shots.

'What was there left to fire at? I edged to the port and, keeping cover, I looked along the edge of the hull and on to the lighters below. The sea, that beautiful Aegean turquoise water, was red with blood. Men were piled up on the decks, some screaming, others twitching, but most dead. One or two, still alive and unwounded used the dead – and probably the wounded – like sandbags to give them cover as they kept up rifle fire towards the Turkish positions that were given away by muzzle flashes and smoke. A handful were ashore but pinned down behind a sand dune. How they were still alive was a miracle.'

There was silence between them. He was not looking at Rose but out of the window. The drumming of a spring shower on the window was the only sound.

Rose spoke. 'The man with the pistol was Cousin Robert?'

Julian nodded. 'I didn't see him again as I was taken off to the casualty station and when I'd been stitched up I was posted back to my original ship. I saw myself in a mirror before they cleaned me up. It was a mess so I'm not surprised he hasn't recognised me.'

He pursed his lips and hesitated. 'But I recognised him. Hard to forget. It's also hard to forget the man I killed. Ironic isn't it? The only man I've ever killed was on my side. Not a Turk nor a German – but an Irishman. Not even an Englishman. After that conversation I had with your cousin today, he would probably say "good riddance". Bastard!'

The last word was said with more emotion than Rose had ever heard from him before. When she looked at him in surprise she saw a pair of tears rolling down his face. One caught on the indentation of his scar and was diverted as a rivulet over the bow of his upper lip. He made no attempt to wipe it away.

'That bastard made me a murderer.'

8

Paris, March 1919

The British delegation to the Peace Conference had taken over the Hôtel Majestic, not far from the Quay d'Orsay where the daily rounds of negotiation took place between the victors. Its lobby, a pre-war favourite of Francophile Brazilian women, was decorated with onyx and smelt of jasmine. Isobel was surprised by the security: two young officers wearing Guards' regimental flashes carefully checked their bona fides before allowing them in. A murmur of industry echoed amongst the palms of the atrium.

In front of Isobel and Robert Granville, as they waited their turn at the reception desk, was a short man in an army uniform wearing Arab headdress. He clicked worry beads between his fingers and stared at the skylight three stories up, as if making a study of the towering cumulous above. Others chatted to their companions or smoked, but he seemed content and settled with himself in his own world. Robert Granville leant close to Isobel's ear.

'Lawrence. He was with Allenby in the Middle East, stirring up the tribes in Arabia against the Turk. I'd heard that he was parading around looking like something out of a music hall. I don't know why he's allowed to dress like that. He seems to have gone native and forgotten who's shilling he's taken. Interesting man though.'

A man dressed in a morning coat and wing collar halted in recognition.

'My dear Granville, how good to have you here. I was told you were arriving today. And you must be Isobel Richmond. I met your father once at the Atheneum. How is he?' Isobel began to reply. 'Good, good. I am glad; we need all the help we can get at the moment. We seem to be fighting on more fronts than in any war. The ones that really concern us are bad enough without the

Poles, Greeks, and the flotsam left by the Ottoman all over the Near East.'

He stopped as the vitreous blue eyes of Lawrence settled on him. 'I mean they are obviously all important... but it is difficult to keep one's eye on the ball with so much vying for your attention. I'm exhausted – as is almost everyone here. Oh, I am sorry, my dear; my name's Nicolson; Foreign Office for my sins. I should have joined the Exchequer and had a quiet life of interdepartmental infighting and long weekends.'

He smiled a rueful grin that made him appear only a boy. 'Enough of that. All rubbish of course. I must keep reminding myself that we're making history here. It's just difficult to remember that when you've gone ten rounds with some ragamuffin from Serbia over the same point for the fifth time. That's diplomacy for you, I suppose. How's your French, Miss Richmond?' He quoted a stanza from Verlaine and waited for her reply. She blushed as she answered with its matching refrain. 'Well, well, a scholar as well as a linguist. Very useful. Our erstwhile allies will appreciate that.' He caught her surprised look. 'Erstwhile? I'm being ironic of course – but only a little.'

He stepped slightly closer and dropped his voice. 'You'll find out soon enough that the Germans are not our enemy here. They will just have to chew whatever bitter pill we decide to force down their throats. They have no power. No. The battle here is with our allies: with the Americans who want to give every ethnic handful their own state and the French who seem to be determined to feed on the last toenail of the German corpse. The Greeks are my particular cross at the moment – though Venizelos is more than charming.' He hesitated. 'Dinner? Not here, of course. For some reason it was decided to bring English cooks to Paris; a dark lining brought to a silver cloud, so to speak. Whose idea was that, do you think? It has to be some idiot in the security services.'

He raised an eyebrow. 'How useful to have you here, Granville. With your influence, you might save the British Empire from its own food. You would certainly have the eternal gratitude of the entire British delegation.' He waved to another man of the same age who was beckoning him from across the lobby. 'I have to go. Another Serbian rock laid across the track, I suspect. Dinner in a week or two? I'll send a message to confirm.'

They watched him sidestep his way across the room, weaving through the crowd.

'Nice chap. And intelligent too. Married to Lord Sackville's daughter – who writes, I believe. Now let's find your room and my office. I can see we're going to be busy.'

They were directed out of the main door and down a side street to an annex at the back, into the administrative offices of the hotel where all refinement and glamour was absent. After ten minutes of waiting, a woman strode into the room dressed in black with hair tied in a bun. After a cursory greeting, she ignored Robert Granville.

'Miss Richmond, I am Miss Radcliff and I'll show you to your room – which you will be sharing with two other young ladies. We're packed in like sardines, I'm afraid – but both your companions are educated and well brought up. Mr Granville will have a rather better room I expect.' She gave Granville a look. 'We are working from seven in the morning until seven at night at the moment and you will be transcribing memoranda both ways between French and English. We normally have Sundays off – but not always. It goes without saying that all our work is top secret and the assumption is that we are still at war and the Official Secrets Act applies. Do I make myself clear?'

There could have been no misunderstanding. Isobel nodded.

'You will eat with the other girls; and you must ask my permission if you wish to go out. Please say goodbye now and I will show you to your room.'

She was heading towards the door before she had finished.

'Well, my dear, you'd better be off. I will let you settle in tomorrow and get in touch about our dinner with young Nicolson. Au revoir!'

She hesitated before leaning over to kiss him on the cheek and almost ran after Miss Radcliff who was already half way up the stairs that she climbed two at a time. Isobel's room was in the attic and had three beds in a space barely enough for two.

'Miss Harper and Miss Dunlop are your roommates. Miss Dunlop is hard working and sensible. I'm less certain about Miss Harper. Those deplorable Pankhurst women have turned her head, I fear. I will have a porter bring your trunk and you can unpack in time to join the others for lunch; in the servants' hall I'm afraid: the dining room is reserved for officers and diplomats.'

She was gone without waiting for a reply. Isobel looked around her new home for clues about her companions. There were photographs by each bed. One was of a couple in their forties, unsmiling and framed by palms. She was sitting and he had one hand on the back of her chair, the other awkwardly by his side. By the other bed was an image of two men, in uniform with their arms around each other's shoulders, smiling. Brothers? They did not look alike but there was a familiar intimacy. Whose was whose? There was a crucifix above the bed with the formal couple and a sachet of lavender next to the young men. The room was devoid of other clues. She lay on her bed and closed her eyes for a moment. She was glad to be here – away from Dorset, her sisters and the responsibly for her father and also, now the war was over, from the tedium and back-breaking work that she had undertaken as a Land Girl.

She had come down from Cambridge when the war was three years old without regret: Cambridge was a shadow of itself. At the beginning of her second year it seemed as if the entire undergraduate population had presented itself at the recruiting station – too many never to be seen again. The younger dons and college staff went with them, leaving a place synonymous with youth repopulated with the retired – and latterly the wounded who were unable to fight further. Inevitably this aging of the population and loss of so many young men left a shroud of melancholy over the city and much of its academic life, with the result that Isobel's finals had been a relief. She opted for agriculture only because the alternative, a factory production line, had little appeal.

The work had been monotonous and exhausting, but she enjoyed its physicality, the beauty of the Northamptonshire countryside and the company of the disparate women with whom she was thrown. On the debit side she found the paucity of educated conversation trying and the crude advances of the older men both tedious and sometimes frightening – particularly when fuelled by alcohol. After one harvest festival, a drunk had ambushed her on her way home and she only got away when he attempted to pull his trousers down and ended up tripping himself up. It was the only time she had seen an erect penis which, in the circumstances, had seemed a weapon of violence.

When she had unpacked, she navigated her way to the dining room by sound; the clink of china and women's voices carried to the top of the stairs. She stood by the door looking out over a sea of heads, not knowing where to sit or what to do. A woman stood up and waved to her – beckoning across the room. Isobel picked her way around the tables until she was close enough to talk. She had dark hair pinned up, a rounded, freckled face and a slightly cleft chin.

'I'm Emma. You must be Isobel.'

There was something about her manner that told Isobel that Emma must be the Miss Harper so disapproved of by Miss Radcliff. They sat opposite each other and exchanged information about journeys, beds and food.

'Don't worry about Miss Radcliff,' she replied in answer to Isobel's nervous enquiry, 'she's a man in a dress – but not nearly as bad as she pretends to be, especially if you make her laugh. But her sense of humour doesn't extend to work; so choose your moment. But that's quite enough about her. Why are you here?'

She listened well, with her chin resting on her hands and periodic nods of her head. She seemed slightly older than the rest of the women in the room and there was a tiredness around the corners of her eyes that contrasted with the vivacity of her manner.

'Which is Miss Dunlop?' asked Isobel when she had finished the account of the odyssey that had taken her from Cambridge to Paris.

'Gillian? Over there. Next to the pillar.' She pointed to a woman in black reading by herself. She had the first finger of one hand on her lips and the first of the other tracing the print of her book. Her hair, cut fashionably short, contrasted with her dress – cut unfashionably long. 'She doesn't talk much – but it's generally worth listening to when she does. She doesn't work with us and won't tell us anything about what she's up to. Codes probably. Something secret. Her father was killed last year. Too old to fight – but blown up in the armaments factory where he worked.' Isobel remembered the photograph of the couple framed by palms. 'What about you? Did you lose anyone?'

Isobel told her about her brother and her mother. 'And you?' she asked in return.

She hesitated and her smile fell away. 'No. Nobody. My brothers are younger and the eldest only got called up in '17 and sent to Palestine. Lucky. Papa was conscripted in '16 but was in army supply and never got sent to the front.' Her gaze had fallen on to the plate in front of her. 'It also meant that I haven't had to get God, like poor Gillian. That's a book of psalms she's reading. I prefer the *Tatler* myself.' She looked up at Isobel with a glance that was laying down some sort of marker. 'Sorry, I shouldn't say that to a parson's daughter, should I?'

It was Isobel's turn to smile. '*Tatler* every time. Or *The Sketch*. Or the *Suffragette*. Though I might not tell Miss Radcliff that. She thinks you're going to be a bad influence on me – which I hope you will be, by the way.'

They shared a conspiratorial moment of silence as they both looked around the room.

'Are there many others here?'

'Suffragettes? All of them,' said Emma, 'at least I hope so. If we're good enough to work here, we should be good enough to vote – you'd have thought anyway.'

'You've got the vote.' Both women started at the sound of Miss Radcliff's voice behind them. 'You got it before the war.'

There was a silence where Isobel could hear every scrape of cutlery on china. Her heart sank at the prospect of stepping off on quite such a wrong foot.

'Actually Miss Radcliff, you got the vote then,' said Emma, 'we didn't. We'll have to wait until we're thirty; or we are married; or become householders. Is that fair?'

'Rome wasn't built in a day.'

'It wasn't. It was built two thousand years ago and we're still waiting for something Australian women have had for twenty years.'

Isobel was aware that the background noise in the room was reducing to whispers and individual clinks. Miss Radcliff was staring at Emma. When she replied the silence was total.

'Of course you should have the vote. It's a disgrace that you haven't. But it's better to get it by showing that we are worthy of it rather than breaking windows or throwing ourselves under the King's horse. I am aware, Miss Harper, that you think my views are antediluvian, but we have all seen where violence leads. We are on the same side, by the way – but we'll have to differ on how we resolve it. Now, Miss Harper, I think Miss Richmond here needs to have some lunch, don't you?'

There was a collective outing of breath and a resumption of conversation as Miss Radcliff marched towards the door with her customary vigour.

'I told you her bark's a lot worse than her bite.'

'I wouldn't have had the nerve to take her on like that.'

'But it was fun, wasn't it?'

'Yes. I suppose it was.'

'I like to push things. See how far I can go. If you step back fast enough when you've overdone things, you normally get away with it.'

'And when you don't?'

Emma shrugged. 'Deal with it, I suppose. But don't worry; I'm not a high stakes gambler. I just like tweaking some tails. Or sticking pins into pomposity. Doesn't make me very popular with the likes of Miss Radcliff – but I can live with that.'

'Miss Richmond?' Isobel turned to find Gillian Dunlop standing behind her. 'Hello, I'm Gillian Dunlop.' She held out her hand formally and though she was smiling it was a more guarded expression than the same in Emma Harper. 'I see you've already met Emma and Miss Radcliff. You've certainly had a baptism of fire.'

Isobel stood to shake her hand. 'It was a bit more… interesting than I was expecting in my first hour – but I did come here for some excitement so I can't really complain? Will you join us?'

'Thank you, but no. I've already eaten and my hours are slightly different from the other girls so I have to get back to my room at the Hôtel Astoria before two.' The Astoria was the other of the two hotels occupied by the British legation. 'We'll have plenty of time to talk tonight, I hope. I'm glad you're with us even though it will be a bit of a squash. I was at Girton too – but we missed each other by a year. Plenty to talk about later.'

She gave a half wave as she turned to go. Unlike Emma, she occupied the space she inhabited lightly.

'Let's get you fed and watered.' Emma stood up and waved at a waitress. 'Then I'll show you the place where, after a while, you'll wish you were a galley slave instead. At least galley slaves got a chance to see the world – even if they were chained to an oar.'

*   *   *

Emma's description was apt. In a room that reminded Isobel of the gym at school, dozens of typewriters clattered and pinged all day. Miss Radcliff patrolled her domain like an exam invigilator, collecting manuscripts as they appeared and handing out replacement work. It looked as tedious as a production line, though Isobel found it anything but as she realised that accuracy of translation could have international ramifications if she got it wrong in tone or nuance. The language of the conference was English and French – at the insistence of Clemenceau. There had been a half-hearted attempt by the Americans and British to insist on English but the scornful insistence by 'The Tiger' that French had always been the language of diplomacy, and the fact that they were in Paris, carried the day. Interpreters and translators swelled the ranks of each nation's delegation: no country wanted to be at a disadvantage so the standards were high. This kept Isobel fully engaged in spite of the punishing hours that Miss Radcliff had promised.

Despite sharing a tiny room, it was only on Sunday that the three women had the time or the energy to talk: falling into bed after dinner was all that they could manage after such long days. The first free Sunday was a bright early spring day and they headed for the Tuileries Garden. A few crocuses showed their heads but the dominant hue was brown – mud with the barest leavening of grass. It was cold and only a scattering of the beau monde were in evidence – still in furs as they took the air in mostly feminine pairs: France had suffered an even greater cull of its young men than their allies across the channel. The detritus of that decimated generation was on display on park benches: limbless men, some wearing masks to hide disfigurements. Others, with sightless eyes, looked directly at the spring sun. They crossed the river and near Les Invalides they found a café viscous with tobacco smoke. Emma ordered Pernod and they laughed as the water turned the clear spirit opaque.

'Have you ever tried absinthe?' asked Emma. 'I ordered some a couple of weeks ago but the waiter wouldn't serve me. He muttered something about it not being suitable for ladies. A drink for prostitutes apparently.' Isobel's expression must have given away her shock. 'He was probably right. Look over there. Don't stare. In the corner.'

Three women, one barely more than a girl, were sitting at a table. They were talking, but as they did so their eyes were scanning the room. The youngest smiled as she caught a man's eye and her smile was accompanied by a raised eyebrow that could never have been innocent.

'Is she proposing to him?' whispered Isobel.

'Propositioning is the correct word,' replied Emma.

A red-faced man, cigar working round his mouth, leant close to the girl. Her expression didn't change as she replied to his question while her finger touched his beard. She nodded and stood, blew a kiss to her companions and took the man's arm as they headed towards the door; close enough to their table that they could smell her cologne – and his sweat.

'Not very glamorous, is it?' Gillian sipped her drink.

'Well she's not exactly a courtesan, is she?' said Emma, 'and he isn't the Duc de Guermantes either. I'm sure if you went to the opera and saw some of the comings and goings in the smarter motorcars you'd have a different viewpoint.'

'Of prostitutes?' said Gillian.

'Of men and women.'

'Are you saying that just because it's a lord and a courtesan, that paying for... love... is acceptable? Really?'

The air between the two women was suddenly charged. Isobel glanced anxiously between them.

'I don't see the difference...'

'... between prostitution and marriage? Oh please, Emma, don't start on that again. It's ridiculous.' Gillian had, up until this moment, read quietly or demurred to Emma's opinions that habitually sought out a reaction. The exasperation and irritation in her voice was something new.

'I didn't say marriage and prostitution are the same.'

'But you implied it.'

'I simply said that both are where money and... love... sex... meet.'

'Which is like saying that a bottle of absinthe is the same as a glass of cordial. A rather obvious difference, I would have thought. What do you think, Isobel?'

Isobel had no desire to take sides. She fingered her glass. 'I don't know. The thought of allowing that man to...'

'That's not what we were talking about. Emma seems to think that marriage is just a respectable form of selling your body; the man pays and the woman sells. I don't believe that. I refuse to believe that.'

Her voice had risen and heads turned towards them. Gillian sat back in embarrassment. She stood suddenly and picked up her bag.

'I need to be out of this smoke. Sorry. Would you mind if I walked back on my own? I need to clear my head and take some exercise.' She paused. 'I'll see you later.'

Isobel and Emma watched her negotiate a drunk leaning on the doorway and said nothing until the door was closed.

'I touched a nerve there,' said Emma.

'You did – but I'm not sure why.'

'God probably.'

'I'm not so sure. I don't know her – but there was something that was more personal. You've obviously had that argument before. Did she get so upset last time?'

'Today was worse. I don't think she really approves of me. Rather like Miss Radcliff.'

'But what have you done to make her so upset?'

'It's more what I'm not doing. Or what I'm not going to do.'

Something changed in her voice. Until that moment it was upbeat and challenging in tone. Now there was a thickness and emotion to it that hooked Isobel's attention. She stared towards the door and Isobel could see her eyes were filling. 'She thinks I am not behaving as I should – and I disagree.' Her mouth was working. 'She thinks I should marry him. But I can't, can I?' The question did not require an answer and Isobel stayed silent as her companion swallowed and pursed her lips. 'I told you I hadn't lost anyone. Well that was true – up to a point. No one killed anyway. You've seen the photograph by my bed? The one on the left is Rufus.'

Isobel remembered a smiling man, not much more than a boy, with fair hair and a gap between his front teeth. 'Cambrai, '17. He stood on a mine and it took off his leg. And everything else. Everything. He's out of hospital and back with his parents. He has a bag I'm told. He won't talk about it though. As if it doesn't matter.' She wiped away a tear. 'As if it doesn't matter that there can be no... no sex and no children. A leg would be fine. I could live with that. But we aren't married and I... I can't go through with it.

'Is that so terrible? Is that something that I should feel so guilty about? Of course I feel guilty about it. I'll always feel guilty about it. And maybe I'll regret it. There aren't exactly dozens of other men to take his place. Maybe no one. Damn Gillian. What does she know about what it's like? How dare she!'

She looked at Isobel with tears running down her face, shook her head and gulped her drink. 'I expect you think the same. I don't blame you. Why should I? I'm just a woman who wants... not a lot really: love, companionship, married love and some children. Not money. Is that so bad?'

'Do... do you love him?'

The cloud that swept across Emma's face made Isobel regret her question.

'Love? I don't know what that means any more. Really. We were children when we got engaged. He was nineteen and I was eighteen. We did all those things that people in love do. Kissed. Lay around in long grass. Laughed. Went to the beach. That was… six years ago.' Wide eyes, brimming with tears, blinking. 'Now? He doesn't say much. Stares at the wall. Says "hello" when I get to his parents' house and asks me how I am. That's it. We kiss goodbye. On the cheek. Love? Love? No. I don't. I'm there because I have to be. Actually, I wish he were dead. Gillian doesn't know that; that I actually want my fiancé dead. Really. Dead.'

The dam had broken and the tears gushed down her face. Isobel shifted along the bench and put her arm round her heaving shoulders until Emma reached into her bag for a handkerchief, blew her nose and rubbed her eyes.

'I hardly know you and I've told you something that I barely even dared to tell myself. Well, you know me now. I should be grateful, shouldn't I? To have someone. But when I think of him now I actually feel hatred. I hate him for putting me in this situation. Why can't he be the one that breaks it off? Why do I have to be the one that abandons a war hero – be the one who everyone thinks of as heartless and cruel.' She looked at the ceiling as her mouth worked with emotion. 'Well I am, I suppose.' Her gaze came back to Isobel. 'What would you do? If you were me?'

Isobel was dreading this question. She knew what she should say – but what came out was visceral.

'You can't marry him; not if you don't love him. Certainly not, if you hate him. But you don't hate him do you? Really?'

Emma was looking towards the door and rummaging around in her bag for a cigarette. She lit it with shaking hands and exhaled, following it with a gulp of her drink. She continued to look away as she spoke.

'No. I don't hate him. I just hate what he's made me. You know the picture by my bed? That's the man I wanted to marry. If he was still that, even without his… bits… then I think it would be… alright. But he's no longer that man. No fun. No laughter.

Not much to say about anything. Except football. And even then, if Villa loses, he sulks for a week. He's a different person. Not someone, even if he hadn't been injured, that I would want to marry. His real injury is to his mind. I know that sounds as if I'm making up excuses. Maybe I am. But I have thought about it. I never stop thinking about it. But that's just as bad according to Gillian. It's in sickness and in health as far as she's concerned.'

'But you're not married to him. You're only engaged. It's not the same.'

'Not according to Gillian.'

'Well she's wrong.' The vehemence with which Isobel said this caught Emma by surprise and she looked up and at her companion with surprise.

'I don't think your father would say that.'

'Do you know, I think he would. Especially if the *him*, the inner person, was different. No one should criticise that.'

'They do though. They really do. His parents... they refuse to acknowledge that there's any change. They carry on as if we were still eighteen and he's still a sunny, funny boy on the edge of life. Maybe they just want me to take him off their hands. If I don't, then they'll have a morose cripple for the rest of their lives.' She hesitated and pulled on her cigarette. 'That sounds cynical.'

She was no longer crying but her eyes were red and there were damp patches on her blouse. Isobel leant over and took her hand.

'You're not alone, you know. There are thousands of women faced with the same choices. But most of them are already married. You're not. You can walk away.'

'That's kind. Very kind.' She looked around the café. One of the other women on the corner table was now sitting next to a man in a bowler hat – the same drunk that had been by the door. He was trying to put his arm around her shoulder against her wishes and the barman was looking over with concern. 'I think we ought to go. We need to be out of here before it gets nasty.' She pushed a pair of coins on to the table. 'I owe you that after ruining your Sunday.'

* * *

Isobel was focusing on a draft memorandum on the disputed status of Danzig when Miss Radcliff placed an envelope on her desk without comment. She recognised her cousin's writing and the message inside was to the point: instructions to meet at a restaurant on the Champs-Élysées that evening; neither pleasantries nor endearments.

The restaurant was full. When she was ushered to the table she saw that there was a middle-aged woman sitting next to her cousin. The diplomat, Harold Nicolson, stood.

'My dear Miss Richmond, may I introduce you to Madame Aurigny?' The woman made a neck bow towards her, murmuring a greeting and fixing her with a cool, smiling gaze. 'Madame Aurigny is an old friend of mine – but has known your cousin for even longer. Please... sit. Wine?'

Isobel concurred and used the bustling of the wine waiter to gather her thoughts.

'We were talking about President Wilson, Isobel. Have you caught a glimpse of him yet, or of his fat little wife? No? You girls are worked much too hard. He still gets mobbed in the streets – which sadly does nothing to puncture his sense of self-righteousness. He's come to save the world, he thinks, or at least to save us from ourselves. He's as high-minded as our prime minister is cunning – which makes our meetings interesting.'

'He's actually very charming, Harold,' said Madame Aurigny, 'but he's better with women than men. You could learn from him, Robert, if you could leave some of your English reserve behind.'

Her English was nearly without accent and her expression was of amused interest. Her eyes were heavy lidded and gave her a languid aura.

'You know him?' asked Granville.

'Of course. Philippe met him when he was at Princeton. We had dinner in New York and went racing with them; with his first wife that is. Quite flirtatious for someone who appears so buttoned-up. Highly intelligent. But doesn't listen. Very sure of himself. Phillipe – that's my late husband, Miss Richmond – was always surprised that he went into politics: more suited to sermons than speeches he used to say. I agree. Now, you two men chat amongst yourselves for a few minutes while I find out more about Miss Richmond.'

Isobel found herself in a bath of charm. The Frenchwoman rested her chin on the palm of her hand and asked her questions, probing to find common ground. 'Robert says you are a sculptress. That's an interesting hobby for a woman.'

'It is a hobby now – but I want to make it my career. Better than a secretary which I suspect I'll have had quite enough of by the time I get home.'

'Do you like Rodin?'

'My hero.'

'Mine too. If you would like to see some of his work then you have timed your visit to Paris well. They've made the Hôtel Biron into a museum for him and it's opening any day now. The curator, Leonce Benedite, is a good friend. It will be too trying if we have to fight our way through the crowds that will descend on it for the opening day – and subsequently – though you would have some fun observing the beau monde at play. Now tell me more about your work.'

Isobel told her of her fascination with bronze and the technical difficulties she had experienced in casting. She became aware, as she was talking, that the two men had become silent and were listening to her – her cousin for the first time with genuine interest. Their attention put her off her stride.

'Well, well.' Nicolson was smiling. 'Granville, you didn't tell me that your cousin was not only a linguist and scholar – but also an artist. We will need to get you launched into a more creative milieu than the Miss Radcliff's typing pool, won't we?'

'But I'm not very good.'

'I doubt that. Painting is one thing; a dab of paint here and there is in anyone's repertoire. Casting bronzes is only for the committed and skilled – so I suspect that your modesty is false. I'll introduce you to some of my wife's friends who are artists and writers when we were are back in England. Everyone needs a hand to get them going.'

'You seem to have a rather powerful one already,' said Robert Granville, 'very powerful. The Prime Minister in fact.' The other three looked at him in surprise. 'I received this today and I have to say I was rather taken aback.' He held out an opened envelope. 'It was given to me to pass on to you. Your sister may have had something to do with it.'

'Rose?'

'Davina. It would appear that she made good on a promise to let the PM know that you were in Paris and that your skills were going to be vital to the furtherance of world peace. He wants to meet you and has asked you to tea tomorrow – if Miss Radcliff can spare you, that is. I have a feeling that even the redoubtable Miss Radcliff will find that hard to refuse. Even our up-and-coming diplomats like Nicolson here hardly ever get words addressed to them from such a height. Or such depths – this is LG we are talking about after all.'

'Come, Granville, he's not so bad,' said Nicolson. 'He has just won the war for us after all. Without him I don't think it would have ended as it did.'

'The man's a Bolshevik.'

'What you mean is that he's not exactly a Tory peer – which isn't a surprise as he comes from a Welsh valley. The roof hasn't fallen in yet despite his attempts to take rather more money from us than we would like – or you would like anyway; I don't have any.'

Isobel took the letter from her cousin and read it. It was addressed to her, handwritten and to the point. The LG signature contained a distinctive flourish. Madame Aurigny placed a hand on her arm.

'Would you like me to accompany you? He does have something of a… reputation.'

Isobel smiled at her gratefully. 'I think I can look after myself – but thank you. I would dearly love to visit the Rodin collection with you though. I could think of nothing in Paris that I would like to see more.'

'Then we shall do it. Now, Robert, do you have any further surprises for poor Miss Richmond?'

'I think that's quite enough for one day. What is he playing at though? You can't say that he isn't worked hard enough: not even I would claim that.'

'But he's a politician, and no one kisses more babies or turns the charm on better than he does,' said Nicolson.

'And no one kisses more women than he does.'

'You exaggerate. He's the statesman here in Paris and he's got his daughter and mistress with him.'

'Miss Stephenson?' queried Madame Aurigny.

'The same.'

'I thought she was his secretary.'

'She has two jobs.'

'All the safer then.'

'The old goat is quite incorrigible.'

'You've spent too much time being suspicious of everyone, Robert. I think Harold is right. It's much too public here for that sort of thing.'

'In Paris? It's the home of that sort of thing, isn't it?'

'Should I be insulted – as a respectable Frenchwoman?' She said this with a smile.

'More to the point,' said Nicolson, 'is that we shouldn't make Isobel nervous. It is tea with the Prime Minister after all – and there aren't many girls coming to Paris to labour under Miss Radcliff's regime who will get the opportunity to meet the great man. It's an opportunity that I wouldn't turn down.'

'And nor will I,' said Isobel. 'It's why I came to Paris in the first place; to be part of the biggest event since… of course I'm going.'

'Bravo, Miss Richmond,' said Nicolson. 'You must report back to us peons at the coalface what's going on in his mind. I've certainly got some questions I would like some answers to – as I'm sure you do, Granville. How clever of you to bring your own secret agent with you. We must have a debrief next week without fail.'

9

Scapa Flow. Orkney Islands, June 1919

Julian walked into the sunshine, shading his eyes against the glare from the oily calm. Kittiwakes squabbled on the foreshore and the fins of a pod of porpoises sliced the surface in the middle distance. Beyond, black silhouettes of warships squatted across the anchorage up to the far shore nearly five miles away. Drifts of smoke from their funnels lay in tendrils of dissolving mist. Behind the cottage the clatter of a hay-turner, hauled by a horse, was the only sound competing with the seabirds.

He pulled off his shirt and felt the sun penetrating his winter-white skin. He stretched in exaltation, massaged his face and dipped a saucepan into the water butt, pouring it over his head in one movement. The shock and the sensuality of the water coursing down his naked body stripped away his drowsiness in an instant. He wiped the water from his eyes and ran his fingers through his dripping hair, conscious of every rivulet as it ran down his back and buttocks. His head was musty with the after-effects of whisky – but he had not enjoyed such an elevated sense of physicality for a long time. He sat down on the sofa that they had dragged out the previous evening in order to imbibe the night sky that had pulsed with starlight. It was damp with dew but warmed already by the sun. The hum of bees mixed with the regular clack-clack of the hay-turner. He ran his hand over the head of his penis. It was tender to the touch but he felt a twist of arousal at the memory.

How did he know? You always do, he thought. Was it something he had said? A hint? Or was it a glance, that sideways look that was ambiguous, but with enough in it to make you sure that some other – tiny – suggestion was made certain; a dance of sorts; a minuet of moves that led towards the touch where the full power of mutual desire became extant. He remembered the first time at school when the boy in the next bed in a darkened dormitory had brushed himself against his hand, leaving it there for just long enough for its meaning to be apparent – but able to retreat if the advance was unwelcome. He remembered the bolt of arousal, his hand enclosing the hot tumescence only inches from his face. He remembered manipulating it and feeling the hot ejaculation into his palm and the swimming waves of his own orgasm that seemed to ripple on forever.

He heard the squeak of the brass bed within the cottage. A hessian sack formed a curtain of sorts. There was the slap of bare feet on wooden boards, the irritation of a badly oiled hinge and the pumping of a primus-stove. Would he regret it? How would they deal with the day after, without the lubrication of whisky? It had not been his first time either – that had been obvious. Would he retreat into an angry denial – it would not be the first. Or, as he hoped, would he treat it as a sensual experience; of pleasure given and received allowed by drink and circumstances. He felt no desire to hold him or kiss him, only to have the unbearable pleasure of a tongue circling the tip of his penis – and to reciprocate. No woman had done that to him. He had exulted in their bodies – their breasts, the curve of their buttocks and the silk of their sex – but the carnality of his fantasies were still rooted in the intensity of that moment in the dormitory. There was the bang of plates; Julian could visualise the ritual of the teapot and milk churn and the spooning of sugar. He remembered his own nakedness and pulled the towel that was hanging over the door around his waist. Why? He could not say. A foot hooked the door open and Lt Ranald Godwin squinted into the sun that was now high in the midsummer sky.

'What a morning!' He was wearing a night-shirt and carrying two enamel mugs of tea. 'Tea?' He stared out to sea where two seals were rippling their clumsy way on to a sunbathing rock. His hair, normally plastered down by hair oil, was now sprung into curls. He was in his mid-twenties though his red-cheeked complexion made him look younger and belied that he was the naval lightweight boxing champion. Julian had seen him knock out his opponent during the first seconds of a fight on the quarterdeck of Admiral Beatty's flagship. He sipped his tea and stretched so that Julian could see the outline of his penis against his nightshirt. Julian felt another twist of arousal at this unconscious sexuality. 'What a morning,' he repeated. 'I've never seen a day like this here; have you?'

He hadn't. Four years of mist, gales, snow and the sort of rain with which he was familiar on the west coast of Ireland, had been the constants of his shipboard routine, his adversary on an open bridge as he had swept the harbour through his binoculars for the thousandth time in search of the overfall that might be a periscope; or the streak of white against the grey of the surface that would frame the run of a torpedo. Scapa was never a homecoming into a friendly port with the prospect of a run ashore; only a place of greater safety – and calmer waters – than the wastes of the North Sea. He was cured of the sea. He could speak the language and communicate with its natives – but it was business, not affection. It was the same with the Orkney Islands. Until now. For the first time he saw their beauty; in the desolation unbroken by trees or mountains; in the pellucid light; in the contrast between the new grass and rocks – and the smell of newly cut hay. Perhaps it was peace that did it: a relaxation from nagging danger, a raising of the siege of the nerves.

'Our guests are arriving in Stromness on the lunchtime ferry,' said Julian.

'Time for breakfast before we go. Have you got a hangover? I should have. You've had a shower? Do me the honours will you?'

Ran put down his tea, stripped off his nightshirt and stood by the butt with his head thrown back and his eyes shut. Julian swept his muscled body with a glance, fighting the desire to reach out and touch the head of his circumcised penis, red in contrast to his white skin. He filled the saucepan and stood behind him, pausing with it over Ran's head.

'Fast or slow?'

'Slow. Dribble it.'

He splashed the top of his head, working it round in a circle. As the water trickled down his back Julian could not resist following the stream down with two fingers, slaloming down his spine down to the cleft of his buttocks.

'Heaven.' Ran's eyes were still closed as he swept his hair back with Julian's hand resting on his thigh. 'What could be nicer?' He turned round. 'I know what, but we haven't got time, have we?' Julian swallowed hard before replying. His companion's penis was swelling with a bold vein pulsing along its length.

'No. Sadly.' He stretched out and held it, feeling his own pushing against his towel. 'But tonight, I hope.'

'Perfection!' Ran grabbed Julian's towel and flicked it playfully at the protrusion.

*   *   *

They followed the path that snaked through the low walls that delineated fields to the edge of a crag where the path became one for sheep rather than humans. As they breasted the shallow summit the anchorage behind came into view. Below them, much closer than the ships they could see from their cottage, lay the German battle cruisers, the nearest ship only half a mile away. In the calm they were lying to the local current rather than to the wind that normally scarified the anchorage, the faux bow-wave giving an impression of movement. The sound of activity floated across the water as a lighter came alongside the nearest ship. They could see a group of sailors smoking and leaning over the stern rail. Rust streaks waterfalled down the line of rivets and two warps lay hanging over the side. An officer walked behind the sailors but none saluted nor even acknowledged his presence. Julian glanced at Ran. Such insolence in the British navy would have had every sailor under arrest in an instant. They had heard that discipline had collapsed throughout the fleet and that officers could not safely patrol the lower deck. There were tales of sailors' soviets and violence to officers left unpunished.

The two men sat in the sunshine and, eyes closed, allowed the solar fireflies to dance in their vision. Two weeks of rain and gales had kept them indoors apart from their daily hike to the radio station where they were in charge of signals coming in and out of the harbour. The urgency of wartime had evaporated. Then, the whole Home Fleet, apart from a permanent screen of cruisers and minesweepers patrolling the approaches to the Baltic, had been corralled in this perfect natural harbour. Vigilance had been its *raison d'être*, waiting like a hawk in a tree to swoop on any attempt by the German fleet to attack the English Channel and the flow of men and ordinance to the meat-grinder of the Western Front. Constant feints by the Germans drew the hawk from its perch. The nexus of the intelligence machine that watched and waited day and night had been the radio operations on the island of Flotta. There, every intercepted signal was analysed for clues as to where and when the Germans might appear. Through the radio station flew signals that, as Churchill said about Admiral Jellicoe, could lose the war in an afternoon. That knowledge had given an urgency to its activities that Julian remembered with pride.

Now they were jailers of sorts. After the Armistice of the previous November the German admirals had wanted a *Götterdämmerung*, with the fleet sallying out to confront the enemy in a suicidal last show of force. Their crews, hungry, demoralised, war-weary and infected with the bacilli of Bolshevism had other ideas. They had refused to sail and mutiny had broken out across the fleet. When the Kaiser fled to Holland, the purpose of an imperial navy rang hollow even amongst its aristocratic leaders and, in accordance with the terms of the Armistice, the German fleet surrendered itself to be interned during the peace talks in Paris.

The place chosen was Scapa Flow in the Orkneys, the centre of an archipelago of low islands about as remote as possible from the European landmass, fortified and enclosed as the home of the British fleet during the years of danger. Though the Royal Navy watched over the German ships, they remained a sovereign fleet, supplied entirely from Germany with their own officers, naval laws and customs intact – though chronic low morale, homesickness, indiscipline and lassitude made it a shadow of its former self. The ships themselves were filthy – the smell drifting across the harbour and wrinkling noses of crews in the lighters that plied between the guarding British ships.

A skiff was tied up against the pier where a lighter was being loaded, men hauling on a derrick and winching pallets into its shallow hold. A sailor was sitting on the step, his sole job being to slip or tighten the dinghy's lines with the ebb and flow of the tide. He saluted as the two men approached and began to untie the lines. Ran stepped aboard and began to raise the gaff-rigged mainsail which slatted back and forth in the breeze that was now rippling the water. Julian took the helm, the rating pushed the bow out and the skiff began to move – faster as the jib was raised.

On a gentle reach they ran down the line of German ships, vast slabs of steel streaked with rust, their turrets like turtle shells. There were no flags apart from Admiral Richter's fleet flag on the cruiser *Emden*. They were observed by listless groups of sailors, many sunning themselves on top of turrets. On the other side of the harbour, smoke was rising from the British squadron tasked with guarding the German fleet – a fleet that was essentially disarmed as they had surrendered their guns' breech-blocks. They were preparing to go out on exercise and were raising steam. The funnel smoke was drifting sideways to the advent of the breeze. They crossed under the bow of the *Nürnburg* heading for the small town of Stromness on Mainland, the biggest of Orkney's islands, which was the nearest approximation to a town other than the city of Kirkwall amongst the shake of islands.

Wartime, and the presence of the British Grand Fleet and now the German High Seas Fleet, had made it a gold-rush town with its shops the only source of any luxuries for a hundred miles. The breeze stiffened as they moved out of the lee of the land, the skiff heeling and accelerating in a direct line towards Stromness. Ran leant outwards, holding the jib sheet and grinning with sun and wind beating on his face. His exhilaration was infectious and Julian laughed with delight as he strained against the tiller, the rudder stirring a wake that was trailed by two gulls whose beady eyes scanned the boil for a potential meal.

The dominant hue of Stromness was grey; grey stone, grey slate – and normally a grey sky. Today the blue of the sky was reflected in the sea and the reds and whites of the fishing boats gave the town a jaunty air. Even the narrow streets, as they climbed the short hill to the town's only hotel of any size, seemed altogether of another world of seaside and tearooms in the sunshine. Julian saw Rose, Ariadne and Davina with their faces pressed against the window of a bookshop. They were still dressed in their travelling clothes and their delight at Julian's greeting was unfeigned. Even Ariadne's reserve melted. The women were full of their journey: the sleeper to Wick and ferry ride through the vast fleet that lay at anchor in the Flow. Rose caught Julian's eye while introductions were made to Ran.

'We have three day's leave,' Ran announced, 'and you have brought with you the loveliest weather we've ever seen here. I hope you have your walking shoes with you. We have a skiff for some sailing and we are going piggyback on a children's sightseeing trip around the German Fleet tomorrow. You only saw the destroyers on your way in. I can tell you the battleships are quite something. But that's tomorrow. We've arranged lunch. Fresh caught fish and a potato and onion salad. How does that sound?'

*   *   *

The following day, the *Flying Kestrel* was lying against the quay with children pushing their way up the gang-plank, their chattering overwhelming the shouted instructions of their teachers who corralled them into the seats either side of the superstructure. The ship was a tug on charter to the navy, but being used for a school outing from Stromness School. Tendrils of smoke spilt down the side of the funnel and occasional sparks drifted like dying fireflies. Julian felt Rose grasp his arm in happiness as seagulls swooped to scraps being thrown to them by the children. The engines churned the water as the shore-lines were released. As the slight breeze caught the bow, it swung towards the fleet that was beginning to reform into lines imposed by the wind. The shriek of the ship's whistle echoed over the harbour as the speed built and the apparent wind flicked hat brims.

Julian recited the names as they steamed down the rows of battleships. They sat squat in the water, their plumb bows giving them the appearance of a fort rather than a ship, platforms for the huge guns that dominated their decks. As they rounded the stern of the *Keiserin*, her name framed by rust streaks, they saw three sailors carrying a canvas-covered roll towards the ensign staff that sloped over the stern rail. The children waved at the sailors, but none waved back. Julian glanced past the cliff of the stern towards the *Derfflinger* where a similar party, supervised by an officer, had a sailor shinning up the pole to release a jammed halyard. Ran pointed to the stern rearing above them where the black and red of the imperial battle-flag, its creases visible, flopped and then twisted into the faint breeze.

'What's happening? Is everything alright?' asked Rose.

'I don't know.' Julian chewed his lip. 'Those are battle flags – illegal under the armistice. It can only mean two things: they are preparing to make a run for it while our squadron is out on exercise – but I doubt it as they don't have steam up; but they wouldn't run out the flags unless they were about to move. Maybe they have heard something from Paris. Maybe the negotiations have broken down and they could be about to scuttle.'

'Scuttle?'

'Pull the plug. Sink themselves.'

'Why would they do that?'

'To stop the fleet being surrendered – or sequestered.'

The *Flying Kestrel* steamed on regardless, past the last of the battleships and into the channel between the islands of Hoy and Fara where the destroyers were lined up in rows. There was abnormal activity on the smaller ships. Julian glanced at Ran who nodded. 'We have to see the captain. I'm sure everything is fine – but there's something going on. It's not dangerous, so don't be worried.' His voice failed to carry conviction. They climbed the ladder to the wheelhouse where the captain was staring through his binoculars at the small collection of British ships, all that remained of the squadron that had left the Flow the previous day on an exercise. If a scuttle was taking place there was little that the Royal Navy could have done at the best of times. With only a handful of ships in the anchorage, and only supply vessels and lighters at that, their capacity to influence events was negligible. The captain barely acknowledged them. 'There's a signal being raised on the *Victorious*,' he nodded towards another set of binoculars in front of the coxswain, 'use those and check what's being said.' Julian focused the glasses on the flag halyard. He read slowly. 'Fear fleet scuttle imminent. Return to Stromness. Disembark passengers. Return immediately. Prepare for tug action.' The captain kept his binoculars to his eyes. 'Coxswain, make course for Stromness. Full speed.'

The tug leant out of the turn as it swung round, its screws thrashing as the slight swell lifted them momentarily out of the water. In the few minutes that had passed all had changed. The lines of destroyers, whose funnels had been arraigned with the order of the parade ground, were listing at madcap angles. One rolled over with a suddenness that did not seem possible, water streaming off its weed-covered hull, its screws white with barnacles. Another settled by the stern like a dog shifting on to its haunches. Lifeboats were pulling away as the ships groaned, hissed and settled. A cat was being lowered by a sling into a boat as its mothership listed, threatening the crew below. The sailor on deck let go of the halyard and the cat disappeared into the forest of hands outstretched to catch it as the sailor jumped over the lifeboat and into the sea beyond.

Julian and Ran remembered their visitors and climbed back down to the deck where some of the younger children were crying and being shepherded below by their teachers while Rose comforted Davina who, they were relieved to see, was more fascinated than frightened by the scenes unfolding around them. As they cleared the channel where the destroyers were moored, this time at full speed, they steamed down the line of capital ships in their death throes. The first was down at the bow with its stern high out of the water. As it slid forward steam hissed out of its sides and it gave off a subterranean groan that echoed from its bowels. A slick of black oil, the lifeblood of a dinosaur, spread out around it in a skirt. The *Nürnberg* merely settled, upright and steady with only the gap between the deck and sea diminishing slowly as its ship's boats pulled away.

As they drew opposite the *Derfflinger*, she listed towards them so that from the deck of the tug they could see down her funnels that acted like a megaphone for the hissing, rattling of chains and gurgling emanating from below. She seemed to hesitate – and then rolled over, setting up a wave that surged towards the *Flying Kestrel*. Its upturned hull appeared in one movement as it slid below the surface leaving a momentary calm that was eviscerated by a bubble that erupted in a gulp of oil, steam and detritus. The smell of oil, sewage and coal steam scorched the air that had only half an hour before held the scent of hay and kelp. All around steel castles groaned, leant, pitched, rolled and sank in an anarchy of dying, like brontosauri trapped in a pitch lake. They sank with the exhausted sigh of drained beasts, either captured, twisted and consumed or in quiet acceptance of their fate as the sea claimed them and they bled to death. As the *Flying Kestrel* approached the *Baden*, still upright with no sign of anything untoward other than a flutter of boats pulling away from her sides packed with her crew, they saw a sailor, in white summer uniform, climb on to the roof of the forward turret and dance a hornpipe. Who was his audience? He danced as if the world would never end and was still moving as they lost sight of the ship that, alone in the fleet, still retained the solidity of an island.

The *Flying Kestrel* swung alongside the quay with elan and barely were the lines secured than the gang plank was thick with children running on to the quay. Ariadne and the Richmond sisters followed them and in less than ten minutes, engines at full power, she surged out of the harbour in full working mode as a tug. The *Baden* remained upright with no sign of settling or change other than the absence of the dancer on top of the turret. Around her the carnage was nearly complete with upturned hulls or the top of superstructures indicating the final resting places of the High Seas Fleet. The usually pristine waters of the Flow were black with oil and rubbish. To the south-east, the entrance to the harbour was stained with smoke and the silhouettes of the British battleship squadron as it returned to its base to slam the door of a stable from which the horse had long gone.

The *Flying Kestrel* turned toward the *Baden* and nosed alongside where the departing crew had left a boarding ladder. Half a dozen sailors swarmed up, passing a rope hand over hand towards the fairlead at the bow. Once secured, they hauled the huge towing line off the aft deck of the tug and out of sight on to the battleship's foredeck. A minute later the roaring rattle of the anchor chain being let go echoed across the Flow and with a final whip-flick the bitter end joined the anchor on the seabed. The *Flying Kestrel* gunned its engines and let the towing line flake behind it, slowing down as the tension firmed. The cable visibly stretched as the aft deck was cleared of crew; a lethal place if the line should break and the towing cable scythe the deck. Slowly, and it seemed imperceptible at first, the bow, with its ram visible as the ship settled at the stern, began to swing round and forward movement was discernible. He could see where the captain was heading – a shallow bank by Mainland where he could beach the battleship to facilitate a later recovery. It was a race against time: Julian could see the gap between deck and water narrowing. Two sailors, with axes, stood by to cut the towing cable if the *Baden* showed signs of capsizing. Whether the ship had sunk faster than the bank had come up to meet it was a moot point as the tug was throttled back. The captain lent out of the bridge window.

'She's well aground. Gentlemen, would you please take the *Kestrel's* spare ensign and run it up. She's now a prize after what can only be construed as an act of war and she needs a prize crew. If you would do me the honour, I would be obliged. I suspect this is the only time you will be able to do this in your naval careers. There will be others to salvage so I need to get moving. Keep the half-dozen men already on board with you.'

Both men saluted and prepared to board as the *Flying Kestrel* came alongside the ship's ladder once more. As they climbed they wondered again at the vastness of the steel cliff and the unearthly noises that were emanating from within. Layers of steam washed over them coming out of hatches and vents in the deck but the usual bustle of a battleship was missing – the noise of boots on ladders, the slamming of metal doors and the vibration from turbines, whistles, bells and the barked orders of petty officers. The ship moved – but unnaturally as her hull shifted on the sandbank below. The sailors from the tug formed up for orders – relief on their faces on realising that they were now safe from capsizing; the thought of being on the deck of such a monster, if that occurred, was terrifying indeed. With the sailors, they made their way to the stern, part of the way in the shadows of the massive guns. This was the last and mightiest of the dreadnought class of battleships that had only been commissioned in the last two years of the war – too late to take part in the Battle of Jutland. Despite the rust streaks and lack of paint the boarding party were impressed.

It took them less than a minute to change the flags, making sure that the German ensign was carefully folded – a souvenir to treasure. They knew that the rest of the British fleet would have too much to do in rescuing German crews and salvaging what ships they could for them to be picked up soon. The ship felt solid and aground and the tide was falling, so their fears of a sudden capsize were allayed – enough to consider exploring the ship. They first climbed up to the bridge which gave them a panoramic view over Scapa Flow. The ships whose names Ran and Julian had ticked off on their outward journey were all scuttled. Some were down at either bow or stern with airlocks holding the other end out of the water to expose propellers or the bulb of their bow. Others had disappeared altogether. Yet more had turned turtle but lay afloat resembling sounding whales. The *Hindenburg* was aground but with only her funnels, fighting top and bridge out of the water. Oil, pieces of wood, boats and assorted rubbish covered the sea that was unnaturally calm, the oil blanketing any wavelets that might have formed in the breeze. Bubbles of air would burst the film on the surface marking a ship's grave and sinister bellows, muffled in their echo, groaned out of hulls that were still visible.

It was dark below decks with no generators to provide power. With three miner's lamps between them, the party split, Julian taking command of one and descending the superstructure into the entrails of the ship. Strange sounds accompanied their progress, made more ghostly by the surrounding blackness. He checked the captain's cabin for anything of obvious interest. It was immaculate – and the safe empty, with its door open. As they descended downwards and into the crew's quarters, the smell and the filth became almost overpowering. Rats fanned out in all directions and cockroaches gave every footfall a crunch. Clothes, possessions with no value and rotten food covered the floor. The boarding party were surprised at the lack of any permanent accommodation with hammocks slung randomly from any possible point. They remembered that this ship had never been designed for living. Its home was the Baltic and its sphere of operations the North Sea. Its crew had lived ashore and were on full operating alert during their occasional forays to sea. It had not been a fleet, like the Royal Navy, designed for the maintenance of an empire. A mutinous crew, boredom and rock-bottom morale had left the most modern battleship in the world a stinking slum.

With relief the boarding party returned to the deck. By now the anchorage was beginning to fill again, this time with British ships. The capital ships had dropped anchor and their boats fanned out across the Flow. Destroyers were rounding up German crews whose hands were in the air as they came alongside the grappling nets lowered from the ships' sides. Rifle and small arms fire crackled across the rubbish-strewn surface. The flagship was only a mile away and its signalling lamp was flickering almost continuously as the admiral tried to limit the disaster that had occurred in his absence, but on his watch.

Ran shook his head. 'What a mess. What a bloody awful mess.'

*   *   *

It was a subdued party that met for dinner in Stromness. Julian and Ran had checked into the hotel having spent the afternoon assisting the *Flying Kestrel*'s captain as he attempted to move ships that had scuttled but not sunk. They had managed to drag one destroyer on to a sandbank where it lay, partially capsized. The others had been a lost cause: most had disappeared completely with only burps of oil or other flotsam to mark their grave. Some were settled down to their funnels – but solidly aground. They had assisted in rounding up the German crews who, for once, seemed cheerful as they looked forward to a long awaited repatriation to Germany and their families. Some were less so, nursing the marks of blows from British sailors who had anticipated resistance and struck first with rifle butts and boathooks. They were corralled into churches and redundant storage sheds. The sound of drunken songs drifted in the still evening air. It was close enough to Midsummer's day and far enough north for only partial darkness to punctuate the gap between one day and another and the sailors had left their ships with all the drink that they could carry.

It was this sound that accompanied Julian and Ariadne as they strolled along the quay after dinner. The two sisters and Ran were playing cards, which had no appeal to either of them. They sat on the outer end of the mole and watched the signal lights blinking across the anchorage as the unfortunate British admiral counted the cost of the day's debacle.

'Were you frightened?' asked Julian.

'At the beginning – when we had no idea what was going on. You might have told us more, by the way. I could see the size of those ship's guns and you don't have to be in the Navy to know that one shell would have blown us apart. As they say about hunting, all the excitement of war and only a tenth of the danger.' She had a way, inherited from her mother, of tilting her head back as she spoke. 'Were you?'

Julian considered before replying. 'Not really scared. I knew that none of their guns worked – which I should have told you, I'm sorry. I suppose it was more a fear of doing the wrong thing. Believe it or not we'd never practised for a scuttle. Plenty of training for what would happen if they tried to break out though. We'd discussed the possibility of a scuttle in the mess – but that's all. Rather amazing, don't you think?'

'The Navy's not known for its imagination.'

'I suppose not.'

A foghorn sounded across the Flow.

'So what happens to you now? No German fleet left to guard. Will you be demobilised?'

'Not immediately: too much of a mess to clear up in the short term. But I was due to be given indefinite leave from the reserve next month anyway, so I should be back in early August, or a bit before. Does that suit you?'

She offered him a cigarette. 'Why are you asking me? It's nothing to do with me what you do; Ralph or Papa – but not me.' She left a silence that was punctuated by another horn echoing around the anchorage. 'Unless I actually mean anything to you.'

Her face was discernible but the subtleties of expression lost to the twilight. This caught him by surprise but he hoped the gloaming would have hidden this from her. She had always treated him with cool reserve – and in the building closeness with Rose he had failed to notice any change. He cast his mind back for clues that might have warned him of this development.

'You run the hunt... I know not officially. Of course I'd ask you.' He knew this sounded evasive. 'And I... and we get on well. Friends I hope. I think. Aren't we?'

The flare of her lighter lit her face – but her expression wasn't readable. 'Friends? Yes of course.' There was a testiness in her voice. 'So why don't you talk to me? Not about hunting but about... books... or politics. I'm not Isobel. I haven't been to Cambridge but I do have other things to talk about. Just as much as Rose.'

Julian felt an urge to put his hand on her arm to reassure her, but there was something in her natural aloofness that checked him. The glow of her cigarette created light enough to illuminate a tear running down her high cheekbone. He reached out and put his hand on her arm. She did not pull away. He heard her breathing deeply.

'I like men. I like men's company – and I like your company. It's in short supply at the moment – as you may have noticed. Papa is Papa and Ralph is not really one for talking. So you're my best bet. Sorry to make it sound as if I wouldn't have anything to do with you if there were better alternatives. I don't mean it like that. And I'm not trying to get between you and Rose.'

'There isn't anything between me and Rose.'

'Of course there is.'

There was no credible response.

'I'm sorry, Ariadne. Really, I am. And of course I would like to be friends with you – but I thought we were already.'

'Not really.'

'Not through lack of trying.'

'Why do you say that?'

'Because you don't say very much and I have no idea what you're thinking.'

She was silent for a few seconds.

'I suppose that's fair. But you don't do your bit either, do you?'

'It's difficult.'

'Meaning?'

'I have to be careful what I say. I'm a single man. It sounds an enviable situation. It might have been before the war but now there's too much at stake and I don't want to make things awkward.'

'That sounds pretty smug and self-satisfied.'

'I know.'

'And I never asked you to feel sorry for me.'

'I don't; and I don't want to be in a situation where I could feel like that. Can you understand that?'

'Sort of – but not really. You're saying that you don't want to be friends with me because I might take it the wrong way. So if I've told you that I won't take it the wrong way, what's the problem? I can't see one. But maybe I'm being stupid?'

He knew resistance was pusillanimous.

'Of course I want you as my friend. I feel bad that I was so… aloof.'

'Aloof? That's what I do. I know that. But I'll try to do better. I don't really do jolly and jokey so I might not try and go that far; but I think I have a sense of humour.'

'Sometimes,' he could sense her smiling, 'when you're not being aloof and fierce that is…'

She kicked him; not hard enough to hurt.

'I'll do it properly next time.'

'Then I'll stay up here a bit longer. Safer.'

She stood and lent over the iron railings, throwing the end of her cigarette into the sea. She was facing away from him as she spoke.

'Rose is in love with you; you know that, don't you?'

There was a silence.

'I'm very fond of her.'

She snorted. 'Oh, come on! Don't be so pompous; it doesn't suit you.'

He felt a tinge of irritation.

'I'm not sure how you know how I feel in such detail. It's not as if I've confided in you – or you in me. I can't answer for Rose.'

'Well I can.' She had turned round to face him and he could sense the long haughtiness of her gaze looking down on him. 'She's told me how much she loves you.' There was a pause. 'But she hasn't got a penny. And she knows you haven't either. So you probably can't afford to love her is what she's thinking. Probably rightly.'

The air was thick with the brutality of her words and Julian was glad of the chorus of a drunken song from across the harbour that filled the silence.

'That's a… pretty… cynical thing to say.'

'True though.'

He didn't know what to say – glad only that the gloaming was now so on the side of darkness that she could not see his discomfort. He was about to reply when they both heard laughter approaching them up the pier. Julian made as if to say something but thought the better of it.

'There you are!' Rose's voice was closest.

'We walked up to the top of the town to see if you were there,' came Ran's voice just behind, 'but Davina said you'd be down on the quay. How right she was.'

'So what have you two been talking about?' asked Rose, 'it must have been interesting.'

'It was,' said Ariadne. 'It was about the exchange rate between love and money.'

'And what is it?' asked Ran.

'That depends,' answered Ariadne, 'on supply and demand.'

'And did Julian have any insights for you? He spends enough time with his nose in a book.'

Julian could sense his companions looking at him. He was still taken aback by the harshness of Ariadne's remark. 'Actually we were talking about friendship. Ariadne thinks I've been aloof with her. Maybe I have. What do you think, Rose? Guilty?'

'More than with me and Dav? Probably. But you're a bit like that with everyone. Too much time on a ship, I expect. Though Ran seems pretty normal.'

They laughed and Davina spoke. 'I think Julian is very nice. And so is Ran. And so is Ariadne though she doesn't talk as much as Rose. Is that what aloof means?'

'Pretty well. It also means that you might think yourself a bit superior,' added Rose, 'a bit above everyone else. I don't think Julian's like that.'

'What about me?' asked Ariadne, 'I know I can appear like that – so I won't be offended.'

'You're an honourable – so that makes you superior to all of us. We should all be glad that you speak to us at all.'

'I may be an Hon. but Mummy was hardly born to the ermine. Grandpapa owned a string of foundries in the Black Country; lots of money but not a lot of class. Which is the right way round, by the way; it's kept the roof on the house and the hounds in their kennels.'

'So is that your exchange rate then?' asked Julian. There was a pregnant pause.

'It worked for them. Or not. They're pretty miserable, as you know.'

'So you wouldn't advise it?'

'Love and money?'

'Who would object to that?'

'Exactly.' Ariadne stood suddenly. At that moment a searchlight beam swept over their heads. 'I don't know why we are even discussing it. I'm getting cold. Shall we have a glass of port before we go to bed?'

10

Paris

The Rue Nitot was a short walk from the Hôtel Majestic. The Prime Minister's secretariat had been set up apart from the rest of the British delegation – not least because the usual machinery of government had to continue alongside the business of the conference when both the Prime Minister and the Foreign Secretary were away from Westminster. Isobel had chosen a simple brown dress and the gold cross that was her mother's last gift to her. She wore her hair pinned up. She had paced up and down the corridor outside her shared bedroom in an attempt to master her nerves, rehearsing her words of greeting and imagining avenues of conversation that might open.

She was shown to the third floor and ushered into a suite of rooms containing two civil servants and three secretaries. One of the women took her coat and the other steered her into an anteroom where she sat nervously on a chaise longue with the muffled sound of conversation emanating from the other side of a set of double-doors. It was stuffy; her mouth was dry. There was nothing to read or occupy her mind other than some fine eighteenth-century paintings; she recognised a Hoppner and a Lawrence, remembering that the apartment had been a gift from a wealthy Englishwoman. She stood and looked out of the window and down towards the boulevard clogged with traffic and pedestrians. The sun was out and the trees were throwing their first buds. She longed to open the window and inhale the spring air.

The door opened to reveal two men talking. Lloyd George was nearest to her but facing away and she immediately recognised Clemenceau as his companion. The Frenchman was speaking English and his hands, encased in grey leather gloves were gesticulating to make a point. He caught sight of her and halted, bowing slightly. Lloyd George swung round in surprise. In an instant he checked himself and held up a finger.

'Miss Richmond? I do apologise for keeping you waiting. Will you excuse me while I escort the Prime Minister to the door?'

Clemenceau bowed without speaking. He was physically small but the gleam in his eye was of a knowing worldliness as he glanced at Lloyd George before going through the door.

Isobel fingered her cross as she heard the bustle of the secretariat. After a minute of instructions and consultations, Lloyd George reappeared with his hand outstretched. Her first impressions were of hair – white and wild on his head, in his moustache and sprouting from his eyebrows. He was inches shorter than her, but shared with Clemenceau the same glittering eyes that had seemed faintly sinister in the Frenchman but radiated an intelligence and energy in the Welshman. She had seen his photograph countless times but the physical presence carried all before it. He took her hand and kissed it while holding eye contact.

'Please forgive me for keeping you waiting, Miss Richmond.' He stood back and waved her towards the doors. 'When I have the Prime Minister to myself for a couple of hours, we get more done than in a week with everyone else in Paris. We don't always see eye to eye, Monsieur Clemenceau and I, but we have worked together for so long now that we can cut to the chase on most things.' His accent was strongly Welsh and every word accompanied by a hand gesture. 'The Levant is our current bugbear. If only it didn't matter so much… but now that we are all so dependent on oil. The curse of the internal combustion engine – and fleets.'

The room into which they had entered was like the lobby and as stuffy as the antechamber, with linear proportions not matched by the ceiling heights. He waved towards a sofa.

'I have ordered tea, my dear. It's a bit early for champagne – but we could bend the rules?'

'Thank you, Prime Minister. Tea would be… delicious.' Her mouth felt dry and she wished she had asked for a glass of water as well. Before she could speak he was off again.

'How good of you to come at such short notice, Miss Richmond. Your sister was very persuasive of your abilities…' he was smiling… 'and I felt I had to make your acquaintance given our temporary proximity. She had not told me that you were such a beautiful woman – which is an added bonus from my point of view.'

Isobel felt herself blushing. She hated this in herself.

'You are very kind to ask me, sir. Davina, my sister, said that she was going to write to you before I left Dorset. I had no idea that she would actually do so. She is… some would say… simple. She is grown up physically but with the mental age of a ten-year-old and easily impressed. She thinks that because I went to Cambridge I'm a genius.' She felt the heat rising in her hair. 'As you can see, I'm no such thing; just a secretary in the translating and typing pool. Not very interesting at all.'

She had been looking at the carpet while she said this; but conscious that he was watching her. She glanced up at him to see him smiling with his hands on his hips.

'It had crossed my mind that, while you might have some great talents, Miss Richmond, solving the intricacies of the shape of nation states may not be the greatest of them. But I was amused by her letter that I just happened to see on a desk with a reply on my behalf. It tickled my interest. And if you don't mind entertaining someone who is getting rather worn down by the non-stop business here in Paris, I can assure you that you will only find gratitude on my part. Tea it is.' He nodded to the maid who was standing by the door. 'And some champagne – on ice for later – if, that is, you can spare me the time.' His hands were off his hips and opened as if to aid his question.

He sat down beside her and began to converse. He was a good listener and asked questions that were searching and direct. She found herself flattered by his indiscretions and laughing at his imitations of public figures – in particular of his languid foreign secretary, Arthur Balfour. It was charm; and she knew it. But there were barbs in his exasperation with the American president and distain for Orlando of Italy. She began to relax and found wit drawn out of her that she did not know she possessed. As he laughed at one of her tentative sallies, she began to see him differently. The initial impression of hair, wild and unkempt, ebbed away. She found herself fascinated by his pale blue eyes as they laughed or held her gaze with unblinking attention as she spoke about her life in Paris and her sculpting ambitions, or she replied to his questions about some of the areas with which she had a partial knowledge through her translations. German reparations came up.

'So what should the Germans pay, Miss Richmond?'

She hesitated.

'I'm interested. Really. Should they pay to repair the damage to northern France? Or towards the cost of the war? Everywhere? That's impossible of course – so what is reasonable? And even if it is reasonable from our point of view, how can they pay? There are starving children on the streets of Germany.'

'I suppose they must pay what they can.'

'Or what we tell them to? We still have armies on the frontier – and what was agreed last November is only a truce. Marshal Foch is all for pressing on to Berlin and wringing every last ounce of coal and gold out of them. Insane, of course. But the French are our allies and they see the world differently. Look at Monsieur Clemenceau. A force of nature. A wonderful Frenchman. But he has one big idea that was formed in his youth and has been confirmed all his life. It is that the world is a Manichaean struggle between light and dark; the light for him being France – and the dark, Germany. It's not too surprising: he was a young man when the Prussians took Paris in 1871. He was there. He also knew men who had been with Napoleon at Jena and had seen the Prussians in Paris in 1814. This time the boot is on the other foot – his foot – and he intends to stamp down as hard as he can until there is as little life left in the German corpse as possible. He wants to make sure that generations pass before the German bulldozer rolls over France again. Me? Like countless British statesmen before and, I dare say, after me, I want peace – which simply translates as a balance of power: no one able to dominate the continent. But you can see what I'm up against, can't you? You saw him today. He's not a man to be swayed: certainly not by pieties – which is what our American president is offering. He's an old man. Maybe the work will kill him before we are finished here in Paris – but I can't bank on that; he's a tough old gamecock.' A weary note had entered his voice. 'My challenge is pushing hard for something that is, after all, rather nebulous. I'm always in danger of our allies accusing me of being "*perfide anglais*" if I plead the case for a Germany left standing. Doubly hurtful if you are a Welshman. Winning the war may prove to be the easy bit.' He scratched his eyebrow and was silent for a moment.

The cloud cleared in an instant, and he smiled again. Even at this short acquaintance, she understood that his core strength was optimism. This was what made him such a formidable politician, a restless mind that saw mountains not as obstacles but as challenges – of the intellect and of the will. She saw why he aroused such mistrust, as this could so easily be seen as opportunism. He was a pragmatist with a finely tuned sense of what was possible, for whom motion and direction was everything. Reflection and self-questioning were not in his nature. He was also a man who clearly loved women: Isobel was aware of his eyes glancing down her body, flickering occasionally from the otherwise intense concentration with which he held her. She had never had any man, let alone one of such confidence and power, treat her in this way. It was flattering – and attractive. She no longer saw an older man, or the hair; only his eyes and the hands that constantly made circles and gestures of emphasis.

A knock on the door interrupted him in full flow. He halted, put his hand on her knee in a way that was intimate – and just avuncular.

'My dear, I fear that business intrudes. I have enjoyed myself more than you can imagine. Would you give me that pleasure of your company again? Very soon? Will the fearsome Miss Radcliff spare you again? I do hope so.'

They both stood as the door opened to reveal one of the civil servants whose expression gave nothing away.

'You asked me to interrupt you ten minutes before the queen of Romania is due, sir.'

'Now there is an interesting woman, Miss Richmond. But I have to prepare my ground as one needs to be on one's metal when dealing with Her Majesty – more than a match for any politician here, I can assure you. À bientôt, my dear. Coleman, please would you do me the kindness of escorting Miss Richmond to the door and provide her with a taxi if she needs it. And please send my thanks to your sister, Miss Richmond. I am in her debt.'

As she was escorted to the lift, she could hear his voice behind them issuing instructions and demanding answers. When the lift arrived she turned to the civil servant.

'Thank you. I can see myself out and I won't need a taxi as I am only going round the corner.'

'Very good, madame.' He looked around to check that they were alone. 'Madame – maybe mademoiselle would be more appropriate – may I say something?'

She looked at him in surprise. 'Of course. Please do.'

'Please be careful. Not least with your reputation. I know the Prime Minister well. He has many fine qualities. But also some weaknesses.' He paused. 'Have a very good afternoon, mademoiselle – and enjoy Paris. There is nowhere more beautiful at this time of year.'

He gave a half bow and turned back into the suite.

*   *   *

A note was waiting for her on her return to her shared bedroom. She had decided that her sojourn with the Prime Minister would absolve her from yet another long evening in the memorandum factory and she lay on her bed enjoying the solitary pleasure of silence. The only sound was the whirring of lift machinery. She felt weary and allowed herself to doze for some minutes. She awoke refreshed and leant on her side to read the letter. It was from Madame Aurigny and as she read, she imagined the half smile and languid eyes of her correspondent.

My dear Isobel (if I may call you that),

I do hope your meeting with Mr Lloyd George was interesting. He is a fascinating man but I have to admit that I have been feeling guilty that I did not insist on accompanying you today. He has a reputation; and while someone of my age is well able to look after herself, I was concerned on your behalf. I would be grateful if you could reply to this as soon as possible to put my mind at rest.

I have engineered an invitation for us both to visit the Hôtel Biron next Sunday. The opening night is the following Thursday, so we have been warned that there will still be workmen preparing for that while we visit. As this is likely to be many less than the huge crowds that will be there for weeks after the opening, I am assuming that this will suit you as much as it does me. Perhaps you can confirm this when you assure me of your continued wellbeing? I will pick you up in my motorcar at noon, if that suits you.

Your concerned friend,

Sophie

She read the letter again and recalled the parting words of the civil servant. She lay back on the bed and parsed the time that she had spent with Lloyd George to try and judge from her experience whether the warnings were justified. She recalled his hand on her knee and his close proximity – but had felt only charm and kindness. She found herself smiling at the recollection and laughing as she remembered one of his imitations. With this in mind she balanced her letter-writing box on her knees and wrote a reply to Madame Aurigny, accepting the invitation and assuring her that nothing untoward had occurred. As she did, she thought again about the man she had met that afternoon. She realised, to her surprise, that he no longer appeared old to her, certainly not young but somehow of no particular age. She felt a stirring of desire that astonished her. All her previous fantasies had been of boys and men of her own age; romantic crushes. This was unsettling and unexpected. She glanced at the door before lying on the bed, reaching down into her underwear and running her middle finger between her legs. This pleasure was not new to her but the extent of it was, as she felt an exquisite tension rising up her groin and a warm wetness soaking her fingers. She stopped, almost in fright. At the same moment, a door opened on the floor below – and the thread was broken. She lay still on the bed with her back to the door and safe from any observation, hand still in place and a warm pulse of echoed pleasure flickering through her.

*   *   *

The following Sunday, Gillian was out of the building before either of her roommates were out of bed. She had given no indication as to where she was going. In another this could have been seen as aloof or rude; in her it was self-containment, part of her natural demeanour. Emma lay on her bed reading a romantic novel as Isobel dressed.

'I think she's a spy,' said Emma, putting down her book, rolling on to her side and cupping her chin in her hand. 'Why else won't she tell us where she's going?'

'She might just be private,' replied Isobel, 'and not want to spend her day off with us. You don't exactly see eye to eye.'

'But she hasn't fallen out with you. I can see why she doesn't want to be with me – or you for that matter; but I don't understand why she has to be so secretive about where she's going. I think she's hiding something.'

'What sort of thing?'

'A lover?'

'A lover?' In her mind's eye Gillian was the woman in black with a finger on a psalm. 'Gillian?'

'Maybe that's why she's such a prig.' Emma swung her legs over the side of the bed, her book forgotten. 'She's a double agent. You know; make a song and dance about what a moral beacon you are while sneaking out for an assignation with a depraved lover – maybe an oriental – who you seduce with all the powers you have learnt from… who knows where?' She warmed to her theme. 'It all makes sense now. Throw your schoolgirl roommates off the trail by dressing like a widow and wave the Bible at them so that they don't realise what you're really up to.' She was now standing. 'And at the same time she's probably an agent for the Bolsheviks. Even better, an anarchist, whose friends are assembling bombs and practising an assassination attempt on all the heads of state here in Paris. I have you now, Gillian Dunlop! I will unmask you to the authorities and you will be guillotined for your crimes.' With that she flopped on to the bed laughing.

Isobel laughed too. As Gillian had withdrawn into her polite carapace, Isobel and Emma had become close. They were different in temperament but the revelation in the bar had opened up an intimacy that Isobel had rarely shared with another woman.

Emma rolled on to her back and stared at the ceiling, suddenly serious.

'I'm going to find myself a lover. Here in Paris. It's the perfect opportunity: the capital of love and no reputation to worry about. No guilt and men who understand and appreciate women.'

'Have you… have you had a lover before?'

'Only Rufus. Before he went to the front. I couldn't exactly refuse him, could I? And I didn't want to. I wanted to know what it was all about. The first time it was painful – and he had no idea what to do. Not much more idea the second time either – but it wasn't painful and he was very sweet. And then it happened. So only twice. And unless I manage to find someone temporary here…' She let the words hang. 'And you? Please tell me you've had a string of lovers.'

'Hardly. Cambridge should have been where I spread my wings – but I was at Girton – which is miles from the centre with a mistress who would have been at home running a convent. Not unlike Miss Radcliff. And it was mostly during the war – so the only men left were too old or too sick to fight.' She paused. 'And there aren't many left for any of us now, are there?'

'Are you serious about finding a lover?' ventured Isobel.

Emma considered this. 'Yes. Yes, I think I will. Not a lot to lose really as my virginity has gone already. How I'll meet someone is anyone's guess – especially with Miss Radcliff breathing down my neck. And you? What about Nicolson, the diplomat you met?'

'He's married.'

'The best lovers normally are.'

'How do you know that?'

'I don't. I heard it said once – and it sounded good.'

'I wouldn't tell Gillian that if I were you.'

'I'm in bad enough odour as it is.'

Isobel put down her hairbrush. 'But what makes a good lover?'

Emma laughed mirthlessly. 'I'm not sure I'm the one to ask as I've only had the one and I don't think he fitted that definition. But that was probably because he knew even less than I did. How was he to know anyway? I suppose it's experience. But then maybe not, as there must be bad lovers who are experienced. It's probably about caring. I think Rufus would have become a good lover because he wanted... he wanted me to have a good time.' The pain that came into her voice when discussing her fiancé was there again. 'I suppose there are men – maybe most of them, I don't know – who just want their own pleasure. They can't be good lovers can they? No matter how much they know about women's bodies? What do you think?'

Isobel shook her head. 'Why are we so ignorant? How are we supposed to find out unless someone tells us or we learn by trial – and probably error. And if we make a mistake then we're saddled with it forever. Look at that book you're reading: it's romantic fiction, about men and women falling in love – but it doesn't have one word in it about sex. I don't have a mother – but even if she were alive I don't think that she'd be very enlightening. I'd like a lover too. But I yearn for someone to tell me what I need to know; about what men want and how it works and about how to... how to avoid getting pregnant.'

They both were silent and now serious. Emma knelt down, rummaged under the bed and pulled out a small trunk. Out of it came a small plain covered book which she handed to Isobel.

'It's by Mrs Stopes. Have you heard of it?' Isobel nodded. 'Then you'd better read it as it's certainly the best advice you're going to get. I wouldn't let Gillian see you reading it though; it isn't exactly the Bible.'

Isobel looked at the blank cover, nodded and slid it under the mattress of her bed without comment. She walked over to the window and contemplated the Parisian roofscape outside. The spring sunshine was shining obliquely on to the cheeks of the dormer.

'Thank you. My sister talked about that book – but I had no idea where I was going to get it.' She paused, still looking out the window. 'But it's only going to tell us how to avoid getting pregnant. Who's going to tell us about men? And how are we going to find a man? Or at least one who is…'

'… intact?' interjected Emma.

'Not dead is what I was going to say. Wounded would be alright. It really would. One leg would be fine. Even disfigurement. A companion.'

'We were talking about a lover,' said Emma, 'not a husband. I'd like a husband too – and I'm happy to compromise as long as he's interesting and kind. But what I want now is a lover; a Parisian lover for pleasure; someone to make love to me. I don't want to possess him. I want a shallow relationship. I want to dine at the Ritz once before spending the rest of my life at home, cooking. Is that so shocking? I didn't want it this way – but now I want to steal the opportunity while I can.'

Isobel glanced back into the room. Emma was still looking at the ceiling.

'What about disease?'

'I'll have to hope not.'

'And love?'

'Optional. As long as he pretends, that's fine.' Emma rolled over and observed her friend. 'What about you? If that was on offer, would you take it? It might be our last chance.'

Isobel looked out of the window again, hesitating before replying. 'Why not? I don't want to become an old maid before I'm old. And who's going to know – or care? I've only got one life and if there is a God maybe he will take it into account as he certainly has been hard at work giving us more crosses to bear than our mothers ever had to carry. I don't think that particular theology would stand up to much of a challenge – but you know what I mean.'

'Sort of, but I don't believe in God I'm afraid.'

'Hard to throw off if your father's a vicar. But hard to see God in many places after the last few years. Mysterious ways, Papa would say.' She sighed and shook her head. 'I'm not going to plan anything, but if something comes up, I won't say no.'

'There's something else I've been thinking about,' said Emma. 'Not about Paris and lovers – but husbands. We're going to have to fight for them, aren't we? For every one of them, there are going to be what? Seven? Eight? Nine of us? We'll either have to compromise or use everything we've got to get what we want. I don't think that I'm naturally ruthless – but maybe I'll have to be.'

Isobel was shocked by this. 'That's not very romantic.'

'Nor are the odds; the odds of any of us finding anyone who isn't like Rufus.'

'So what are you saying?'

'That every woman of our age is going to have to not only find the man she wants – but also fight off other women who'll want him too. I don't think there will be much sisterly goodwill.'

'So if I had a fiancé, would you try to take him from me?'

There was a pause. 'I hope not.'

*   *   *

Madame Aurigny's car was as chic as its owner. She was driving with her chauffeur sitting next door to her in the passenger seat. He ran round to open the driver's door and she stepped out wearing a large black hat festooned with feathers and a skirt that revealed laced-up boots. It was practical – but stylish in a way that made Isobel conscious of the workaday limitations of her own clothes.

'My dear, you look wonderful.' She gave her a kiss on both cheeks. 'No wonder the Prime Minister is so keen on your company. I only hope mine will be interesting enough in comparison. I'm so looking forward to hearing all about it over lunch. Guerlin will sit in the back while you, my dear, will entertain me in the front. I have booked us a table at Verochios – very close to the Hôtel Biron.'

She drove with panache and liberal use of the horn, oblivious to the shouts that followed in her wake – indeed she appeared to treat every waved fist as a triumph of sorts, laughing and slapping the wheel with satisfaction. Isobel was aware of the chauffeur's hands gripping the back of her seat – but she only felt elation in the speed, at being out in the spring sunshine and away from the Hôtel Majestic – which she now felt to be a prison.

'Do you know the story of the Hôtel Biron?' asked Madame Aurigny. 'Why should you?' she carried on without waiting for an answer. 'It was built by a wig-maker who managed to get out at the top when Law's Louisiana speculation went so wrong. The Faubourg St Germain was out in the country then – about 1700 or thereabouts – so it was built as a chateau. It became a school at the end of the last century but when that was closed down, Auguste – Rodin that is – took it over and used the downstairs as his studio. I visited him there with my friend Rose who became his wife at the end. It was nearly a slum and the garden was overgrown but it's a wonderful building and even then Auguste was trying to persuade the government to take it on as a museum for his work. Look ahead, it's round the next corner.'

Despite it being Sunday, workmen were all over the courtyard in front of the soon-to-be museum. The windows were open to the spring sunshine and sculptures were being hauled up to the first floor by block and tackle attached to derricks rigged from inside the windows. Other workmen were painting the window frames and yet more cutting back the parterre hedges that had the leggy straggle of long neglect. Madame Aurigny made no attempt at parking but simply stopped in front of the house and, before her chauffeur had a chance to open the door, was out of the car, taking off her gloves and untying the scarf that was holding her hat in place. In repose her manner was languid; in action it was purposeful. Isobel observed her with added interest as she strode up the steps without a backward glance at her car and driver. She halted in the rocaille hall amongst the criss-cross of workmen before spotting a man wearing a top hat and frock coat who was directing the placing of a bronze pietà. He stopped when he saw her and his smile of welcome spoke of an old friendship. He had a pointed silver beard with turned up ends – in the style of the Kaiser that had recently become unfashionable – a pronounced widow's peak and naturally mournful aspect.

'My dear, may I introduce you to my old friend Monsieur Benedite who is Auguste's executor. Leonce, this my new friend, Isobel Richmond from England. She is a sculptress, as I mentioned to you.'

He bowed as he kissed her hand. 'Welcome to the Hôtel Biron, Miss Richmond. If you love sculpture, we are hopefully creating a corner of heaven for you here.' He waved in the direction of the swirl of industry going on round them. 'I would have loved to have taken you round when it's finished but in some ways, when everything is still unformed, it's more like the days when Auguste was here and surrounded by his work.'

'I hardly recognise it,' said Madame Aurigny. 'It was very shabby then. It had its own charm though; sunlight filtered through windows that haven't been cleaned is rather wonderful as long as it's not taken to an extreme – as it was then. I knew it even before Auguste. It was quite an artists' colony – Cocteau and Matisse were here for a time. And Isadora Duncan, who was my friend then.' She halted and looked across the hall, seemingly moved. 'She used to dance over there, in that corner; before drink turned her into the monster she is now. Have you seen her, Leonce? No? I don't think anyone has for some time. And if they have, I suspect it was probably a matter for regret.'

'Don't dwell on the past, Sophie *chérie*. Our friend here from England is the future. As is what we have here. I know it is the work of Auguste – but it will be an inspiration for anyone with aspiration to create things of beauty. Come.'

He led the way through the interconnecting rooms on the ground floor, backing against the walls to avoid the delicate placement of a ton of marble. It was a thing of wonder for Isobel to set eyes on pieces that she had only seen in photographs, their planes and angles accentuated by the sunlight and shadow and their texture and colour in a different dimension. They paused by a pair of marble hands.

'May I touch them?' she asked.

'Do more. Stroke them.'

She did, running her hands down the grain of the marble, circling the tips of her fingers around indentations and the subtlety of protrusion. The heat of the sun on her back and arms was a delicious contrast to the chill of the stone. Her eyes were closed and when she opened them she found Madame Aurigny staring at her with a look that took her by surprise. There was an intensity to it that threw her. She dropped her hands to her side in embarrassment. Benedite smiled at her. 'Don't worry, my dear. Auguste has that effect on people. Particularly women. And in person it was even more so, was it not, Sophie?'

It was Madame Aurigny's turn to look discombobulated – to Benedite's amusement. 'I think it was Robert Browning who asked "whom does one care to tease that one does not also care to kiss?" I tease you more than I kiss you – but who would not wish to do more of the latter?' They both laughed with the ease of old friends and she took his arm as they moved to the next room. Isobel followed, still taken aback by the expression that she had seen on the older woman's face – but not enough to spoil the enjoyment of the rest of the rooms.

*   *   *

They returned to Madam Aurigny's apartment at dusk. They had supper by candlelight that accentuated the height of the room and cast deep shadows into the corners. A single servant waited upon them and disappeared in between courses leaving them to their conversation. With wine, the conversation became more intimate.

'My dear, I gather your father is a clergyman. My parents had not a drop of religion between them, so I'm always intrigued by anyone who has to live with it daily. What about you? Are you a believer?'

She considered. 'I was. But I can't quite give up the idea that there has to be some purpose to it all.'

'After what's happened over the last four years? Seems like the work of the devil to me, but maybe I shouldn't be so sceptical. We have to deal with an infallible Pope here in France. Your Archbishop of Canterbury makes no such claim. Wise: infallible is a high standard and leaves you something of a hostage to fortune given some of history's popes. Is your father a bishop?'

'Just a parson. He's been given a living in Dorset by Cousin Robert's brother. Since my brother was killed and my mother died, he's been a husk: sweet and amiable but no more capable of being a bishop than a whaling captain. His faith is what keeps him alive. I have to admire that, even if I don't share it. I don't think I want to live my life as if the only thing that matters is what happens when I die. If there is nothing then I've wasted my only chance.'

'So you're an atheist?'

'Agnostic. I think of it as a camera where someone is opening the aperture; more; then more; then more – until the whole camera is flooded with light. That's what I know; all that I can know. But there may be something outside that box that I don't know. So to that extent I'm an agnostic. Is that too simplistic?'

'Far from it. Elegantly put. I would have to agree with you – though I'm more in the atheist camp. It's not an easy choice though, as it implies that you're responsible for your choices and your life is the sum of all those choices. It has to come from you, not God. Sometimes I envy my mother-in-law who's rarely off her knees. How simple that would be, that unconditional faith. No decisions to weigh up; no choices. It's a gift – but not one that's been given to me – or you, from what you are saying. I have made my choices and I can't complain about the consequences. How can I?' She raised her glass to her companion. 'It must make for a more interesting life though, don't you think? I could have hung around the Faubourg, married a rich count and died a death of gossip. Instead I've had friends like Auguste and Leonce – and many a good deal more disreputable I can assure you.'

'Madame, I…'

'…Please; my friends call me Sophie. You must do the same.'

Isobel nodded acknowledgement. 'Thank you. I was wondering about you. You have been so kind and made me feel a more interesting person than I really am – and I have had such a day. I will never forget being able to touch the work of such a genius. Ever. But you? What has happened in your life? What happened to your husband? I feel I know nothing about you and you know everything about me.'

Her companion didn't answer immediately but pushed her food around her plate as she weighed her words. Isobel was struck again by her heavy-lidded eyes and the half-smile that was her natural state of repose. The lines on her face that puckered around the edge of her mouth accentuated the sensuality.

'I was lucky in my parents. My father was rich; my grandfather was what you in England would call a nabob. His fortune was made in Indochine – supposedly silk but I suspect opium may have had a part in it. It did enable my father to live a life of the beau monde and marry well: my mother was the daughter of a count – Napoleonic unfortunately, so despised by the *Ancien Régime* families – not that that worried my parents. My father was a director of the Louvre but had tastes that were more bohemian in private. He supported Degas early in his career and it meant that I was brought up knowing and appreciating things of beauty and have been able to live in Paris most of my life. I married Phillipe when I was twenty.' She paused and sipped her wine. 'He was… he shared your Oscar Wilde's tastes – about which I only found out a few years into our marriage.' Isobel felt herself blushing. 'Don't be embarrassed. I'm not. Phillipe was a sweet-natured man – and apart from that, he was a perfect husband. Everyone knew, of course, but in Paris these things don't matter as much as they seem to in New York or London. No scandal was all that mattered and, apart from a small problem with a soldier in London that we managed to hush up, he was discreet and gave me no cause for complaint. But I had to go elsewhere for my pleasures.' She paused and held Isobel's eye. 'Does that shock you?'

Isobel shook her head.

'That's a surprise. I've never met an English person that didn't find discussing sex difficult. Maybe it's the climate. Or the Scottish Calvinists that you have to put up with. Americans are the same, I've found. And that's between men and women. The thought of two men… well we know what happened to poor Wilde. I met him when he was living in Paris after his fall; probably rather nicer then than when he was famous – though habitually drunk, I'm told. Paris didn't seem to mind as much as London – though he wasn't exactly welcomed into the beau monde, I grant you.' She paused. 'So what about you, my dear? Will you take a lover here in Paris? It's a good opportunity.'

Her companion found herself blushing again.

'I hadn't thought about it.'

'Really? I find that hard to believe. Surely no one comes to Paris on their own, and doesn't think about it? At some point anyway. You should – if that is not too forward of me. Life is about taking opportunities, no? Well that is what I have always thought. And I used the… difficulty… between me and Philippe to have adventures of my own. I was not able to have children – so that gave me something of an advantage with the lovers that I took.'

'But Madame…'

'… Sophie, please…'

'… Sophie; even if I wanted to find a lover, it'll be the same in Paris as in London; all the men are dead. Or wounded. Or suffering dreadfully in their minds from the things that they have seen. And… and I…'

'… you're a virgin? Everyone is at some point. The secret is to find someone for the first time who is considerate and kind. Don't go for a boy; they have no idea. You need an older man. Not an old man – but one who knows his way around.' She smiled at Isobel. 'There aren't many of those, you are right. But I'm sure I can find one for you – if you would like that, of course.'

Isobel shook her head. 'I… I suppose I thought it would be more romantic; that I would find a lover who would sweep me off my feet.'

'You will, my dear, in time. The first time is something that you have to go through, I'm afraid.' She halted as the door opened and the servant stepped into the room almost without a sound and stood without expression. 'Davout, would you clear the table please? Are the candles lit in the library? Good. Then shall we go through?'

The library had deep sofas and a fire that competed with the candles to shed an orange light over bookshelves that rose to the ceiling. It was a room clearly well used, with books and pairs of spectacles on every surface. Madame Aurigny, dressed in a loose gown of variegated silk and her long black hair hanging loose, took a box out of a drawer and perched on the edge of an ottoman to open it. Out of it came a decorated pipe into which she scraped the edges of a brown block with a knife whose handle was a pair to the pipe.

'Have you heard of hashish? I smoked it first when I went to Morocco and gained something of a taste for it. Will you try some?' Isobel's alarm was obvious. 'It's very pleasant, I promise you. It lifts all your senses – taste, smell, sound. I used to smoke it with Auguste and he would make me feel his sculpture as you did today: every gradient of temperature and change of plane coming up through your fingertips in a way that you have never felt before. And then you sleep like a baby. Though I love champagne, I'm afraid it has the opposite effect on me and I always wake nursing a dull head.'

'Will it make me…'

'… addicted? No. It isn't absinthe – or opium. I do know about opium as my grandfather became dependent on it when he was in Indochine. Not that it stopped him from becoming very rich and buying one of Baron Haussman's first *hôtels* in the Faubourg. But it didn't do him any good and his life on his return to Paris didn't amount to much – according to my father, that is. He always seemed perfectly healthy and content when I saw him as a child. But then you always remember fondly any adult that treats you as an intelligent and worthwhile person when you're young.' She halted her ministrations and pressed a thin metal gauze into the pipe. The weight of the pipe on her lower lip gave her face a palsied look.

She took a long match and let the flare die down before teasing the bowl with the resultant flame. She held it away from her as she exhaled, holding Isobel's eye. 'You could use the pipe... or you could inhale as I exhale... let's do that.' She shifted from the ottoman next to Isobel. Her scent, heavy with lilies, combined with the velvet smoke. The candlelight rippled the silk of her gown into a voluptuous sheen. She drew on the pipe and leaned forward, flaring her lips slightly. Isobel, lying back on the sofa, opened her mouth and allowed her to slip out of focus as she felt the first waft of smoke against her face before she inhaled. She mastered the urge to cough and held her breath.

'Good. Now breath out gently.' That will probably be enough for now. See how you feel in half an hour.'

They both lay back on the sofa, the shared pipe an intimacy that had subtly changed the rapport between them. They both gazed at the play of light on the bookshelves without speaking, the older woman twisting her long hair into ropes and then slowly shaking them out.

'Do you feel lonely?' Isobel glanced at her companion to judge the tenor of her question. Her expression was pensive. 'I do. It's not that I don't have friends and those that love me. It's just that when I come back here, or wake up during the night – it's only me. And I used to feel the same when Philippe was alive. Maybe it's just the natural state of us humans – or any creature for that matter. It shouldn't play on me but it does – and it makes me sad; though I have little enough to be sad about, surely; certainly less than any men or women of your age. It's not that I feel bad – far from it. I think of myself as happy. But I'm just more and more conscious that our existence is solitary – and now that I no longer have Phillipe I suppose I'm ever more aware of it. I would like to have someone to do nothing with. The nothing seems to be more prominent now, that's all. Sorry, my dear. I don't know why I'm loading these dark thoughts on you. We hardly know each other – but that is maybe why I can say this to you. Do you mind?'

'No. Not at all. I'm flattered. Really.'

'And you?'

Isobel hesitated. The words she had just heard had struck a chord and she felt a closeness to this woman whom she hardly knew – but who reflected the thoughts that she guarded to herself in the long hours of half-sleep before dawn. 'I have the same thoughts – but had hoped that if I was to find someone to share them with that they will... that I won't have them any more. But maybe what you are saying is that they won't go; they will still be there whatever happens. Why should I be surprised about that? You're right, it's just what happens to us, isn't it? The human condition. Normal.'

With almost a start, Sophie sat up.

'Would you like some music. I have a gramophone and Davout has just sharpened the needles. I was thinking of Puccini – something beautiful and also slightly sad... Or maybe something for dancing? Let me look.'

The gramophone with its serpent horn was in a shadowed corner. She rummaged around a box next to it and pulled out a disk.

'*Butterfly*. The first act. Are you happy with that?'

She wound the handle and lifted the needle on to the groove of the disk and stood, waiting amid the crackle and clicks. With the first notes, she swept her arms in the motions of a conductor and the grace of a dancer. In the firelight she was a beautiful witch conjuring up music from a dark well, music that seemed to rise out of the shadows, flow over the dappled ceiling and run down the walls as an aural waterfall. Isobel lay back in the sofa, aware of the sink of the cushions and a sense of being suspended.

Even through the crackle, Butterfly's voice had a luminosity that she had never heard in any recording, each surge of music a wave that rose and subsided with no break. She closed her eyes and let the music wash over her, feeling and seeing the sound as if her senses no longer occupied their delineated cells. She was aware of the magus's presence on the sofa next door to her, a soft wave that undulated the cotton wool cloud on which she was floating. She kept her eyes closed as she felt her hand being taken and the brushing of finger tips along the palm of her hand keeping time to the music.

'Would you like some more?' She lifted up the pipe. Isobel nodded. She felt a strong urge to touch and reached out to stroke her companion's hand which opened to take hers, entwining their fingers together. 'Again', she heard through the sweet-smelling smoke and once again she parted her lips in preparation. 'Now inhale.' She felt the warm smoke over her mouth and breathed in deeply with her eyes closed. She felt the draft of breath halting and exhaled, aware that the mouth that had fed the smoke was only a finger's width from her own. On an impulse, she raised her head slightly and pressed her lips against those above her, marvelling at their softness as they yielded to her kiss. Again impulsively, she circled the tip of her tongue around that of her companion, teasing and stroking with a sensuality that sparked a surge of arousal. She kept her eyes closed, afraid that if she opened them the spell would break – but it held and their kissing became more intense and she became aware of the other's body against her, the curve of her breasts and hips, of her fingers teasing round the line of her jaw and lips, manipulating her ear lobes and stroking her hair. She lost all sense of time until she was aware of her partner disengaging. Reluctantly she feathered her eyes open to see the Frenchwoman slowly undoing the sash that held the silk gown and parting it to show her breasts, orange in the candlelight with dark and pointed nipples. She held one in her hand while the fingers of her other hand manipulated an earlobe.

'Happy?'

Isobel nodded.

'I said I would find you a lover.'

11

Isobel awoke with sun streaming into the bedroom. She felt saturated with sleep and it took her some time to remember where she was; with that realisation came a rising panic. There was an indentation on the other side of the bed but no sign of the person who had formed it. The ormolu clock on the dressing table indicated that it was just after nine o'clock. There were footsteps the other side of the door which opened to the leaning of Sophie Aurigny carrying a tray that contained coffee and fruit. She was wearing a silk robe and a scarf that she had wound around her head as a turban. Without makeup and her customary slash of scarlet lipstick, her face had a flatness that entirely altered her appearance. Her voice was reassuringly the same.

'Good morning, my dear. And before you worry yourself into an early grave, I have already spoken to Miss Radcliff – who it turns out is a crashing snob. It's always surprising how snobs melt when you drop the right names. I told her that I had insisted that you stay after a disagreement with some oysters last night. However, I did promise her that, whatever your stomach was doing, I would have you back this evening.'

She considered Isobel from below her heavy eyelids. 'How are you feeling? With the hashish I always enjoy the sleep of the just; but maybe after such a delicious evening that should be the sleep of the wicked!' She placed the tray on a stool by the side of the bed and sat on its edge, taking one of Isobel's hands in hers. She kissed it. 'You? Did you have as special a time as I did?'

Isobel rubbed her eyes. She shook her head as if to clear it. 'Wonderful – but I still feel half asleep; as if there's cloud in my head.' She squeezed the hands that held hers. 'How did you know about Miss Radcliff?'

'Your cousin. I don't think much scares him – but Miss Radcliff seems to have made an impression. I remembered the name and got one of the servants to go round to the hotel to find out how to get hold of her. She was perfectly reasonable – which she jolly well should be; after all you are neither a child nor a slave, so why should she treat you as either?'

'She does run it a bit like Girton.'

'Girton is for girls; you're a woman.'

Isobel shrugged. 'It's not as if I'm here forever; only until the treaty is signed. I just don't want to get on the wrong side of her as she'll make life difficult for me. She has a thing about "bad influences". My friend Emma is one in her mind – and she has her eye on everything she does. I'm not sure what the sanctions might be, but I don't want to be the one that finds out.'

'You're in the clear – for today anyway. Enough of Miss Radcliff; what are we going to do – assuming you really aren't too ill of course? There's a restaurant on the Île de la Cité next to Notre Dame which is famous for its foie gras – or was before the war. No livers for the last four years but apparently they've made a return. The drive there will blow the cobwebs away.'

The restaurant looked over the Pont St Louis and they were shown to a table upstairs looking down on the tables on the terrace below. It was warm enough just inside the room for them to be comfortable with the windows fully open. The sun was bright and they were glad of their hats. The outside tables below filled slowly as the inside of the restaurant reached capacity. Both men and women wore coats against the sharp wind.

They laughed at the idiosyncrasies of their fellow diners, one of whom was a grande dame dressed in the fashion of the ante-bellum Faubourg. Her companion, sitting on the chair opposite, and being served without a blink of irony on the part of the waiter, was a pug of impeccable manners. It barely flinched when a soldier with one leg and the worse for wine, lurched against the table with the clumsiness of a neophyte with crutches. His apologies to the lady were sternly directed to her companion who accepted them with a cocked head and mandarin inscrutability.

Yquem and sun brought with them drowsiness and peeled away Isobel's inhibitions. 'I loved last night. Thank you. But I'm worried that I'm now,' she hesitated, '... only going to be interested in women?'

Isobel shook her head, embarrassed and uncertain. She felt herself blushing.

'Maybe you will; but I doubt it.' Sophie laid her hand on Isobel's. 'I can only speak for myself of course but, in my experience, circumstance is everything. My lovers have nearly all been men, but occasionally,' she raised her glass, 'someone who happens to be beautiful and *sympathique* makes their way into my life and affections. How lucky am I? And nearly all those lovers were married – happily as far as I could tell. So count yourself blessed, as I do, to be able to enjoy so much.' She observed Isobel. 'Are you feeling guilty? Regrets? A daughter of the vicarage indulging in the sin of Sappho?'

'No. Not really. Though it's been a bit more complicated than I thought. I had only just got used to the idea of a lover in lieu of a husband.'

'Why in lieu?'

'The war.'

'Of course. I'm sorry. But I think you are being too pessimistic. There's always a shortage of interesting men. Most are boors and stupid – and a goodly number don't really like women. Not that they are sodomites – but they just prefer other men's company. You – beautiful, somewhat bohemian, and intelligent – will always be of interest. No need to tie yourself down...'

'But I would like children.'

'That does complicate things.'

'But it wouldn't be a tragedy if that wasn't possible. It's just a fact of life for all of us who are young now. We've had plenty of time to work out the odds – years now – and I know that it's just unlikely, that's all.'

They contemplated this in silence with the hum and clatter of the restaurant going on around them.

'I know that. Of course I know that. And I shouldn't belittle the issue – not least because I couldn't have children anyway. I would have loved them – but there it is. All I'm saying is that there is another life than the conventional; there's going to have to be after what has happened. You're starting on that road – and I think it will suit you. What I hope is that the road will come up to meet you. A few years ago it would have been more difficult, so there is something for you – particularly you – to celebrate. I don't think I am being too Panglossian about it, or at least if I am – then it's because I believe it. *Courage mon amour!'*

She raised her glass and they held each other's eye. Isobel sat back and glanced down at the scattering of tables below. She started. Facing towards her, but oblivious to her presence in the window above, was Robert Granville. His hat was off but his coat was buttoned against the spring chill. He was smiling and leaning forward with a woman's hand in his. Her hat obscured all but the outstretched hand; an unremarkable scene on a Parisian pavement. The woman disengaged, picked up her bag from the floor and stood. They said something – an endearment from the look of the body language – and she turned towards the restaurant. It was Gillian Dunlop.

*   *   *

As Sophie Aurigny had promised, she delivered Isobel back to the hotel at dusk just as the gas street lights were hissing into life. Miss Radcliff was sitting in a cane chair in the hall reading a book. Isobel greeted her uncertainly. The reply was brusque.

'Have you seen Miss Harper?' Isobel shook her head. 'She hasn't returned since she left yesterday morning. Should I be concerned – or angry?'

'I don't know. She said she was meeting a friend. That's all I know. Do you think she is alright?'

The older woman considered her coldly. 'She had better not be alright. I will have to notify the gendarme later if she fails to appear. And if she does turn up, unless she has a very good reason, there will be hell to pay.' Her foot was tapping in exasperation. 'I have always felt that Miss Harper was… headstrong. I won't deny that she is conscientious and hardworking but I will not tolerate her wilful disregard for my rules. Not at all. And you? A Madame Aurigny called me this morning. I had assumed Miss Harper was with you. You look well; not like a girl who has been laid low by oyster poisoning.'

Isobel had seen her reflection in a glass before leaving her lover's apartment: her complexion was one more likely to bring a summer holiday to mind than a sickbed. She had anticipated this. 'I had a bad oyster at lunch yesterday and couldn't move for over ten hours. I woke late this morning and Madame Aurigny took me to an outside restaurant where they gave me something that looked like porridge. It was the only thing I could swallow. I've never had oysters before – and I don't think I'll ever be able to face them again.'

There was a long silence. 'I'm sorry if I caused you any worry, Miss Radcliff.'

The older women waved in dismissal. 'Off with you. Miss Dunlop is back. Why can't you two be as easy as she is?'

*　　*　　*

Gillian was lying on her bed reading. She sat up.

'Where have you been? Miss Radcliff is in a fine fury; with Emma mainly – but she wasn't too pleased with you either.'

'Ill. Oysters. I was nursed by a friend as I couldn't move all night. What about you?'

'Today? I met a friend for lunch. We ate outside.'

'How lovely. Where did you go? When my friend finally got me out of bed, we went to a restaurant on the Île de la Cité.' Isobel looked away as she said this – but could see, out of the corner of her eye, a twitch of alarm.

'We were near there too. Poor you with the oysters. I've never been tempted by them; the texture. It sounds as if you were lucky to be with someone who could look after you.'

The memory of Gillian's priggishness with Emma came into Isobel's mind. 'Yes I was. My friend, Madame Aurigny, said she saw my cousin, Robert Granville.'

If Isobel had been expecting a blush or denial she was disappointed. 'I know him. He's in my office; but I didn't know he was

143

your cousin. We came down in the lift together last week and we spoke. I wasn't too sure about him, but he's very polite and always raises his hat to me whenever I see him.'

'Good. He's not much liked in the family – but his wife is.' She watched Gillian carefully. The memory of Emma's unhappiness acted as a goad. 'Apparently he was with a woman. Do you think he told her that he's married?'

Gillian shrugged. 'Who knows? This is Paris after all; hardly the global capital of chastity. It may have been perfectly innocent.'

'Cousin Robert? I doubt it.'

Gillian looked, for the first time, disconcerted. 'How do you know that ? I haven't heard anything like that about him.'

'How would a collection of girls in a typing pool know anything about him? But I have to say that whatever his reputation, he's been only kindness to me here in Paris – even if we got off to a bad start when we first met. He introduced me to Madame Aurigny.'

'And that's how he's been to me on the few occasions we've spoken. A gentleman.'

'I don't know about gentle. He's something to do with security. A spy? I don't know and he won't tell – but it gives him a rather sinister reputation – but you would know more about that.'

'Hardly. We're not allowed to discuss anything we do even amongst ourselves, let alone about what goes on in other departments.' She paused, and changed the subject. 'What about Emma? Do you know where she is?' Isobel shook her head. 'I hope she's alright.'

'She's a grown-up,' said Isobel, 'but I'm guessing that Miss Radcliff won't treat her like one when she shows up. Whatever happens please don't make it any worse for her than it will be anyway.'

Gillian looked at her with surprise – and what looked like hurt. 'What do you mean by that? What she does is her own business and nothing to do with me.'

'I don't know – but she may have met someone. A man.'

'But she's engaged.'

'Yes.'

'So if…'

'What?'

'Well, if she is seeing someone…'

'I thought you said it was none of your business.'

'Yes… but…'

'But nothing. It is none of your business.' Isobel's voice was raised a tone.

Gillian broke the quiet. 'Emma's a friend.'

'Then treat her like one… rather than giving her sermons. I'm sure you are pure enough to throw the first stone – but don't be surprised if it gets thrown back at you. You treat her as if she's some sort of modern Messalina – rather than a woman who's in an impossible situation. If you really are her friend, help her; don't make her dilemma worse than it is already.'

There was a shocked silence.

The door into their room was still open and they could hear a voice three floors below; angry. The lift machinery hummed. The voice, muffled, rose in volume with the lift and belonged to Miss Radcliff.

'Disgraceful! I have never had such a thing happen to me.'

There was a clunk as the lift halted and whoever was inside wrestled with gates. Isobel and Gillian watched in appalled fascination as Miss Radcliff appeared, supporting Emma, whose head lolled and whose eyes were half closed.

'Come on you two, help me. Quick. Miss Harper is drunk. Disgracefully so.'

They grabbed an arm each and manoeuvred her, like a disjointed marionette, on to her bed where she slumped with her face to the wall and her legs drooping on to the floor.

'Disgusting behaviour. Absolutely disgraceful.' Miss Radcliff shook her head. 'I'll deal with her in the morning.' She took the half-dozen steps to the lift unsteadily – having to hold on to the gate for a second or two. Emma and Gillian looked at each other.

'She may be sick,' said Gillian. 'I'll get a bucket.'

*   *   *

The next morning Emma refused to move. Isobel and Gillian had breakfast and, after checking that she was still asleep, they went about their work overseen by Miss Radcliff who said nothing about the previous day nor asked about Emma.

At lunchtime Isobel returned to the room to find Emma dressed and sitting on the edge of the bed. She was pale. Isobel sat next to her and took her hand.

'How are you feeling?'

'Dreadful.'

'What did you drink?'

'More a case of what I didn't. Absinthe and brandy were the worst of it. God, I've made a fool of myself. But I don't regret it, though I'll miss you.'

'Miss me?'

'My suitcase is packed,' she indicated to the end of the bed, 'as I don't think Miss Radcliff is going to want me here any more, do you?'

Isobel's silence signified a similar conclusion.

'Have you seen her?'

Emma shook her head. 'No. But I would like to apologise to her.'

They sat in silence.

'What happened?' asked Isobel.

The whir of the lift machinery and pigeons gurgling above the sound of Parisian traffic seemed unnaturally loud. Emma sat back against the wall and drew her legs up to her chest resting her chin on her knees.

'It was an adventure. Whatever happens now, it will have been worth it.' She smiled ruefully. 'And I'm not just saying that to make my conversation with Miss Radcliff easier. I'm not exactly going to get a glowing reference after this.' She paused. 'It was unexpected. But then I suppose I was looking for it. You knew that.'

She reached out and squeezed Isobel's hand. 'Where do I start? Well, I went exploring. I wanted to see a different bit of Paris so I took myself to Montmartre: I was getting a bit bored of smart Paris and thought I'd try something a bit more bohemian. It didn't disappoint, though the number of beggars – poor wretches with terrible injuries – were everywhere; and it was dirty and seedy. I went round the new basilica which has only just opened – a Byzantine wedding cake – and sat in a cafe in one of the streets below it where I could be in the sun and out of the wind. There were two men on the next table arguing. Well they weren't really arguing, but talking about Delacroix and I was enjoying the banter. One was Spanish and the other French. Then they were joined by another who was called Brissaud – I knew that because they called out his name when he came in. I found out later that he's an artist – as were the other two. I was pretending to be interested in the street life when suddenly I was sprayed with wine.

'I didn't see it but apparently the Spaniard had made some point with a hand gesture which caught the carafe on their table and the whole lot ended up over me, well it felt like that anyway. They were wiping me down with napkins and a towel brought by the waiter and insisted that they bought me a drink. They probably did it on purpose. The Spaniard was difficult to understand: he spoke French but with a heavy Catalan accent and his new wife, who is a Russian ballerina, turned up later. They were all in each other's pockets and well-known in the bars on the hill and around Pigalle. Gillian wouldn't have approved of most of the women we met. If they weren't prostitutes, they were dancers or actresses – which no doubt her holiness would think were one and the same. They were fun though – and we all were pretty drunk from the first spray at about three o'clock until we dispersed...'

'... which was rather later than Miss Radcliff's curfew,' interjected Isobel.

Emma nodded. 'Unfortunately. But by that point I wasn't really caring. Brissaud – Pierre – was particularly sweet. He told me about everyone we met, their work, their affairs and illnesses. We played card games and watched dancers performing – not in the Moulin Rouge which they said was now only frequented by tourists – and drank far too much. I tried hashish.'

'So did I!'

'With your friend? What's her name? Madame Aurigny?' Isobel nodded. 'Well we've certainly tasted Paris haven't we?' A bilious look came over her again.

'Brissaud? What happened?'

'When we parted company it was way too late to make it back here. And I didn't want to. Sheep as a lamb and all that. He asked me back to his studio. I was expecting a garret – but it turned out to be a proper studio: he's successful – though I've never heard of him, have you? We drank some more and went to bed together.'

Emma looked at Isobel. 'Are you shocked? I am.'

'It is what we talked about.'

'And do you know it was even better than I hoped it might be. It was as if all that he wanted to do was to give me pleasure – and he did – with his tongue and his fingers for what seemed like forever. There was no pain – none – and he told me how to how to use my mouth on him. He wasn't circumcised. Rufus was. That was a surprise as I'd never really thought about it.'

Isobel had never heard sex being spoken about so frankly and was more shocked than she would have expected.

'What about precautions?'

Emma shook her head. 'None. I ought to be worried shouldn't I? Nothing I can do about it now so I'll just have to hope.'

'But why did you get so drunk last night?'

'Stupid. The night before we drank wine. I was on such a cloud the next day that I didn't want it to end. I insisted on trying absinthe and I really don't know what happened next. I remember getting into the lift with Miss Radcliff – but that's about it. Was I sick?'

Isobel nodded. 'In a bucket, luckily.'

'Oh God, I'm sorry.'

'It was Gillian who looked after you. She checked on you all through the night.'

'I wouldn't have expected that. I don't think I'll be telling her the details though…'

'Maybe not. Though I don't think she's quite the nun that you think she is.'

Normally, Emma would have been curiosity itself, but she closed her eyes as a wave of nausea rolled over her. She swallowed and held out her hand again which was taken by Isobel.

'Thank you. I am going to have to ask you a favour. I don't have any money. I lost my purse yesterday and I'll need a hotel for tonight and enough for my fare home. I don't think Miss Radcliff is going to pay for it in the circumstances. I can repay you when I get home?'

Isobel squeezed her hand. 'Of course.'

*　　*　　*

Still pale, Emma left the following day. She and Isobel hugged before she stepped aboard the tram for the Gare du Nord – both women with tears in their eyes.

The working week reasserted itself. From the fragments that came across Isobel's desk and the gossip she received from Sophie and Harold Nicolson, there was a sense of affairs of state moving towards resolution. Increasingly the memoranda tied up loose ends rather than addressed principles. The fluid state of the war-ravaged continent began to coalesce around linguistic ties and geographic realities. The purity of the realignment envisaged by President Wilson met the practicalities of politics and diplomacy, and disappointed minorities emerged as the great powers did what they had always done; impose a peace that suited their interests rather than the Wilsonian ideal.

The work remained unremitting; typing, translating, amending and polishing – with Miss Radcliff pacing up and down her rows of charges. As May slid into June, familiarity with each other and the foibles of their fierce charge-hand became normal life. Miss Radcliff's bark became something they observed with amusement rather than terror – particularly when it was accompanied by an affectionate hand on the back.

Isobel saw Sophie Aurigny every weekend. In public she was her protégée, a young artist to be introduced to Sophie's circle of writers as well as grander friends from the Faubourg. In private they were lovers of increased intensity as Isobel's natural sensuality was teased out by the older woman until it was Isobel who became

149

the leader in their erotic adventures. Their finite time together was an added stimulus, as was the attention paid to Isobel by Sophie's male friends who were intrigued by the striking young woman who spoke perfect French. Both women enjoyed these flirtations. Without Sophie, Isobel would have taken one further – but she appreciated the freedom she had from fear of pregnancy and disease and contented herself with a discreet kiss. She had almost forgotten about her meeting with Lloyd George when another note arrived on her desk – hand delivered. It was in his scrawled handwriting and asked her to join him for lunch in two day's time. Miss Radcliff raised an eyebrow when she was asked for her permission to spare Isobel for an hour or two.

'You have a chaperone, I presume?'

Isobel nodded and took back the proffered letter.

It was unseasonably cold and windy, with showers raking the boulevard as she walked the few streets to the Rue Nitot with one hand pulling her coat tight around her and the other holding her hat in place. The civil servant who had seen her to the lift on the previous occasion greeted her with inscrutable politeness and escorted her to a suite of two interconnected rooms, one of which had a table laid for two and the other a sitting room of empire clutter and palms. The scent of flowers was overpowering. She was nervous; not the disquiet of her previous visit where awe of the office was the main emotion. This time it was anxiety about the situation into which she was placing herself. She had not told Sophie and the parting words of the civil servant, along with the dubious look of Miss Radcliff, had her rubbing her hands together and biting her lip as she waited.

In his customary gale-like manner, Lloyd George stormed into the room, his hair if anything more startling than at their first meeting. He grasped her hand as she stood to greet him, slightly longer than mere gallantry would have dictated.

'My dear Miss Richmond, how good of you to do me this honour. I have been much looking forward to it – and it should have been earlier. But business...' he made a gesture of dismissal... 'always seems to get in the way. But today is Friday and I insisted that we all needed some rest. Enough of me and my trials. What of you? Paris has worked its magic I can see. You are even more beautiful than I remember.'

Once again his energy and charm carried all before him. It made him ageless and drew the eye to his eyes that were brighter than any she had come across before; sometimes holding her with a steady stare; at others flickering disconcertingly up and down her body as she spoke. This time his mimicry was directed at President Wilson but the mockery had a serious edge.

'He has made a terrible strategic mistake, I fear,' he shook his head, 'in coming here with only his cronies – Colonel House in particular – and only Democrats. He's weak in Congress, so the ratification of any treaty is going to be an uphill task at best. Senator Lodge and the Republicans can't wait to humiliate him. He thinks he'll be able to appeal over the heads of Congress directly to the people.' He shrugged. 'We have a different system, of course, but I fear for his chances – and for his precious League which will lose its backbone, not to mention its teeth, if the Americans retreat into their shell.' He smiled. 'But that is only speculation, of course. For every cloud, there is a silver lining. For every former empire licking its mainly self-inflicted wounds, there is a new country we're delivering blinking into a new world – like Poland. I wish you could meet Paderewski. He's the personification of that country; an artist and a statesman. I wish I could have been that too.' His eyes moistened at the thought. 'It is strange though, when I think of what we are doing, the three of us. We sit in a room and play with countries and people like...' he struggled for the right simile, '... like librarians recategorising a library. Is it history? Or biography? Or geography? Everyone has an opinion but something nudges the decision. It might be a personal like or dislike. One of us may be ill, so the others get their way. We've tried hard – but our judgments are just that, judgements. We can't always get it right – and indeed there may not even be a right answer, just the least bad. But books don't care what shelf they're on; people do. Empires can be quite useful, I'm beginning to realise, as they stir everyone into a porridge on to which they force a lid. Unstirring that porridge can be messy, as even our idealistic American president is beginning to understand. But I hope our blunderings will be less catastrophic than those of the wretched Kaiser, the Tsar or old Franz Joseph. We have to hope so anyway.' He paused. 'We've done our best – but only time will tell if that's good enough. Good enough? What does that mean? We can't please everyone so I'll settle for no war. And you? What do you think?'

His question was delivered with no hint of condescension. Isobel considered for a few seconds.

'What about the Germans?'

He stared at her before replying. 'Hard. Very hard. My worry is that no self-respecting German government will willingly sign such a treaty. I wouldn't if the boot was on the other foot. Clemenceau is implacable though. He really believes that Germany will be France's nemesis if it is ever too strong again and that he is acting in the common good by holding her down. The facts are that we can force the Germans to sign: they have no choice. But it will be through gritted teeth and enforcing the terms will mean armies on the Rhine, if not forever, then for at least a generation – and a state of mind that is about war rather than peace. Not the stuff of a lasting settlement, I fear. The problem is that most back at home feel the same as our French allies: in January, it was all I could do to stop a lynching party heading off to Holland to hang the Kaiser – not that he didn't deserve it, mind. But a lynching really wouldn't be the done thing – even Clemenceau agreed with that. Ah, here's lunch!'

The blanched asparagus with mayonnaise and the tournedos were epicurean delights unknown to the rest of the British delegation. Isobel was careful only to sip first the champagne, then the white burgundy and finally the Haut Brion – but even so, by the time they were on to the culminating sorbet, she was light headed. The wine softened her nervousness, as did his charm, but failed to dispel it completely. She knew she was being seduced – but dimly.

Effortlessly he moved the conversation on to her and her time in Paris, and their situation to the small drawing room where they sat together on the chaise longue. He asked her about Sophie Aurigny with a hand on her knee, left there for too long to be avuncular but not long enough to be overt. As he filled her wine glass he edged closer to her so that his leg was touching hers, again on the far cusp of the affectionate, enough for her to be disconcerted but not enough to take offence. Anyway, such were his powers of beguilement and fascination that, despite her better, if impaired, judgement, she felt a familiar stirring of desire. Suddenly he was close enough to her to feel the warmth of his breath. His words changed too; florid compliments that she only half heard. Then, suddenly, his lips were on hers. His tongue lunged into her mouth as his hands grabbed her face. She froze. The insistence of his tongue and rasp of his moustache were abrupt and threatening. Still she hesitated, not knowing what to do. His hand was on her breast while hers were still at her side, uncertain. Any desire was gone. All that was left was a violent physicality as he shifted round with the insistence of his erection pressed against her leg. She squirmed away from him pushing as she did so. Still he clasped her, his breath coming in staccato hisses through his nose as he pulled her towards him. There was unexpected force in his grip and she felt a surge of panic at the same time as she heard the sound of knocking on the door of the connected dining room.

Instantly, he let her go and sat up, running his fingers through his hair. Instinctively, she wiped her mouth with her sleeve and stood up, taking a step away from him. Before he could give the command to enter, the door opened and standing in the doorway was Robert Granville. His raptor eyes blinked in the scene and he made a slight bow.

'Please excuse me, Prime Minister, but I have urgent news from home about my cousin's father who has been taken ill. She had told me she was lunching with you and I hope you will excuse my unannounced entry. Your staff are not to blame as I insisted that I tell Miss Richmond the news myself.'

Lloyd George's sangfroid was intact and he was concern itself.

'My dear Granville, of course you should have come here directly. We had finished our lunch and I was hearing some of her perceptive views on the political landscape at home. When we finally get her, and her fellow young women, the vote that they so deserve, us politicians are going to have to take note of their views.' Without missing a beat he turned to her as if the previous five minutes had not occurred and took her hand. 'My dear, thank you for taking the time to entertain and enlighten an old man who has had too much of presidents and other prime ministers over the last few months. Your company has been a tonic and I am so sorry to hear about your father. I hope to see you before we leave but if not my best wishes go with you and your family at such a difficult time. À bientôt, I hope.'

As they left the inscrutable civil servant saw them to the lift again. He and Granville shook hands.

'Thank you, Coleman. I'm in your debt.'

'Not at all.' He turned to Isobel. 'Au revoir, Miss Richmond. I hope the rest of your stay in Paris is enjoyable.'

They walked out into the rain-soaked streets where her cousin took her arm.

'Coffee? There's a cafe over there.'

He ordered and they sat in silence until the pot and cups were in front of them. He looked at her with a raised eyebrow.

'I hope that my entry was welcome.' She nodded, still shaken – and embarrassed. 'You have Coleman to thank for that. We're both members of the Turf Club and he had the wit to send a message that you were lunching alone with the old goat. My entry was probably not ideal for my career – but I don't think it's the first time he's been thwarted – and everyone got away with their honour intact, I hope.' He looked at her with genuine kindliness. 'Are you alright?'

She nodded and unconsciously wiped her mouth with her sleeve again to rub away the memory. 'Yes. I'm fine. Just embarrassed; that I let myself get into such a situation.'

'You won't be the first – or the last. He's quite incorrigible and very charming – as you have found out on both counts. Not many people get the chance to have lunch alone with the Prime Minister, so don't be too hard on yourself. You presumably didn't tell Sophie? I thought not. She would have stopped you if she'd known. Anyway – no broken bones, or worse. And the good news is that I have a pass to the signing of the treaty – if it ever gets agreed, that is – in the Hall of Mirrors at Versailles. Clemenceau has insisted it takes place there as it was where the old Kaiser was acclaimed as emperor in '71. The symbolism is too perfect to ignore. And the even better news is that I have a pass for my wife – who isn't here. Would you like to accompany me?'

*　　*　　*

He was true to his word and, on the day of signing of the treaty, she was picked up early by Sophie Aurigny's car that contained her cousin, her lover and Harold Nicolson. Within minutes they were in a traffic jam that reduced them to a crawl, creating a smog of exhaust fumes that settled on the convoy, reddening eyes and irritating lungs.

'They can't all be going to Versailles, surely,' said the diplomat.

'Why not?' answered Sophie, 'it's the biggest show in Paris since Napoleon crowned himself. But something of a nightmare for you, Robert?'

He shrugged. 'We've done what we can. It's now down to the French police to make sure that no madman has a go. We've isolated and locked up all the anarchists and Bolshevists who might fall into the category of sane and dangerous. But lunatics are another matter. We just have to hope.'

'If we ever get there,' said Nicolson. 'We've been party to the biggest international conference since Vienna in 1814 and we're going to miss its culmination sitting in a traffic jam. That would be the anti-climax of a lifetime. Not something I want to tell my grandchildren, though I do have a horrid feeling that watching the humiliation of the poor German delegates isn't going to be something to boast about. The Coliseum would have had more blood – but only been marginally less cruel.'

'Come, Nicolson,' replied Granville, 'anyone would think you were talking about throwing some Christian virgin to the lions. Those Huns let loose on the world the most awful war it's ever seen. Or have you forgotten that?'

155

'Of course I haven't. But this is supposed to be a treaty – an agreement. The Germans have just had to swallow whole what we presented to them on a plate – without even the pretence of a negotiation. And it's a treaty that's pretty light on Wilson's fourteen points – which was the basis, after all, on which they originally requested an armistice back in November.'

'They were beaten. They'd lost the war. They may have thought that Wilson was throwing them a lifeline – but they were naive if they thought they could get away with a tap on the wrists. Look at the treaty they imposed on the Russians in '17: the Russians lost a third of their European territories and nearly all their coal mines. This is mercy raining down from heaven by comparison.'

'I don't disagree – but it misses the point. The Bolsheviks at Brest Litovsk just needed to end the war at any cost in order to fight a civil war that they still haven't won. This isn't an ugly contest – or shouldn't be. We should be trying to create a peace that will last – and some institutions that might have a chance of stopping it happening all over again…'

'And we have. The League of Nations.'

'And what did you have to say about that the last time we discussed it?'

'A Tower of Babel.'

'Quite.'

Granville lit a cigarette and leant back. 'This isn't very promising is it? Our idealistic diplomat dressed for a wedding but talking as if he's off to a funeral; or maybe a divorce ceremony – if such a thing existed. Even I, a cynical old sceptic if ever there was one, am a bit more cheerful. Ladies? What do you think?'

Sophie, seated next to Isobel and facing forward, pursed her lips and paused before answering. 'I'm a Frenchwoman. We have a different perspective to you Anglo-Saxons. My grandfather and my father saw the Prussians promenading through the Tuileries as if they owned them, and I have been only a whisker from sharing the same experience in '14 – and again in the spring of last year. The difference is only in that if we hadn't won the Battle of the

Marne it would have been the German Empire marching down the Champs-Élysées, not just the Prussians. And what sort of treaty would they have imposed on us if the tables had been turned? I don't think we've gone far enough. Germany is too big and too powerful. We should have started with that in mind and tried to break up the country into the parts from which it was formed – which was only fifty years ago, after all.'

'And how would you have done that?' asked Harold Nicolson.

'There are plenty of Bavarians and Saxons who dislike the Prussians as much as I do.'

'In the same way the Scots dislike the English. Not enough to want to dissolve the Act of Union.'

'If we had lost the war you might not be so certain of that. I suspect if we had offered a generous peace to the individual states then Germany might have fallen apart rather nicely.'

'Wishful thinking.'

'You didn't try.'

'Fair point. It was discussed – but all the advice was that war had welded Germany, if anything, closer together. We'll never know if that might have worked as Clemenceau – and, let's face it, almost every Frenchman,' he made the motion of tipping his hat at Sophie Aurigny, 'and every Frenchwoman, wanted more than a pound of flesh: coal mines, colonies, reparations, the whole gamut of revenge. I saw Clemenceau at work. Implacable.'

There was a lull in the conversation – punctuated by the sound of car horns and frustrated shouts from the now stationary line of cars lining the boulevard. Isobel leaned out of the window, standing to get a better view. She could see down the curve of the river, where two streams of traffic were merging. She sat down.

'We'll be on our way soon. I think we'll make it.'

'Amen to that,' said Nicolson.

'If we survive without suffocating.'

'Fifteen years ago we would have been complaining about the smell of horse dung instead,' said Sophie. 'They were just as noisy, I seem to remember.'

'Hardly,' replied Granville.

*   *   *

When they arrived at Versailles the traffic jam reasserted itself. The parking area near the palace was already full and the gendarmes seemed to be improvising as nearby fields, still with lying hay, were requisitioned to cope with the overflow. They passed a furious farmer who was gesticulating and shouting at the contents of the cars that blithely crushed his crop. There were tourists in boaters and blazers; working families disgorged from buses and open-backed lorries holding bottles of wine and simple picnics; official cars with diplomats and the beau monde dressed formally in tailcoats and top hats. The driver handed a *laissez-passer* to a flustered official, who waved them through while at the same time remonstrating with a grandee who had sought to bluster his way into the official cavalcade. Cavalry and *poilus* mixed with policemen dressed in formal uniforms topped with feathered shakos to hold the crowd back. They created an avenue for the slow-moving convoy of the elect that snaked its way towards the front of the palace, where it bifurcated to allow a quicker disembarkation.

Nicolson was first out and held out a hand for Isobel. She took his proffered arm as they climbed the steps and turned to take in the view. The crowd was the greatest they had ever seen, pressing against the cordon of troops and kicking up a thin mist of dust and humming with the melded sound of thousands of voices and remonstrations. The air smelt of exhaust fumes, sweat and horse dung and a thin patina of dust lay on the black coat of Isobel's companion.

'Look at that,' said Nicolson. 'Try and remember it as we won't ever see anything like this again. Do you realise that it is five years to the day since poor old Archduke Ferdinand was killed? It seems like an aeon ago.'

An official approached them. 'Your passes please.' He was perspiring. Robert Granville pulled out an envelope and handed it over. The official shook his head. 'Ladies, I am afraid that all passes for the guests of officials have been cancelled. There are no exceptions. La Gallerie des Glacés is simply not big enough.'

'But our car has gone;' protested Nicolson, 'what are our guests to do?'

The official shrugged. 'The ladies may stay – but in the vestibule. You may see something there and it is out of the sun. I can do nothing else.'

With that, he turned to deal with the next in line.

'I am sorry, ladies. There isn't much I can do.'

'We can look after ourselves,' said Sophie. 'We are here after all – and present at the great event – just with less fine seats. Thank you for your concern – now off you go.'

Both men lifted their hats and bowed, agreeing to meet on the terrace afterwards. The women joined the ranks of the *refusées* as they crowded into the anterooms to the Hall of Mirrors, stuffy and humid already with the crush. They were in good time and the Hall itself, seen through the wide open doors, was only a quarter full. Sophie took her companion's arm and steered her to the door where another two officials stood guard.

'This is as far as you can go, mesdames.'

'I understand. But could we just have a quick look at the *Galerie*? We may never see the Savonnerie carpets again.'

'But quickly please, Madame. The delegates will be here soon.'

They stood out of the flow to the side of the doors and took in the scene. A bank of tables lined the wall opposite the windows and a solitary *boule* table sat in the middle with the bound treaty open at the signing page.

'Magnificent!' said Sophie. 'Look at the carpets. It's the first time they've been out of store in my lifetime. Maybe since Napoleon, I'm not sure.'

The crowd was still spread thinly enough that the huge fleur-de-lys, crowns and leaves were clearly visible and reflected in the eponymous mirrors lining the walls. The official delegates were streaming through the open windows from the terrace and the sound of the crowd outside created a low hum. It was a cross section of the world – every skin colour – but all dressed as westerners: frock coats, some with formal overcoats despite the heat, others in suits and boaters, many in military uniform.

They recognised some of the dramatis personae from the previous months of the conference. General Smuts, tall and grave with his pointed grey beard and electric stare was talking to the British Foreign Secretary, Arthur Balfour, whose demeanour, in contrast, was of languid boredom. Colonel House, President Wilson's confidant, was sitting behind the horseshoe desk opposite the signing table watching the room fill, his eyes flicking left and right taking in the scene.

The official touched Isobel's elbow. '*Mademoiselle,* you must come back now. The Prime Minister has arrived.'

The two women squeezed round the side of the door against the swelling press coming the other way. They attempted to merge into the wall of the anteroom, almost behind the door, hoping that they might be ignored. The official had higher worries as Clemenceau waved his stick in front of him to clear his passage into the Hall, his hands encased in his customary grey leather gloves and top hat still on his head. The crowd opened in front of him as if in fear of his famous ferocity as much as his growled order to make way and then closed around his short frame, with only the silk of his hat visible, as he made his way to the mid-point of the room.

'*Le president! Il arrive!*' Isobel, the taller of the two, stood on tiptoe, straining to see what she could. The officials were in front of Wilson, parting the throng for him. He was a head taller than the crowd and laughing at the joke of an invisible companion. As he came level with Isobel, she saw Lloyd George by the President's side, his top hat in hand waving good-naturedly either side of him. His darting, restless eyes fixed on her and with no break in his smile or stride, he nodded. Her hand rose to acknowledge him, but before it had reached her elbow, his glance and progress had moved away from her and into the Hall. The crowd in the anteroom slowly debouched behind the two statesmen, leaving a number of men, mainly in uniform, milling around the doors that closed as the last of the elect were admitted. There were two chairs against the wall and windows into the Hall just above eye height. Sophie nodded to Isobel and they stepped up, allowing them to see down the length of the Hall. Apart from the area surrounding the small desk in the middle of the room – 'a scaffold', whispered Sophie – the Savonnerie carpets were now invisible. Clemenceau was greeting his peers and the crowd still milled but with all eyes on the centre of the table lining one side of the room. One of the men in uniform looked up at the two ladies and then opened the door a crack, enough for the sound of hundreds of voices to flow again into the vestibule.

'*Silence! Mesdames et Messieurs, silence, si vous plait.*'

The crowd settled and above the residue of conversation came the rasping voice of Clemenceau.

'*Fait les Allemandes.*'

Next to them the door was opened – fully this time. They had been so absorbed by the spectacle inside the Hall that the two women had failed to see two men in top hats and morning coats standing behind them. They were both pale – one with a thin moustache which he pulled nervously; the other was blinking fast and squeezing his fists. The usher glanced over his shoulder and nodded before he led the way to the signing table in the middle of the room.

'Which one is which?' whispered Sophie.

'Bell is the one with the moustache – I think.'

Both men looked at the ceiling as they were led to their seats. Two thousand eyes were upon them. The silence was absolute apart from the footsteps on the wooden floor not covered by the imperial carpets. They sat and removed their hats. Only the odd cough punctuated the silence.

'*Le séance est overte,*' said Clemenceau. In his harsh voice he said a few more words and on cue with their conclusion, the two Germans stood to sign, all nervousness in the suddenness of their movements. The master of ceremonies petulantly waved them to sit down again. A ripple of voices swept round the room, silenced by Clemenceau's raised hand. An usher approached the Germans and led them to the table. His proffered pen was met by a stare from the shorter of the two delegates and a deliberate reach into an inside pocket from which he produced his own. In a quick movement he signed and handed the pen to his companion. As he straightened there was an audible exhalation around the room; another ripple; another raised hand.

The familiar gravel voice. '*La séance est fermé.*'

The Germans, with great dignity, looked straight at their judges and, like convicted men, they followed the usher the way they had entered, eyes upwards to avoid eye contact. They came close enough to Isobel that she could see the sweat and misery on their faces. Their dignity kept the silence as they passed but in the main Hall behind them the tension evaporated in a murmur of conversations as the international delegates came forward to sign, led by the American president and his French and British peers. As they signed, the sound of guns, fired in celebration, boomed through the now opened doors on to the terrace accompanied by cheers from the crowd outside. The signing became a simple procession as Lloyd George and Wilson gripped each other's hands and shoulders in mutual congratulation and the throng within dissolved into a thousand conversations.

'Quick. Let's go outside to see them leaving,' said Isobel.

The two women climbed down from their chairs and pushed their way across the press that was leaving the Hall of Mirrors. The heat inside was now oppressive and though the day outside was hot, it felt fresh by contrast. They were just in time to see the crowd outside burst the cordon of the police and soldiers that had, until then, held them away from the cars that were below the steps up to the terrace. They hesitated.

Sophie moved decisively, beckoning Isobel. 'By the fountain. There's a step there. We'll see them without getting crushed. Quick!'

They made it almost at a run, before the crowd reached the steps, taking the opportunity to dip their hands into the water and splash their faces. Around them, a head lower, the multitude spilt past them and up to the doors of the hall from whence the trio of leaders was now emerging, surrounded by a posse of police whose every gesture and expression showed that they had lost control. The crowd, good natured though it was, surged around the leaders with individuals trying to pat their shoulders or shake their hands. The bonhomie of the leaders evaporated as they were jostled and hemmed in. Clemenceau raised his stick. They were now opposite the two women and only able to move forward one step at a time as the cordon around them forced the crowd back. Wilson maintained a fixed smile but Lloyd George had a look of fury as he struck away at importuning hands. A surge rippled towards them and the whole party, cordon and leaders, were stuck sidewise with both Lloyd George and Clemenceau picked up in the crush and propelled toward the fountain where Lloyd George stumbled and fell at Isobel's feet. As she looked down on him, two policemen grabbed his arms and pulled him upright. He struck out either side of him and in the small space that cleared around him he raked his mane of hair back into shape, rage in every movement. He waved away his hat and jutted his jaw while the escort created some space around them. For the second time that day Isobel caught his eye. This time he merely blinked and turned back towards the steps and his waiting car.

12

Dorset, August 1919

It was harvest time when Julian returned to Milborne. He had not
seen the West Country in summer before and was entranced by its
beauty. He loved his native Galway – but it was a land of stone walls
and wind-bent trees where summer took only a tentative hold. As
his train wound its way through the chalk valleys of South Wiltshire,
he watched fishermen casting over streams for trout, women and
children forking cut corn into ricks and dust rising out of threshing
machines like smoke to shroud barns and villages in a yellow mist.
As the landscape changed into the pastures, hedges and banks of
the Blackmore Vale, the ricks were now of hay – winter feed for
the cows and beef stock that ruminated under the shade of elms
that formed an almost interlocked canopy along every hedgerow.
Green – sombre in the depths of the woods, vivid in the meadows
and sinuous grey in the pond willows – was the dominant colour; an
overdose of chlorophyll even in high summer. The stone changed
too – from the moss green of the chalk valleys to grey, and then
to russet brown.

The closer he got to Milborne in the car sent by Ariadne to collect him from the station, the more keenly he observed the fields
and lanes that he had known only in winter. As the car disappeared
he stood, with his bags at his feet, on the doorstep of his cottage
and contentedly smoked a cigarette, the smoke of which mingled
with insects and breeze-borne pollen in the mid-afternoon sun.

He had a pleasant surprise within. The kitchen was still primitive
but, in addition to the range, there was now a paraffin stove and
a single tap replacing the hand-pump that had been the cottage's
only source of water. The entire interior had been whitewashed
and windows that had been framed by hessian sacking now had
rough curtains of calico drawn back on wooden poles. The bed

was the same but an eiderdown had replaced the stained blankets. A vase of wild flowers stood in the middle of the kitchen table, evidence of a woman's hand. He imagined Rose, sleeves rolled up and wearing a straw hat, searching the hedgerows for dog rose and mallow, and smiled to himself.

Wearing a light summer suit, he rang the door bell of the rectory. When the door was opened by the maid, the woman standing behind her was not Rose but Isobel. He hoped that his disappointment didn't show as she greeted him with affection and took his hand to lead him out to the garden where her father was sleeping under the shade of a cedar tree. The vicar woke in confusion and Julian stood awkwardly as he apologised for his open shirt and crumpled jacket. Tea was summoned and dignity restored.

'My dear boy, what adventures you've had! We've heard of nothing else from Rose and Davina – not to mention Ariadne; though from her you would have thought that having the German fleet sink in front of her eyes was something that happened every day on the front lawn at Milborne. Adventures all round. Have you heard that my other daughter has been having tea with the Prime Minister?'

Julian looked at Isobel. 'That is news to me. How did that happen?'

'Davina. Do you remember that she said she was going to write to Mr Lloyd George about me? Well she did. And he asked me to tea.'

'And how was it?'

'It was,' she hesitated, 'fascinating. But you; tell me more about Scapa and the fleet. I'd love to hear more about it from someone in the Navy who really knew what was going on: the girls were a bit light on detail – and facts, I suspect. I want to know what happened afterwards when they'd gone home. You've been there for over a month since then. It must have been chaotic.'

As he answered her, he couldn't help noticing the changes. There had always been a challenge to her conversation – but now there was reserve. Before, as Rose's younger sister, she was of interest – but gauche and opinionated. Now she held her council and listened more than she spoke. She had blossomed, but while there was a physical manifestation that drew the eye, there was also an inner stillness that intrigued. He finally asked after Rose.

'She's gone with Dav to Wales – Pembrokeshire – where Cousin Violet's sister has a house on the sea. I was invited with them – but after four months in Paris I wanted to stay here and be with Papa.'

'You should have gone,' interjected her father, 'and not stayed around here with an old man; not that I am complaining about having you back and all to myself. She's very tired, Belmore. Overworked. I had no idea of the hours that the terrifying Miss Radcliff made them work.'

'How long will they be away?' Julian hoped that his question did not sound too eager – or disappointed.

'Ten days isn't it, my dear? They'll be sorry they aren't around to welcome back the returning warrior. Ariadne is here; though not with good grace, I gather, as her mother has insisted she stays on for a house party that she's organised. It appears that, as Ariadne refused to go to the season in London, the season is to be brought to Ariadne. Dear Violet is determined to have her married off as soon as possible. From what I can gather from Rose it would seem that Ariadne has other ideas. It will be a battle, I fear, as neither of them are much given to compromise.'

'To say the least.' Isobel held out the teapot. 'And why should Ariadne have to get married anyway? Especially to someone that Cousin Violet thinks might be suitable but whom neither of them have ever met.'

Her father's exasperation showed. 'Yet, Isobel. Not all customs are useless and outdated. You know, as well as I do, that Ariadne is an heiress – and a particularly eligible one as she has a fortune but no responsibilities: Milborne and the title will go to Robert but Ariadne will inherit her grandfather's money. Violet clearly wants to make sure that the bees around the honeypot have an interest in her daughter as well as the honey.'

'Papa, you are so naive sometimes. Cousin Violet a loving parent with only her daughter's welfare at heart? Really? I don't think she's ever had an unselfish thought in her life.'

'Isobel!'

'You know what she's like. Everything I've ever heard or seen of her tells me that I'm right. What do you think, Julian?'

Julian waved his hand and shook his head.

'Isobel, you're putting poor Belmore here in a difficult situation. He is dependent, as are we I might add, on the Milborne family.'

'On Cousin James, papa. Cousin Violet couldn't give a damn about us – or probably about Julian either – other than flirting with him.'

'Enough!'

'Papa, you were there at that dinner.'

'Violet was a little worse for wear…'

'And she made a pass at Julian…'

'Enough Isobel! This is indecorous and embarrassing for Belmore – and for me. They are our cousins and we are living in their house and taking their hospitality. That's an end to it.' Isobel stared at the table and bit her lip. 'Now Belmore, I would like to hear more about your adventures, and I'm sure you will want to hear something of what Isobel has been up to in Paris. She may tell you more than she's told me.' He eyed his daughter carefully. 'Robert turned out to be a true friend and an ally I gather – though how I'm not being told. She's old enough to do as she pleases and as long as she has come back safe then I'll leave it there and not pry.'

There was an awkward silence; the sounds of insects and birds seemed unnaturally loud – punctured by the sound of the doorbell. They could hear Ariadne's distinctive voice. Julian and the vicar stood as she strode across the lawn in a pair of jodhpurs, brown boots and straw hat. As with Isobel, her welcome for Julian was affectionate, putting him at ease. Their conversation on the pier-head in Stromness was still fresh in his mind.

'Thank God you're back – and just in time. Mummy has arranged a house party and they're arriving tomorrow. I don't know a single one of them.' She reached inside her bag and pulled out a cig-arette which she lit and blew staccato smoke rings. 'I thought it was just going to be Isobel and me against them all. Now I've got reinforcements, I feel rather better.'

'I'm not sure how we are going to be able to help,' said Julian. 'And I don't know whether your mother has us in mind as ideal guests for her weekend to introduce her daughter to society; it's us that she's trying to get you away from.'

'Don't be silly. Mummy will be fine about it. If she's not, then I'll tell her that I'll get the first train to Wales and she can look after these ghastly people on her own. She knows I'll do it, so she'll scream and shout at me – then give in; and not gracefully.'

'So who's coming?' asked Isobel. 'There must be someone who's interesting and entertaining.'

'Believe it or not a bishop.' She suddenly remembered her older cousin's presence. 'Not that there's anything wrong with a bishop, of course. But marrying a bishop twice my age isn't exactly what I had in mind.'

'There are some younger bishops, my dear,' said Isobel's father. 'But young is relative, I have to agree. There aren't many under the age of forty. And apart from the bishop?'

'Two soldiers. Well they're still in the Army anyway. One's an Hon. and the other's from a "good family" – whatever that means. Both young – which I guess means below thirty and there's a politician Mummy's keen on; one of those who had a good war and made a fortune out of it – or so Daddy says anyway. But he may just be a Liberal. Then there's a girl called Lavinia, whose father's a duke and two others; one called Edith who's renowned for being sweet and plain; and Prudence – who's something to do with Cousin Daphne. Mummy wants no distractions so I suspect that all the girls are handpicked to be dull and ugly only to make me appear less so.'

'Ariadne, you're doing your mother a disservice.'

'I don't think so, Cousin Charles. She's spent months cooking this one up and she's determined to make sure I meet people who aren't from Dorset and, ideally, don't hunt.'

'You could just make the best of it,' suggested Julian, 'they may be rather more entertaining than me and your cousins if you give them half a chance.'

'I suppose you're right.' She sighed and looked at her boots. 'I was looking forward to going to Wales – and also to seeing you now that you've finally made it back to civilisation. Also they're starting hunting on Saturday and I wanted to be there to see how the new entry get on.'

'My dear,' said the vicar, 'the hounds will still be there next week – but a potential husband might not.'

'But I'm not looking for a husband.' She rolled her eyes. 'I know; maybe I could divert one of them on to you, Isobel? What about the bishop? You're used to the church.' Isobel made a face. 'You can live in a palace and sculpt to your heart's content. Damn that; what about an earl? And you, Julian...' She paused and something of the Stromness tone infected her manner. '...the daughter of a duke could be just right for you – especially as her father owns a huge tract of Leicestershire and has his own pack of hounds. I'm sure you could ignore her hare lip and moustache in the circumstances.' She dropped her cigarette on the lawn and pushed her heel on to it. 'You've all got to come, including you, Cousin Charles.' The vicar shook his head and raised his hand in emphasis. 'If you insist. But I won't take a no from you two. Now Julian, I want to hear what happened after we went south.'

Julian felt relieved that the previous conversation was at an end. There was always something about Ariadne that was unsettling. He told them about the return of the British squadron too late to alter events and the fury of the English admiral at what he saw as the perfidy of his German opposite number. The German sailors had made no secret of their delight at the outcome and had shrugged off the casual brutality of their captors in anticipation of their return home. The more thoughtful knew that revolution, hunger and unemployment would be there to greet them too. A handful of ships had failed to scuttle and had been commandeered by the Admiralty. Others, like the *Baden* that Julian had nominally captured, were aground and half sunk. Within a fortnight the first of an armada of salvage vessels were surveying the wrecks.

After the the initial chaos, both he and Ran were as good as redundant. No German fleet meant no threat – and the duties of the signal hut were reduced to the point of irrelevance. After some days this was tacitly accepted by their superiors and a bored petty officer was left overseeing a skeleton crew of even more bored ratings who honed their card skills and slept openly next to the radio sets. Both Ran and Julian were volunteers who knew their naval service was at an end, so they set out to enjoy the Orkney archipelago in their skiff, ranging far and wide with a tent and sleeping bags in atypical summer sunshine. The days were long in these latitudes and the sun disappeared for less than four hours at night. Despite the midges, the evenings around a campfire, with a blanket draped around the shoulders to ward off the chill, were peerless in beauty. They bathed naked in the sea and in freshwater lochs in the middle of the less populated islands that were as denuded of trees as they were of clothes. There was a lack of inhibition in their sex together, in their tent and in shepherds' bothies when they were available. The privacy more than made up for the bareness and discomfort and, though they never discussed it, the enjoyment was the more pleasurable for its transitory nature. It was an extension of the eroticism of their adolescence and both knew that it had no permanent part in their future lives.

'So you and Ran were on a glorified camping holiday,' said Ariadne.

'I suppose we were,' said Julian, both looking and feeling slightly embarrassed.

'Will you have to go back?' asked Isobel.

'I hope not. I'm still in the reserve, so theoretically I could be called back – but no enemy fleet makes it unlikely. And now the treaty is signed we can all get back to normal, I hope.'

The same thought passed across the tea party, articulated by Ariadne.

'Normal? What is normal any more? I can't imagine what it was like before? What do you think, Cousin Charles? I wasn't much more than a child when it started.'

The vicar contemplated his shoes and chewed his lip before replying.

'How can it be normal after this... catastrophe? There isn't any better word is there? I see it every day – and hear it from my parishioners: fathers who have lost sons; and daughters who have lost fathers; widows; just about every permutation of loss. I've noticed a change recently – since the armistice. When the war was going on there was a... I think stoicism might be the right word. The grief was more private; internalised. Now I get anger; visceral anger at the waste and stupidity of it all. I feel it myself. For what? I know I shouldn't say this after all the suffering and sacrifices – but for what? Is there anything we've gained other than victory? And victory isn't going to give us back our sons and brothers, is it? At least we aren't Germany – but that's not much of a consolation.'

There was silence again, broken by Julian.

'You were in Paris, Isobel. What did you see or hear that might make it all worthwhile? Have we got a world that's safer or better? I've been out of the swim of things. We did get *The Times*; but two days late and it was difficult to tell what was wishful thinking and what was propaganda.'

Isobel didn't reply at once but looked up at the cedar tree. Her emotions were close to the surface. 'I was in a typing and translating pool so I saw plenty of memoranda and letters. We all did. And though we weren't allowed to talk about it outside, we had a ringside seat where we got as good a view of what was going on as anyone. I was also lucky enough to meet diplomats and hear gossip from Cousin Robert and others. Safer world? Maybe. No one had much time for President Wilson's ideals that we could see; maybe at the beginning in January, before I got there – but not by March. What we saw was a mixture of the larger powers jockeying for what they could get – Palestine, the Saar, a chunk of Poland or an island in the Aegean – whatever was up for grabs. And then there were the new countries, like Czechoslovakia, trying to make themselves viable. But I didn't see or hear much of anyone, other than the American delegation, paying more than lip service to the League. As my new friend, Mr Nicolson, said to me, the trouble with the League is that it doesn't have an army.'

There was silence amongst the tea party. As with most of the world, they had all breathed in the hope that the American president had brought with him across the Atlantic in January. His high oratory and idealism had seemed to offer something better. They had all followed the twists and turns of the Conference – but through the filter of newspapers. Isobel's description of the brutal realities of power was sobering.

'You met Lloyd George, Isobel,' said Julian. 'Did you get any idea of what he thought about it?'

'Some. But he's the prime minister of the British Empire and there's nothing new there. It's the old world: divide and rule in Europe and get what you can across the rest of the globe. Why did we think it would be any different?'

'Doesn't it have to be?' asked Julian.

Isobel considered this. 'I thought so – but now I'm not so sure. It worked for nearly a hundred years. Maybe the reason it will work again is that the cost of war is too high. Ordinary people won't stand for it.'

'If they're given the chance,' said the vicar, 'but they generally have to do what they're told – unless there's a revolution.' The murderous chaos in Russia formed a daily news background along with the street fighting in Germany. It was a bacillus that all but the far left dreaded, even though it seemed a long way from the English garden in which they were sitting. 'I'm not sure anyone would stand for any war, even a small one, after what's happened.'

'Then you'd better start writing to the Prime Minister,' said Isobel. 'They're still talking about force – or the threat of it – to get the results they want. Maybe it's just the way the world works: the powerful take and the weak have to give. Just because we've had a war that we think is the war to end all wars doesn't make war disappear. There are plenty of people who think that all the treaty has done is make war even more likely by leaving the Germans – and I suppose the Austrians – with nothing but reparations and humiliations. We've left them on their backs for the moment – but that won't be forever. At least that's what Mr Keynes thinks – and many people say he was the cleverest man there.'

'Let's hope that that doesn't make him right,' said Julian.

'Amen to that,' said the vicar.

'In the meantime the next war has to be fought with my mother,' said Ariadne. 'She is trying to organise every minute of every day so that I'm always near one of the men she's lined up for me. Not a second spared for me to have a chat with any of the girls – which is, of course, extremely rude. And don't look at me like that, Julian. I know that cosy charm isn't my forte – but even I know that talking to your guests is common courtesy. Mummy doesn't – and I'm going to have to tell her, which she won't be happy with. What was she like when she was young, Cousin Charles? She can't be as bad as she is now.'

'She was rather wonderful actually, Ariadne. Very beautiful and very…'

'…spoilt?'

'No. I was actually going to say vivacious and…'

'…drunk?'

'No, Ariadne,' a cross note had entered his voice, 'I was not going to say that. I was about to say fun. And funny.'

'Bit of a difference then… with now?'

The vicar shook his head. 'I have only the fondest memories of your mother – and she has been more than kind to me – and my family – since we arrived here. I accept that mothers and daughters sometimes don't see eye to eye but your quarrels, my dear, are neither mine nor Isobel's.'

Ariadne laughed and the haughty mien that was her natural state dissolved. 'Oh, Cousin Charles, I was only trying to co-opt you as an ally. I know you have a soft spot for mummy – and she for you. I was hoping that I might be able to harness some of it in my cause.' She stood up suddenly. 'What a lovely tea party. Drinks tomorrow then? And dinner, of course. Mama has had half a dozen frocks made for me and I can only wear half of them. Isobel, why don't you come round to Milborne tomorrow morning and you can see which of them you'd like? We must be almost exactly the same size. Until tomorrow, everyone.'

They sat in silence. Ariadne's manner demanded attention and her absence restored an equanimity that her proximity disturbed.

More tea was poured and they settled back into the shadows and sounds of a summer afternoon.

*   *   *

Isobel felt self-conscious in the evening dress that Ariadne had pressed upon her. She had been right about the size and, despite protestations to the contrary, Isobel enjoyed the quality of the material and the cut that she knew made the best of her figure. Such clothes were new to her and she hadn't appreciated the difference they would make to her confidence – confidence that she needed as they entered the hall at Milborne from where they could hear laughter and raised voices in the drawing room beyond.

'Ah, Isobel my dear, how good to see you.' Violet Milborne was holding her habitual cocktail in one hand and cigarette in the other. 'You look lovely... and that dress looks as if it were made for you. A great improvement.' She turned her attention to Julian who took her outstretched hand. 'And Julian. Our hero back from the war. The tales that Ariadne had to tell after her sojourn in the Orkneys had my hair standing on end. But you're unharmed, I hope.'

'Thank you Lady Milborne; there really wasn't any danger. It's good to be back and I did want to thank you for painting the cottage.'

'The cottage? Ah yes, I remember Ariadne being rather insistent on that. We'd assumed that you didn't mind it too much as it was. You'll definitely hit it off with Lavinia Bearstead, by the way; all she can talk about is hunting – even now, in summer. She's the one in the far corner.' She leant closer and her musk scent filled the air. 'Her mother needs to have a word with her about the moustache – but she's very sweet apparently.'

With that she made a sort of benediction with her cigarette and moved on to greet another guest who was removing his hat. The noise in the drawing room suggested a party that was well underway. Isobel and Julian exchanged glances as they entered a room that was a medley of servants, glasses and cigarette smoke. They caught Ariadne's eye as she glanced towards the door. She made a brief excuse and sidestepped her way towards them. She was flushed like her mother.

'Well done, you two. Thank God you're here. Actually it's been fun. Only a couple of duds.' She dropped her voice and indicated to her left where a sleek man of an indeterminate age was jabbing his cigar at another who had the half-smile of the politely bored. 'And her, I'm afraid.' She indicated towards the window where a girl – she looked young – was studiously examining a leather bound book with the fierce concentration of those waiting for someone to speak to them. 'Edith or Prudence?' asked Julian.

'Prudence. She answers to Pru. You are a darling.'

Julian approached and looked over her shoulder at the book she was pretending to read.

'Wyatt. He was the architect of this house,' he said.

She started at his presence. She was round-faced, pretty rather than beautiful, but there was something about the set of her mouth and the wary way her eyes scanned the room that made him realise that there was more to her than Ariadne had indicated.

'Yes. I was reading about him – and the building of Milborne. Apparently the family regretted hiring him as he was hopeless at business and nearly went bankrupt while the house was being built.'

'You have been busy. I'm Julian, by the way, and I believe you're Pru. Maybe you could tell me who's who as I only know the family.'

She closed the book and looked around the room.

'With the cigar? Evelyn Grumond. He's an MP for somewhere in the Midlands. George Richford – the one who he's speaking with…'

'… talking at, I think…'

'I had him for half an hour non-stop in the car from the station. George says that he made a fortune in black cloth over the last four years. And that would have been a lot of money, wouldn't it?'

'And George Richford?'

'He's the younger son of Lord Someone or Other. He seems nice. He's been in the army since the beginning – and then in the RFC. Shot down twice but survived and has a DSO. He drinks,' they watched him as he swallowed half his cocktail, 'but doesn't seem to get drunk.' She turned back to look at him. 'What about you? Are you local?'

'Well, yes… and no. I'm the master and huntsman of the local hunt and I live in a house on the estate – but I come from Ireland. I haven't been back there much over the last few years as I was detained at His Majesty's pleasure in one of his ships. Just got out – so the beak would probably say that I was of no fixed abode. And you?'

'Rather the same. Except I do have a home – or rather my parents have a house – in London. I've just been demobbed too. I was a nurse. Still am, I suppose. Though I don't think I want to see any more pain and misery for a very long time. I joined up as a volunteer in '15.'

'Me too. But I suspect I had an easier ride.'

She didn't reply immediately, but reached into her handbag for a cigarette.

'Yes. You probably did.' She looked around the room. 'This all seems like a foreign country to me. I think Richford and George Allan… that one over there with the eye patch… probably feel the same way. You too. We've all seen things that no one else here has. Lucky them.'

Julian looked across to where she had indicated, towards the man with the patch. His good eye was taking in the room as he spoke to his companion and, as he turned round to pick up his drink, he showed the other side of his head. His ear was gone and instead of hair above it, there was stretched white and red skin – livid and barely healed. The contrast with the handsomeness of the other profile was doubly shocking.

'In a tank I'm told. He got out at least – which is more than could be said for the rest of his crew – who were roasted alive. We had plenty like him in my field hospital near Amiens.' She rasped the flint on her lighter which flared and then settled. 'Most died from infection. Quickly if they were lucky.' She looked at Julian through the smoke as if to gauge the effect her words had had on him. 'I find people like him,' she nodded towards the man with the cigar, 'hard to deal with. What about you?'

'I only saw some action; at Gallipoli: the only time I saw men killed and got close to bullets. The rest of the time I was on a ship in the North Sea where I was more likely to die of boredom than anything else. I missed Jutland and only had one shell that got anywhere near me. I had an easy ride.' He paused. 'And you? How do you fit in?'

'I don't. My mother's a friend of Daphne Granville and I was called up as party fodder. I make a point of accepting any invitation that arrives as it's better than sitting at home with my mother worrying about whom I'm going to marry. If I'm here it gets her off my back for a few days. I suspect all the girls here are in the same boat.'

'So you don't know Ariadne?'

'Not until yesterday. Hunts, I gather. But doesn't seem to talk about it quite as much as Lavinia over there.'

'She actually prefers to talk about anything other than hunting – which is what I prefer.'

'You'll make a perfect couple then. I've heard that she's very rich – or will be anyway.'

'You heard right. But you'll find that she has rather exacting standards – and I don't think they stretch to an impecunious Irishmen who is employed by her father. A bit like marrying the gardener…'

'Stranger things have happened.' There was an embarrassed silence broken by Prudence. 'And who's the tall girl over there?' She nodded towards Isobel.

'Ariadne's second cousin. Isobel. One of three sisters who are living with their father in the rectory.'

'Very Jane Austen.'

'I suppose it is. But Isobel isn't Fanny Price. Far from it. She's a sculptress, has a degree from Cambridge and is just back from Paris where she was doing something at the Conference. She and Ariadne don't take prisoners.'

'Rather good for you then.' Julian looked at her in surprise. 'Men get away with boring on about themselves too much.'

'Am I doing that badly?'

'You're fine: so far. It does make a change though. Do you know Mrs Granville?'

'Yes. And I like her very much. We're both keen on Thomas Hardy's novels and went to have lunch with him last spring. I don't think she has a happy life though.'

'The husband? Mummy can't stand him. But it's thanks to her that I'm here – and I like her too. This…' she nodded at the party, '…is beginning to improve already. Thank you. Will you introduce me to Isobel. She sounds interesting.'

Isobel was talking with, or being talked at by, a woman who was a head smaller. Julian's heart sank when he saw the dark shadow on her top lip. Within a minute he was hearing about an outstanding run that the Quorn had enjoyed in February and was making a mental note never to describe a hunt again.

Isobel was as relieved as Julian was despondent about their change of conversational partners. But Pru's first question threw her.

'Are you in love with him?' She raised an eyebrow in Julian's direction. 'From the way he was talking, I think he has a soft spot for you.'

Isobel felt herself blushing and wished that somehow she could stop this happening.

'No. Not at all. Whatever gave you that idea?'

'I'm sorry. It was just the way he… forgive me. Stupid. He just seemed rather interesting and I found that… well, a change anyway. He asked about me and didn't just talk about himself.'

'Which most of them do, I agree. I think he's interested in my sister though – and she in him.' A shadow of disappointment crossed Pru's face. 'But they aren't engaged, and he's been away since March, so I don't know the lie of the land.'

At that moment Daphne Granville appeared out of the melee.

'There you are, my dear girl. And you too Isobel, fresh from Paris. How was Robert? I hope he looked after you.' Her expression was one of hope rather than expectation.

'Actually, yes Cousin Daphne. Very well in fact. He was kindness itself. Really.'

'He introduced you to the right people, I hope.'

'Better than that. Two of them are now friends. Do you know Madame Aurigny? Or Harold Nicolson?'

'He's spoken about them – but that's his world, not mine. He doesn't share it with me – not that I'd want it particularly as I prefer the country.' There was an awkward silence. 'But I am glad that he was good to you. I'm particularly glad as he was so rude to you that first evening here at Milborne. Quite out of order, I thought. But you stood up to him – and he likes that. Will you come and have lunch with me next week? Can you stay on, Pru?'

'I would like that very much indeed, Mrs Granville – but you know Mummy. I will need to ask her as she has taken control of my life since I got back from France. Not a moment to myself as she scours the marriage market on my behalf. I suspect you have the same problem, Isobel.'

'Not really. My mother died three years ago.'

Pru looked downcast. 'Golly, I really am putting my two feet in it this evening.'

'You weren't to know.'

'Still, not very clever.'

'It's what I do all the time. I'm known for it aren't I, Cousin Daphne?'

'Not really. But you tell some home truths – and prick some pomposities that need a pin. You two will get on fine, I suspect. I'm sitting next to you at dinner, Isobel, so I'll leave you be for now.'

She waggled her finger as a sort of wave and made a line for Julian who had a fixed smile and nodding head as his companion made shapes with her hands.

'Hello Julian. You've met Lucinda, I see.'

'Yes indeed, Mrs Granville. We were just discussing hound breeding. Fascinating. Lucinda is a real expert.'

Lucinda beamed in appreciation. 'Mr Belmore is an expert too. It's such fun to run into someone so interesting. We've so much in common. I'm hoping to lure him to the shires for some real hunting.'

'I'm so pleased. I haven't seen Julian for months as he's been trying to stop the Germans sinking their fleet.'

Her eyes widened. 'I didn't know that.'

'Well you might have to ask him about it. He does do quite a bit more than hunt.'

She looked disappointed. 'Oh… really?'

'Yes. Rather nice for the rest of us as we are surrounded by hunting all winter. Even the summer sometimes. I can just about do horses – but hounds? No.' There was a strained pause. 'My husband is one of the worst, isn't he Julian?'

Julian's face betrayed that he wasn't sure how to answer that question. 'On hunting? Not at all, Mrs Granville; believe me there are plenty who are much worse. I was meaning to ask if you have heard anything from Mr and Mrs Hardy? I kept thinking about Mrs Hardy when I was in Scotland.'

'Who are the Hardys?' asked Lavinia.

'I'm so sorry. Thomas Hardy, the writer. Mrs Granville introduced us in the spring and we had lunch with them.'

Lavinia brightened. 'I love reading. What sort of books does he write?'

Julian glanced at the older woman. 'Love stories is how you might describe them.'

'My favourite! I'll look out for them. Will they be in a bookshop yet? Would you excuse me for a moment? I need to pass a message from my mother to Lady Milborne.' She held Julian's arm. 'But promise me we can carry on our talk later. I'm so glad you like the Welsh crosses as much as I do.'

'I'll look forward to it.'

They waited until she was out of earshot.

'What a shame,' said Daphne, 'that someone of her background can be so appallingly educated. A disgrace really. Mind you, her parents are no better – either of them. They both seem to take pride in their philistinism. Snobs of course; the last refuge of the truly useless in my experience. Is it the same in Ireland?'

Julian considered. 'Yes. And no. Plenty of drunk and bored people whose only pastime is hunting. But the snobbery is slightly different: more about ascendency and religion; less hierarchical. Socially easier, but politically deadly.'

'I'd like to go there.'

'Not now: it's too dangerous. Now the world war is over we can get down to a serious civil war. It's beautiful... but unhappy.'

'That's what Robert says. You know he was in Ireland after the Rising?'

'No, I didn't,' he lied.

'I wouldn't want to go with him though. He has too many pre-conceived notions and only sees Ireland through the prism of the Empire. He's a harsh man – but you know that.' Julian made no reply. 'He's still in Paris. I'm not sure why, as they must be winding up there after the treaty was signed. He says it's important so I suppose it must be.' They both looked around the room where the volume had risen with the intake of cocktails. She didn't look at him as she spoke. 'It's good to have you back, Julian. You've been missed.'

'I can't imagine who by.'

'I'm sure you can.'

'My hounds?'

She looked at him quizzically.

'I hope you're joking. She's more than fond of you. Look, it's not my business, but I like you both and... I think you're well suited. That's all. I won't say any more. But would you like to come to lunch next week? I've asked Isobel and Pru – if she can stay, that is. I'd like to see you before Robert gets back. His presence does change things and it wouldn't be... well it would be nicer without him.' She bit her lip. 'I shouldn't have to say that, should I? No one should, ever; about their spouse. But there it is.' A tray went by and she reached out for a cocktail. She held it, looking at it as a scientist might examine a test tube. 'Marvellous stuff. Happiness in a jar. I've never liked wine, but I'm beginning to see why Violet likes her cocktails so much.' She looked back at Julian. 'Don't do what I did. Either of you. He married me for my money and I married him for his family. I was only nineteen and I thought that was what you did. One decision as a child that has made us both miserable for life. Too easy to do. Everyone wants everyone else tidied into boxes. Maybe the war has changed that – but I don't

think so: look at Ariadne and Violet – and Pru and her mother.'
She looked away again and around the room. She addressed her
next words towards the self-absorbed party ahead of them. 'Most
of these girls won't have anyone, of course. Their mothers hardly
talk of anything else. But I'm finding that I have to keep my council as I secretly think that not having someone would have suited
me fine if I'd been able to live an academic life.' Julian glanced
at her in surprise. She looked back at him. 'I know. These are just
the musings of someone who's been diminished by her choices.'

Julian found he could not look at her directly. This was a raw
admission. 'Mrs Granville…'

'…Daphne, please. I'm quite a lot less than double your age,
and a friend I hope…'

'Thank you. You've been very… open with me. And kind. To
be honest, I don't know what to do. You… well it feels a bit as if
you are trying to do to Rose and me what Lady Milborne is trying
to do with Ariadne.'

She put her hand on his arm shaking her head. 'No. That's not
the case, I promise you. Violet is trying to put Ariadne in a box.
I am only saying that I like the company of you and Rose together.
It works – or seems so to me as a busybody outsider anyway. That's
all. Just an observation. No matchmaking, I promise you.'

He nodded. 'But you are assuming that Rose might be interested in me.'

'Of course she is.'

'I don't have any money.'

'Money isn't everything.'

'That's easy to say if you have it.'

She sighed. 'That was insensitive of me.'

'And rude of me. I'm sorry.'

'But you do have a job here.'

'Of sorts. And I do have some rents from the farm in Ireland –
but my mother needs most of that. And Lord Milborne is generous – but I am supposed to be an amateur with a private income.
I can get by as a bachelor – just – but it's not enough to support
a wife and family.'

'Have you met Evelyn Grumond?'

'Of the black cloth fortune? Not yet; though he has been pointed out to me.'

'Maybe he might be able to help? Give you a job?'

He hesitated, shaking his head. 'Doing what? I know nothing about money and business. All I have is a degree in Greats from Oxford, some farming experience and a faculty with hounds. Oh, and I can navigate a ship and I'm almost bilingual in morse code.'

'And why does that make you any worse than any number of boys coming out of university or the Army? You're doing yourself down.'

'The difference is that they are twenty-one; and I'm thirty-one. I know the likes of Grumond: all he thinks about is money. He's good at it. I don't think about money: I just worry about it.'

He sighed and his shoulders slumped. He felt her hand on his arm.

'You don't know. You've never tried. Grumond owes me a favour. Don't ask what that might be, but make sure you have a good conversation with him. He's an interesting man; not very nice – but he thinks differently. He's made for this new world we're in – and he knows it. We just need to hitch you to his star.'

There was a short silence between them which was broken by the boom of the dinner gong.

*   *   *

Isobel was seated next to George Richford. He glanced to see which way the conversation was going and then back at her.

'Well?'

'Well?'

He picked up his cocktail and downed the half-full glass in one go. 'Well, what's the thing of which you are most ashamed?'

He stared at her. She felt herself colouring again – mainly with annoyance.

'Aren't you going to tell me your name? Or ask mine?'

'Why? We'll both find out soon enough. And it's not that interesting.'

'But it is normal. And polite; well to me anyway.'

He shrugged. 'Normal? I suppose so. But it's more interesting to find out why it's worth finding out what someone's name is – isn't it?'

'And if I'm not interesting enough?'

'Then no doubt you – or someone else – will tell me your name anyway. So why don't we just cut to the chase?'

Isobel realised he was drunk; deep and intentional. The knowledge relaxed her. 'You may be right. But you start.'

He leant over and picked up a wine glass. 'Well done.' He toasted her. 'I think I like you.' He made as if to swallow it – but checked himself and carefully placed the glass back on the table. 'Where do you want me to start?'

'You said most ashamed. I don't think that means a catalogue.'

He nodded. There was a delicacy of manner about him that wasn't effeminate. His evening clothes were immaculate. He was clean shaven but with a pronounced five o'clock shadow, dark eyebrows and eyes that reminded Isobel of Charlie Chaplin. As he fiddled with his glass she noticed that his fingernails were bitten to the quick.

'Fair enough. But I've a lot to be ashamed about: I've been in a war. So I'll give you a choice. Personal or professional. Or both. I don't really mind. Beyond caring really.'

'Professionally then.' She hoped that he might talk about something other than the war – but knew that it was unlikely.

'Do you have any idea what it was like? Well you can't really. Unless you were a nurse like the lovely Prudence over there.' He nodded in her direction. 'But you weren't, were you? It's funny; you can tell. It's like the Masons – except you don't need a funny handshake to know. Like sex.' He held her eye as he spoke. 'You just know if someone's interested.'

'Are you trying to shock me?'

He shrugged. 'I suppose I am. But I don't think you're going to pour your soup over me in indignation.' He raised his eyebrows theatrically. 'Are you?'

Isobel laughed, and some of the tension evaporated. 'You deserve it.'

'Pour away. It's happened before – but I don't learn.' He held his glass for the butler to refill and sipped it. 'Good wine.' He hesitated. 'I was a pilot, you know: a knight of the air; soaring above the filth and corpses below. Some idiots think it was glamorous.'

'Better than the trenches?'

'In some ways. If you've had Trench Foot then anything's better than that. I had it before I was transferred to the RFC. It was like gout; makes your foot so sensitive that you can't bear anything touching it. Exquisite torture, all day, every day. But did you know that us knights of the air were shitting ourselves every flight? It wasn't because we were scared – though we were – but because we had rotary engines that were lubricated by castor oil. It came out of the engine in superfine mist that you couldn't avoid inhaling. Probably the equivalent of downing half a bottle of castor oil a day. You can imagine what that does to your underwear. Still sound glamorous? Or the cold. I used to cover up every bit that I could and then plaster any exposed flesh with fat. Even so I got frostbite on my nose. A bit fell off.' He pointed to the corner of a nostril that was missing. 'Actually, apart from the occasional foray into No Man's Land and any stupid offensive they came up with, the trenches weren't too bad. Boring, miserable and squalid to be sure – but not too dangerous as long as you kept your head below the parapet.'

He paused, raised his glass in an ironic toast – before gulping it down. 'Where was I? Boredom? Oh, shame. I can do shame. Here's a good one. I got stuck in No Man's Land once: knocked out after a trench raid and left for dead. I woke at dawn in a shell hole and there was just me and a Hun who had taken some shrapnel in his guts. Not in a good way – but compos mentis. And thirsty. I knew I had a whole day with him as I couldn't make it back to my trench in daylight. I had a water bottle and it turned out he spoke English. I was bored and getting fed up with his groaning so I decided we'd have a bet. Heads he gets the water bottle and shoots me. Tails I keep the water bottle and I shoot him.' He contemplated his glass. 'I've always wondered what I'd have done if it

185

had come up heads. Interesting bet though. Interesting chap. He looked me straight in the eye as I did it.' He made a pistol shape with his hand and fingers and squinted as if taking aim. 'Your turn now Miss Whoever You Are.'

Isobel shook her head. There was something about the way he had told his story that made her realise it was true – and that there were other revelations that could be worse. She lost her nerve.

'I… I don't think I know you well enough.'

'If you don't know me then why does it matter? Think of me as a priest in a confessional. Anonymous. You can say anything – and I've probably heard it before. Worse probably. It would be a speaking tube to the Almighty.' He raised his glass. 'When I get drunk, I don't remember anything I've said the next day. Can be an advantage. Sometimes not. A girl that I proposed to, apparently the previous night, wasn't too happy when I didn't recognise her the next day. I can see her point.' He raised an eyebrow. 'Well?'

'Well, I'm not sure I really want to tell you, that's all. I don't really want to play your high-stakes games – because that's what they are, aren't they? I don't need to play them – and you do for some reason.'

'I don't have to. I just enjoy it. Humour me? I can't imagine your sins are much compared with mine after all. Murder trumps most things. Well it did, but war seems to have cheapened the currency. What could you have possibly done? A little adultery perhaps? Stolen something at school? Sorry; I'm being patronising. I may be speaking to a Queen of Crime or Empress of Sin, for all I know.' He hesitated and looked around the table. A look of such vulnerability came across his face that Isobel found herself placing her hand on his forearm which he looked at with surprise.

'You don't need to do this,' she said. 'I don't need to be shocked. And I'm happy to be talking to you. Genuinely. I'm Isobel, Ariadne's second cousin; but I don't have a penny and my father's a vicar – but I don't believe in God. And I want to make a living as a sculptor but haven't yet worked out how to do it. And I've just lost my virginity to a woman – of which I am not the least ashamed by the way.' She stared him in the eye. 'Does that satisfy you?'

He raised his glass. 'Entirely. How wonderful to get to know you, Isobel. I think we're going to get on just fine, don't you?'

*   *   *

As the main course was being cleared the conversation turned and Isobel found herself facing Daphne Granville.

'How did that go?' asked the older woman.

Isobel thought before replying. 'Do you know him?' Daphne shook her head and Isobel lowered her voice. 'He is… damaged. Not on the surface like that poor man over there…' They glanced over the table at the ruins of the face opposite them. '…but in his mind. Yet there is something very sweet about him; almost innocent; which he hides. Or tries to anyway. He wants to shock – and does. Why does he do that?'

Daphne tilted her head slightly so that she could observe him behind Isobel's head. 'Fear probably. No, certainly. I saw it in my youngest brother. He was killed last year but was called up in '16. Not a natural soldier. He was a painter – and a good one. You could see the effect each leave. Jumpy at first. Then nightmares. And then brutal and cynical – as if there was no hope. A sweet man who turned into something else to form a carapace to protect himself; a shell of despair. There was nothing I could do.' Two tears rolled down her cheeks to be quickly dabbed by her napkin. 'What could I do? Stop the war? Help him desert – to be shot? Nothing. That was the worst thing. The sense of powerlessness. Michael didn't make it – but your new friend did and he probably can't quite believe it yet.'

'He's very drunk.'

'It helps.'

'But he can't drink like that forever.'

'How long's forever? I suspect he's not thinking more than one day ahead. And drinking – heavy drinking – is like an anaesthetic; it dulls the pain and puts you to sleep without nightmares.'

Neither spoke as they considered this.

'I like him,' said Isobel.

'I can see that.' Daphne tilted her head again to be better able to observe him as he spoke to his companion. 'But be careful.'

'What about Julian?'

'What about him?'

'He's less complicated.'

'As a person, yes. But you know that Rose is in love with him.'

'She's never told me that.'

'You've been away for four months.'

'And Julian? Is he in love with her?'

Daphne gave her a sharp look. 'I know he's more than fond of her. And as it's your sister, I'd leave well alone.'

'I'm only talking about friendship.'

'Good. But don't let it be misinterpreted. Please.'

'I won't, I promise. But who isn't spoken for? Has Cousin Violet got someone lined up for Ariadne?'

'She wouldn't consult me on things like that. She thinks you and I are irredeemable bluestockings – and probably shouldn't be allowed out in polite society: much too intelligent to be any help with important matters such as matchmaking. Your friend Richford is possible – unless he gets too drunk and blots his copybook. And maybe Grumond. He's rich. But then Ariadne doesn't need money – and Violet is probably keen to get some more rarified blood to mix in with her father's money. Maybe she's playing a longer game. Anyway, Ariadne seems to be enjoying herself.' They looked across the table to where Julian was laughing with her. Isobel felt a pin-prick of jealousy. 'If she enjoys herself, then she might be more keen to do a season and find someone suitable. Who knows? Violet's mind is difficult to plumb. But it is primarily motivated by pleasure – her own of course.'

'You don't like her?'

'Do you? I've been the subject of too many snubs and petty humiliations over the years to have much affection for her. A rich, spoiled woman like that can get through life too easily breaking things and people without a care in the world. Not much to admire and not much to like. But she is my sister-in-law – so I put on a smile and pretend.'

'I didn't know.'

'Good. That was the intention. To show it hurt would be to give her a victory she doesn't deserve. Anyway, I'm not worried about Ariadne. She's able to look after herself and will always find some-one to marry: her money will see to that. I'm more interested in you and your sisters.'

'Cousin Daphne, you're very kind, but you don't need to worry about me. I know what I want and I think I'll be able to get it with a little help from friends like you. And if someone turns up that will be a bonus. But I think I'm resigned to the statistics that don't look good if I want to find the sort of man with whom I would want to spend my life. I don't want to be a nurse. I like children well enough – but some nephews and nieces would be fine.'

Daphne looked at her quizzically. 'Do you mean that? Really?'

Isobel considered the question. 'Yes. I think so. I had a lot of time to think about it in Paris and talk about it with people who, let's say, have a different view. I grew up there: it felt like ten years in six months. Mostly thanks to Cousin Robert.' She caught her companion's surprised expression. 'He gave me some new friends and… well, he saved me from making a fool of myself. I won't say any more.'

Neither spoke for a few seconds and they both looked around the table where servants held trays of pudding to which the diners were helping themselves. The volume was high and the crystal glasses splintered the candlelight.

Daphne raised her glass towards Isobel. 'Good. I'm glad for you. I mean that. If I had my life again I would do what you are doing. It's too late for me.'

*　　*　　*

When the ladies left the table the men clustered at one end. Julian found himself between Evelyn Grumond and the raw profile of George Allan. He found the latter both horrifying and fascinating: his injuries made it look as if discoloured candle wax had been

189

poured down the side of his head. Port was passed and cigars clipped and teased into life. Grumond leant back in his chair and exhaled a billow of smoke.

'Delicious dinner. It's good that things are getting back to normal again.'

'We were talking about normal yesterday,' said Julian, 'and we were wondering what the new normal would be. It won't be the same as before.'

'No,' said the wounded man, 'it won't. It isn't and it can't be, can it?'

'Not now, of course,' said Grumond, 'but give it a few years.'

'And we'll just forget it all? I don't think I will.'

Grumond tapped his cigar on the ash tray. He had curly brown hair and a complexion that was almost childlike with no lines. If he felt awkward about the backhanded put-down he had just received, it didn't register.

'My dear Allan, that's not what I'm talking about. You, and everyone who has been through some terrible things, aren't going to forget them. Of course not. I meant that the rationing and the shortages and the restrictions of the war will soon be over. Businesses can get going again.'

'And you can make more money.'

'If people like me don't make money then people won't have jobs, is the way I look at it.'

'What business are you in?' asked Julian.

'Mainly in textiles. I had a big contract to supply khaki – but that's now over for obvious reasons.'

'And black cloth too, I heard. Profitable I would imagine,' added George Allen.

'Still does well. But I suppose I should be glad that the need for the stuff will diminish. We all should.'

'Amen to that.'

'And to replace it?' asked Julian.

'Aeroplanes. Civilian. Obvious, don't you think? There are hundreds, no, thousands of engines in bombers and military aircraft that are now useless. Not to mention the same amount of men who are trained to fly and don't have any other trade. If I can get the right design then I've got the engines and the men already. We've got a huge empire but it takes months to get to most of it.' He spread his hand out as if to signal that it was a point proved. 'What about you, Belmore? Are you staying here or going back to Ireland?'

'Here? I don't know. Ireland? No. We've just been through one war and I don't have the stomach for another.'

'You think it will get to that?'

'It won't be pretty. The war has been brutalising and the Rising, or rather it's aftermath, has put pretty well everyone in the South behind independence. But if Ulster was prepared to fight over home rule before the war, then independence will spark something even worse: war with Britain overlaid with a civil war. There's not much to take me back across the Irish Sea.'

'It's that bad?'

'Worse.'

There was a short silence while this sank in, broken by Grumond. 'So you need to make it work here.'

Julian nodded slowly. 'Yes. I do.'

'How much do you earn as a huntsman?'

Both Julian and George Allan looked at Grumond in surprise. 'We've only just met...'

'... and gentlemen don't talk about money. I know that. But if you need a job – which I think you do – then money comes into it.'

'I didn't say I needed a job.'

'But you do, don't you? Hunting is fine as a sport but not a way to earn a living – unless you don't have to.' Julian's silence spoke affirmation. 'So I'm assuming that you would like to talk about it and that we can stop pretending that you are rich enough not to be having this conversation.' Both men nodded. 'Good. Do either of you speak another language?'

'French. Fluently,' said Julian.

'Swahili. I was born in Kenya. And German. It kept me away from the front line enough that it probably stopped me getting killed,' said Allan.

'I want my aerial line, if that's what it will be called, to cover Africa and South East Asia, so that's a good start. Are you happy to travel and live abroad?' They both nodded. 'Not married, or planning to be? Carting wives and children with you, or leaving them behind for long periods, isn't ideal.' Both shook their heads. 'Good. Excellent in fact. I need gentlemen to deal with the civil servants and diplomats whose only job, as far as I can see, is to put obstacles in my way. The Empire was formed by and for trade – but you wouldn't know it. Both of you have been in the military. They're even worse and only like to deal with their own. They think the Empire was formed only to employ them.' He held his cigar like a baton and seemed to conduct his own conversation with it.

Julian spoke. 'I don't have any business experience. Does that worry you?'

'Yes. But we'll find out if that's a problem soon enough, don't you think?'

'And I'm Irish.'

'We all have our crosses.' He laughed at his own joke.

'And how much will we be paid?' asked Allan.

'So much for gentlemen not talking about money.' He laughed again. 'I can't afford to pay you a lot – but enough for you to be comfortable and a stake in the business. Not a huge one – but a chance for you to make some capital if it all goes well. It'll be more than any master of foxhounds earns, that's for sure.'

There was silence, broken by Allan. 'I'm interested.' He stood up. 'Excuse me, but I need to speak to Mrs Granville about something.'

Grumond and Julian were left facing each other over the table. 'And you?' Grumond made a question mark with his cigar.

'Probably. I need to think about it and tidy up some loose ends here. When do you need an answer?'

'No great hurry. Write to me. Loose ends? Can I ask what they are?'

Julian returned his stare. 'No. No you can't.'

'Nothing to do with the lovely Hon. Ariadne?'

'If it was, I wouldn't tell you.'

He pursed his lips and nodded. 'Just checking. I wouldn't want to... well, you know...'

'I don't, actually.'

'As you wish.' He rolled his cigar in his pursed lips. 'I rather fancy the mother. But I hear she rather likes you.' His smile more resembled a leer. 'Leave one of them for me will you?'

13

Julian surfaced from a deep sleep to the sound of the knocker on his front door. He scrabbled for the pocket watch that was his father's last gift. It was just after three in the afternoon. The dawn start to autumn hunting always left him heavy-eyed after lunch. Normally a catnap restored him but this had made him fog-headed. He opened the door to a middle-aged man with a beard. His clothes suggested a professional – perhaps a doctor. He raised his bowler hat and bowed slightly.

'Mr Belmore?'

'Yes?'

'I've come from a mutual friend who needs help.'

Julian waved him in with a heavy heart. The Irish cadences were unmistakable. He pointed towards the parlour with its now wilting wild flowers and smell of whitewash.

'Tea?'

'Thank you.'

The visitor sat with his hat on his knees as Julian fiddled with the stove and marshalled his thoughts. Since the midnight visit by Collins back in March this had always been on the cards, though he had managed to persuade himself that Robert Granville's absence would absolve him from any further involvement. This man's presence meant that Granville's return was imminent. He had met men like him before – quiet and unassuming, mild even, but with a talent for violence. He glanced at him through the kitchen door. Where most would be reading the newspaper, picking up a book or pacing the room, he sat as still as sculpture.

He put the pot on the table with two mugs and lit a cigarette while standing by the fireplace. The visitor said nothing.

'What do you want?'

'You know.'

'Granville? But he's not here.'

'I know that.'

'Then what can I do for you?'

'Let me know when he's back.'

'So Collins has sent you over here not even knowing if Granville's in the country?'

'He's leaving Paris tomorrow. We just don't know where he's going. Here eventually, to be sure, but where in the meantime we're not so sure. It doesn't matter; I can wait.'

'Here?'

'No. Dorchester. Far enough away to leave a cold trail. You'll tell me when he's back. Send a letter to this address.' He put a card on the table.

'Then what?' He did not reply and simply stared at Julian. 'Will you be back here?'

'Probably.'

'Will you stay here?'

'No. But I will need to know the lay of the land. You'll provide all the details you have of his routine.'

'I hardly know him – let alone his habits.'

'Then find them out.'

'Without incriminating myself?'

'That's your problem.'

'It certainly is.'

The man leant forward. 'Listen. This man has buckets of Irish blood on his hands. You know that. We aren't asking you to pull the trigger or to hide me. This isn't a suicide mission. The Big Man seems to like you and knows you're useful. It's local detail I'm after, that's all. Play your part and the chances are that you'll never hear from us again. We don't kill bastards like him every day, so look on this as a one-off job.'

'Is that supposed to be reassuring?'

He nodded. 'As much reassurance as you're going to get. It's a war. People get killed in wars – you know that.'

Julian flicked the end of his cigarette into the fire. 'When are you going?'

'When I've had some tea. And discussed the new horse supplement that I have here.' He reached into his bag and pulled out a large brown bottle. 'Brewed in Cumbria and I'm told that Lord Lonsdale swears by it. You've had a visit from a salesman for this stuff. That would be pretty normal for someone like you, wouldn't it? I'll pay you a visit once I've received your letter and we'll discuss the merits – or not as the case may be – of this brew. I'll then leave you and that will be that. And even if they find out that I visited here – which is highly unlikely – you will have the perfect cover story. An Irishman selling snake oil to another Irishman. It's not unheard of.'

'You've thought it all through.'

He nodded, placed his hat on the table and poured himself a mug of tea.

'Milk?'

With some relief, Julian returned to the kitchen, retrieved the miniature churn from the larder and slopped some milk into another mug. He banged it on the table next to the tea pot. The man looked at it with his preternatural calm.

'Thank you.'

'I was going to say you're welcome – but you're not.'

'As you wish.' He took a sip of the tea, put the mug down and sat back observing Julian. 'This could be a lot worse, you know; for you.'

'I fail to see how: accessory to murder; shitting on my doorstep. Have I missed anything?'

'It's not murder. It's a just execution.'

'I don't think an English court would see it that way.'

He nodded in agreement. 'But it's not going to come to that, is it? You're well protected.'

'If everything goes to plan. The only golden rule is that nothing ever goes exactly to plan. Certainly not in war – which you insist this is.'

'Don't you? Have you really gone over that quickly?'

'Gone over? What do you mean by that? I don't think it's unpatriotic to not want to be part of an assassination squad killing a government official.'

'Of an occupying power.'

'The parliament of which has sixty odd elected members from across the Irish Sea – who have held the balance of power here for many years. They may have chosen not to take their seats after the last election – but it's not exactly taxation without representation.'

'But it was – as you well know. Cromwell didn't tread gently.'

'That was a long time ago.'

'Not to us.'

'The "us" includes me.'

'Not from the way you're talking. You sound like them to me.'

'Hardly.'

'You took the King's shilling quick enough: Judas money.'

'There were tens of thousands of Irish volunteers. And Irish regiments.'

'Traitors.'

'That's exactly what Granville called me only four months ago. A bit ironic, don't you think?'

'How's that?'

'He thinks I'm a Fenian pretending to be English. And you think I'm an Irishman who's tacked the other way. Which of you is right? I don't know.'

The visitor didn't reply immediately but maintained his stare. 'It's not important. As long as you do what you're told, I couldn't give a damn what you think. Left to me I'd give you a bullet straight after Granville. You both deserve one.'

Julian stared back and, without saying anything, walked to the front door and held it open. The man stayed sitting, continuing to observe him. He stood, picked up his small suitcase, put on his hat and walked to the door, halting in front of Julian.

'If there is just a hint that you have tipped him off, it won't just be a bullet for you.' For someone so physically unprepossessing he radiated a menace that overwhelmed Julian's attempt at composure. The bowler hat sat slightly too low on his forehead, creating an artificial shadow over his eyes that gave them a sinister cast. Julian found that he could not control the shaking of his leg as the man held his eye before walking slowly out of the door and down the lane without a glance behind him.

*　　*　　*

Over the next three days Julian occupied himself with his hounds more than would have been his custom. He made no enquiries about the whereabouts of Robert Granville and made no contact with either the vicarage or the castle. Any pleasure in the anticipated return of Rose was nullified by the malign memory of the Irishman's words and manner. He lay in bed in the small hours trying to think of some way of absolving himself from his predicament. Could he engineer a recall to the fleet? Was there a way of warning Granville to stay away? At best he could postpone – but not without exposing himself; and he remembered the blood-washed lower deck of the *River Clyde*.

In the event he didn't have to ask. He was counting his hounds into their kennels at noon after a productive morning: hunting at that time of year was about vermin control and they had killed three foxes, earning him the gratitude of the farmers on whose land they had been hunting and whose lambs and chickens had fallen victim to the summer surge in the fox population. He heard a car pull up outside the kennels and, as he was about to drop a bucket into the water-butt, he found himself staring at Robert Granville, who was holding out a cigarette case.

'Good day, Belmore. I'm not completely sure if it's morning or afternoon but it certainly is a fine day. And a good morning, I hear. I bumped into Ralph who filled me in. Well actually he grunted and showed me three fingers – which I interpreted as three kills. Was I right?'

Julian nodded. 'We had the new entry out and they all hunted well. A couple rioted on deer – but Ariadne whipped them back in and they were steady as a rock when they had another opportunity.' He took a proffered cigarette and accepted a light. 'How was Paris?'

Granville's demeanour had not softened. His disconcerting, hawk-like stare accompanied his reply. 'The talks? Some people are happy – Poles, Czechs and all those who've got a new country to play with. The French, who've got their boot on the Hun's neck and are enjoying the experience. The Huns? Miserable, I expect. But then they deserve it.'

'And for you?'

'Nothing went wrong – if that's what you mean. No one took a pot shot at Lloyd George sadly – though personally I wouldn't have wept much if they had – and hit him. The French were on to what we think was a Bolshevik bomb plot.' He drew on his cigarette. 'But I hear that you were present at the most dramatic turn of all. Daphne told me in a letter. You're back for good?'

'It appears so – but the Navy is not entirely predictable.'

'Good. You need to be here if you are going to hunt hounds properly. Mistakes were acceptable last season as there was a war on for some of it. This season has got to be back to our usual standards. My brother will be asking me at Christmas whether we should continue with you as an amateur – or go back to Ralph as a professional. Jury's out after last season.'

'So no pressure then?'

'There's always pressure. Surely you've worked that out by now? If you can't take it then better go back to the bogs, eh?'

Julian willed himself to hold the stare. 'I'm good at this. You know that. It's why Lord Milborne – and you – wanted me here. You know, as well as I do, that getting another amateur as good as me is going to be difficult. They're all dead. Or finding it hard to ride a horse without an arm or a leg. That's not an excuse for second best, by the way.'

Granville smiled. 'Excellent! We understand each other then. I hate the second rate – and so do you it would seem. But if you let me down…'

Julian dropped his cigarette on to the cobbles. 'I won't let you down.' He looked back up. 'You'll get more than you expect.'

*　　*　　*

Julian took as many precautions as he could with the letter to the Irishman. He journeyed to Salisbury and paid a small typing agency to produce a communication that would only make sense to the initiated and held no personal trace. He posted it in the city. He told no one where he was going and gave every appearance of having been no further than Sherborne where he established an alibi.

He was opening the door to his cottage at lunchtime two days later when, in the distance, he caught sight of a bicycle and a distinctive bowler hat. He forced himself to carry on inside and waited until the door was knocked. He knew there was no one watching but treated the Irishman as an unknown visiting salesman until the door was closed behind him. He waved him to the parlour where the visitor sat without a greeting.

'I've sent your letter to the Big Man,' he said. The alarm must have shown on Julian's face. 'Did you really think we weren't going to have something to pin on you if you... let's just say if you decided that you didn't want to help us?'

'Of course not,' Julian replied bitterly, 'though a typewritten note from Salisbury telling you that the cloth you were looking for is now in stock isn't exactly a piece of evidence likely to get me hanged.'

The Irishman considered this. 'Maybe. But there would be enough that was circumstantial to make your life... uncomfortable.' It was true, of course. 'So what have you got for me?'

'Not much. There's no pattern to his day that I can see,' he lied. 'He goes everywhere in his car with a chauffeur. I don't know where; but often to the castle – when I've seen him, that is. I couldn't exactly follow him round the countryside on my bicycle.'

'You've got a perfect excuse with your hunting.'

'Which would suggest that you don't know much about hunting.'

'I don't like horses or dogs.'

'Or know much about how the countryside works. If you did, you wouldn't suggest something so stupid. It may look as if it's only fields and cows but almost nothing happens without someone observing it. It's much easier to hide in a town, believe me.'

'So what would you suggest?'

Julian shrugged. 'You're the executioner, not me. I'm sure you'll work it out.'

The Irishman observed him coldly. 'Don't fuck with me. I meant it about sorting you out at the same time as Granville. The only thing that'll stop me doing that is if I think you're being helpful. If you aren't, then it won't matter a damn how much Collins likes you. He's never going to know how you ended up in a ditch with your balls down your throat, is he? I've done a lot worse.'

Julian didn't doubt it. But something had changed in the few days after he had been left by the Irishman with his leg palsied with fear; a strange courage that felt akin to recklessness came over him. This man was like a shark marooned on a sandbank; out of his element, still dangerous but drained of some of its menace.

'You've never had someone shoot back at you, have you?'

'And your point is?'

'Good luck with Granville; he won't be a sitting duck.'

'He's a bastard.'

'I agree. But a dangerous one. I know how ruthless he can be and I know he can handle a gun.'

'Does he have one?'

Julian shrugged again. 'How would I know? Didn't you get briefed properly before they put you on the ferry? The least they could do, I would have thought.' On the surface the man maintained his cold stillness and his hands remained on the small suitcase on his lap, but Julian could see, with satisfaction, his toes working under the leather of the tips of his shoes. He pressed his advantage. 'You're on your own, aren't you? No backup. No support. It'd better go right.'

'And why shouldn't it? Unless you've tipped him off.'

'Why would I do that? I can't stand the man – and the feeling's mutual.'

'So how's he going to know?'

'He probably doesn't. But a man like that is in permanent danger: Fenians like you; anarchists; Bolsheviks – and probably a jealous husband or two. You'll need to get it right first time – and make sure you can get away; with someone to back you up if there's a problem.'

'That's where you come in.'

Julian laughed mirthlessly. 'How touching; but you really need to work on your charm if you're looking for a friend in need. I'll give you a hint – lay off the balls down the throat bit.' The silence was broken only by the sound of a jackdaw on the roof. 'Now if you'll excuse me, I have a letter to post and tasks to complete at the kennels. And I wouldn't talk to anyone from that bicycle of yours. You look and sound like a pantomime Paddy.' He walked straight to the front door and, pulling it firmly behind him and willing himself not to look back, he strode down the lane.

*　　*　　*

When he returned home later that afternoon, the Irishman had gone and the anxiety of the previous week reasserted itself. Ironically, the exposed weakness of the assassin was more disconcerting than reassuring: so much more to go wrong. Could he warn Granville? Did he want to? As he mulled over the alternatives, his sense of the two Damoclean swords of Granville and blackmail hanging over him became, if anything, more acute and the view from the tightrope he was walking more precipitous. As he paced the parlour, smoking as he did so, searching for a more palatable course, there was another knock on the door that brought him up short. With a familiar sense of trepidation he opened the door, steeling himself for confrontation, and found himself looking at Rose.

She had never looked more beautiful. Summer had given her fair skin a lustre he had not seen before. The light clothes and straw hat, the posy of roses in her hand extended towards him and the smile only added to the effect and he was momentarily flummoxed.

'You don't look very pleased to see me.' He heard the hurt in her voice.

'No. No. I'm so pleased. I was... I was expecting someone else – a salesman who's been hounding me for days. I'm sorry.'

'Do I get a kiss? Or is that too much to ask?'

'Yes. Of course.' Awkwardly, he stepped forward and kissed her on the cheek. He sensed more was required but was also aware of his own discombobulation. 'Come in. Please. I'm sorry. You caught me by surprise.'

'I sent a telegram to Papa three days ago saying that I was coming back today. Did you not hear that?'

He remembered his self-imposed isolation with an added sense of guilt. 'I've been very busy and haven't been either to the rectory or the castle and no one from either has been near the kennels.'

'But you knew I was coming back about now. Papa wrote to tell me you were here – and he said you were looking forward to seeing me. I had hoped you were.'

She wasn't smiling now and disappointment was across her face. Without thinking he put his arms around her. There was no softening.

'Please forgive me. My mind has been on other things.'

'Like parties up at the castle.'

'That was last weekend. This week has been difficult.'

'Not so difficult that you couldn't have lunch with Cousin Daphne and Prudence someone-or-other.'

'I met her at Ariadne's house party and Mrs Granville asked her to lunch.'

He knew that his response needed to tend to the emotional not the logical.

'Please. Come and sit down. I'll make some tea.'

'Tea? Is that all?'

'I've got a cake.'

She pushed him away. 'Cake? Cake? If I wanted cake I'd have stayed at the rectory with Isobel and Dav.' Tears were in her eyes. 'It's two months since I last saw you. You never told me when you were coming back. If you had I wouldn't have gone to Wales; I'd have been here to meet you.' She shook her head in anger. 'And all you say is "cake".'

'You know that's not what I meant.'

'Do I? How? One letter since we left the Orkneys. And I know from Papa and Isobel that all you and Ran have been doing is taking a sailing holiday. You even told them how bored you were. So bored you couldn't write!'

He knew that there was no credible defence. She stood in the narrow hallway, silhouetted against the sunshine outside, deflated, with the posy hanging down and tears staining her face.

'Of course I should have told you I was coming south – but I had no notice of my discharge and a letter would have arrived after me. I should have sent a telegram but, well, I didn't. And as it turned out you wouldn't have been here anyway. And as for the letters – guilty. Though Ran and I were in some very remote places, I should have made more of an effort. It's ironic, because Ran and I talked about you so often.' This last bit was true – but the truth was qualified by the guilty memory of the sensual pleasure between those conversations. But it had a benign effect and Julian was relieved to see her wipe her eyes with the sleeve of her blouse. She took off her straw boater and shook her hair while breathing deeply.

'I'm sorry too. I was just… disappointed.'

He put out his hand and stroked her cheek which she leant into his palm. He took a step forward and placed his other hand on her other cheek pulling her head towards him. They kissed gently, paused and he folded her once again into an embrace and stroked her hair. With relief he felt the anger and hurt percolating out of her. She held his hand and let him lead her to the parlour where she sat in the same chair that had been occupied by the Irishman only an hour earlier. He handed her his handkerchief.

'Pathetic. Why did I get so upset?' Julian didn't answer but squeezed her hand. 'I suppose I… well, I thought that you would have wanted me to be here when you got back.'

'I did. You didn't tell me you were going to Wales.'

'Because I didn't know.' She shook her head. 'So why should you? Of course, I'm being stupid.'

Julian sat down opposite her with his hand still holding hers. 'It's not stupid. Not at all. When I went to the rectory on my first day back I was expecting to find you there. Of course I should have sent a telegram.' He paused and they smiled at each other. 'But we're here now.'

* * *

Julian's cottage lay between Milborne Castle and the kennels, half a mile equidistant around the curve of the valley. His custom was to walk to the kennels – unless he had other business, when he would take his bicycle. Little traffic used the road and he usually walked along the grass strip that centred the single track. He was out of sight of both kennels and cottage when the horn of a vehicle made him step on to the verge. He was aware of it slowing down as it approached and turned to see Daphne Granville leaning out of the rear window. Over the noise of the engine, she beckoned him towards her.

'I'll give you a lift. Come on.'

He sat opposite her.

'Sorry about the smell.' The odour of the flesh-house hung on his working clothes. 'I was on my way home to change.'

'If we were sitting down to luncheon, it wouldn't be ideal,' she replied, 'but I'm used to country smells and this isn't the worst.'

'Pretty bad though. And almost impossible to wash out. I put myself in the tub afterwards.'

'Are you on your way home?' She leant forward to open the glass panel between the enclosed passenger compartment and the driver. 'Jason, please could you stop by Mr Belmore's house.'

Over the engagement of gears Daphne Granville asked, 'Did you make contact with Grumond?'

'I've written to him but haven't heard anything yet.'

'I think he'll be helpful. You can't be doing this,' her nose wrinkled slightly, 'for the rest of your life.'

The car braked, causing both of them to brace themselves. There was a hay cart lying across the road opposite an open gate: an unexceptional sight in a rural lane in September. The car came to a halt and the driver waited for the appearance of a pony or donkey to be yoked into the shafts. They waited and at the point where impatience trumped the customary pace of rural life, the driver sounded his horn.

Later, when trying to recall events, Julian was not sure whether his first sight of the bowler hat was before or after the horn. The Irishman came out of the gateway at a run. He saw a pistol in the man's hand as he leapt on to the running board. Before Julian was able to shout to the driver, the Irishman had thrust his arm and upper body through the window of the rear compartment. In a frozen moment, Julian caught the expression of consternation on the Irishman's face as he realised that Granville was not there. Knowing in an instant he would be a dead man if he did nothing, Julian threw his weight on to the extended arm, pulling the man's body almost into the car and eliciting a scream of pain that coincided with the crack of the pistol going off. He felt fingernails raking his face, but bore down as hard as he could on the arm. There was another report. And another. The smell of cordite filled the car. The arm slackened and the fingers probing for his eye sockets quivered and softened, turning from a gouge into a smear. Julian bore down on the arm until all movement ceased – even the quivering – and he fell back into the rear-facing seat panting, every limb shaking with exertion and fear. On the seat opposite Daphne Granville was staring at the roof with her head slightly to one side, facing away. She slid sideways on to the seat. As the other side of her head was revealed there was a bloody hole where an eyeball had once been; over the rear window were brains and blood.

*   *   *

Above Julian's head a pistol was knocking against the frame of the partition window as the hand holding it shook. Julian was sick between his legs.

'You alright, sir?'

Julian retched again and recovered. 'I think so.' The Irishman was jackknifed over the window with blood pooling below him. 'Is he dead?'

'He's not moving.'

'And Mrs Granville?'

The voice above and behind him was unsteady in its pitch. 'It was me, sir. I did it. He hit my arm.'

'He fired a shot.'

'It went through the door.' There was a neat hole just below the door handle. 'I killed her.'

Julian turned round to speak to the driver whose pistol was waving alarmingly, as if he had forgotten it was in his hand. Julian reached up and took his wrist in one hand and the pistol from him in the other. 'It's Jason, isn't it? Jason, you didn't kill her. He did. Whoever he is. Do you know him?'

The driver's face was ashen. His jowls quivered with shock. 'No sir. Never seen him before.' He shook his head. 'Mr Granville insisted I carry a gun. He showed me how to use it. But I never thought I'd have to. What's he going to say, sir? I've bloody killed his wife.'

'You tried to save her. You did your best.' The driver was oblivious to his blandishments, shaking his head with shock. 'Can you drive?' asked Julian. The driver nodded. 'Good. Help me to get him out of the car.' He didn't move. 'Now! Pull yourself together, man.' As effective as a slap, the impact of the order was instantaneous.

They got out on opposite sides and met where the rear half of the Irishman was hanging out of the window with his feet six inches clear of the running board. Julian felt faint and had to support himself against the side of the car. 'You take his legs, and I'll pull him out.' He wiped the blood that was dripping from his eye on to his sleeve as they manhandled the body out of the window before it collapsed on to the road in a backwards sprawl, revealing a hole under the right armpit. His face still held an expression of ferocity that death had failed to extinguish.

'We'll leave him here and get the police. By the side of the road. Help me.'

They dragged the body between them to the verge and stood over it, panting. The driver kicked the corpse before getting back into the car which was still running. Julian leant into the driver's pod. 'Is Mr Granville at home?' Jason nodded. 'Then to his house now – and I'll do the talking. Understood?' Julian put his hand on his arm. 'You did your best – and saved my life. What happened to Mrs Granville was as if that bastard had shot her – and I'll make sure that Mr Granville understands that. You have nothing to fear.' The driver nodded again – but without conviction. 'Let me arrange Mrs Granville and then please drive to their house as fast as you can.'

He climbed into the passenger compartment and lifted Daphne's feet on to the seat and arranged her arms across her chest. A pool of blood and brains was coagulating on the leather seat below her head. When he had done the best he could, trying to ignore the wrecked eye socket, he signalled to the driver to proceed. Only then did he weep for his friend lying on the seat opposite; grief, guilt and shock combined.

Julian's mind galloped during the ten-minute journey to the Dower House. Should he admit to knowing the Irishman? Who might have seen him at his cottage? The horse-tonic story felt weak. He imagined Robert Granville's predator eye on him and knew that it would elicit a line of questioning that could be fatal. He must be a victim, an accidental participant.

Granville was sitting outside in the late summer sunshine with a small vice attached to the garden table and the tools for fly-tying spread in front of him. He held up his hand as Julian approached and he saw that he was using his teeth to tension the line as he fingered a knot.

'Morning Belmore. I'm fishing on the Tweed next week and this is my favourite fly. Do you like it?' He held it up for judgement and caught Julian's expression and saw the blood on his face. 'Are you alright, man?'

'Granville, I have bad news. Terrible news. Your wife is dead.' The grey eyes squinted and the mouth compressed to a line. 'She was shot. In your car – just now – fifteen minutes ago.'

Granville said nothing for what seemed an age. 'Who did it?'

'I don't know. He was shot by your driver. We left him by the side of the road.'

'And my wife?'

'She's in the car. I am dreadfully sorry. She was hit in the head and died instantly.'

He considered this for a moment, then stood and walked through the house to the drive at the front where the chauffeur was standing nervously next to the car. Granville opened the door and climbed in, sitting on the seat opposite his wife's corpse. He contemplated it for a moment before putting out his hand to touch her cheek. Julian knew that she was already cold. Granville closed her remaining eye, leaving his fingers there for some moments. He leant forward and kissed her on the forehead.

He sat up and, without turning round, said, 'Help me get her out please. And tell Mrs Redfern to prepare the chaise longue in the drawing room.' Julian looked round to see that three of the staff were looking on in shock. One began to cry. Between them they manhandled the corpse, that was already beginning to stiffen, on to a blanket that the butler had brought out. The blood had ceased to flow from the back of her head and had already gone the purple-brown of coagulation. They laid her out with her arms crossed over her chest and tilted her head to one side leaving an unmarked profile of seeming sleep. The sobbing was infectious amongst the rest of the servants who now gathered in the door-way – and the more so for being genuine: she had been well loved. They stood around her as Granville held her hand with his own tears running down his face. Abruptly, he wiped them away with his handkerchief, recovered himself and tilted his head towards Julian and the chauffeur indicating that they should follow him. He lead them to his study, shut the door behind them and, leaning against the desk, observed them both.

'What happened?'

As instructed, the driver stayed silent.

'Between the kennels and my cottage. On the bend.'

'I presume it's a he.'

Julian nodded. 'We left him by the side of the road. Neither of us have seen him before.' Julian knew that this committed him. Anything that connected him with the corpse on the side of the road would now lead to the gallows.

'Did you search him? For identification.'

'No.'

'Tell me what happened.'

Julian recounted in as much detail as he could remember. On this he had nothing to hide. When he came to the fatal shot he paused to see Granville's reaction. He merely nodded, then reached out to grasp the driver's arm, looking him in the eye. The fear on the man's face was palpable.

'You did well, Jason. Please don't blame yourself. Without you there would have been three people murdered. Now let's go back to the body before any evidence is removed.'

By the time they arrived at the scene of the crime two young men, grasping bicycles, were standing over the corpse. They doffed their caps at Granville who walked around the body.

'I don't recognise him.'

He squatted on his haunches and reached into a breast pocket from which he removed an envelope. A punch of panic hit Julian as he imagined its contents. Methodically Granville worked his ways through the pockets, removing change and a money clip as well as a rosary. 'Catholic. Fenian probably. Nothing much to be drawn from the letter though; probably from his wife.' He handed it to Julian. 'Have a look.' He unlaced the man's shoes and examined them carefully. They were new and of good quality. 'Here we are, under the tongue. C&S. Curran and Slane – one of the best shoe-makers in Dublin. He wasn't a poor man; but maybe he was a good thief. Not some peasant from the bogs though; look at his hands; they've never seen a spade in anger. Where's the gun?'

Julian took his handkerchief and opened a box under the seat in the rear of the car. He held the pistol with the handkerchief and passed it to Granville who regarded him with a raised eyebrow.

'Have you handled it with bare hands before?'

'Only the barrel.'

'Good.'

He examined it carefully.

'Mauser C96. German. Probably part of the cache that Casement brought into Ireland during the war. I think we can say he's a Fenian.' He beckoned one of the two men standing nearby with their bicycles, barely more than boys. 'You're Rob Wilkes's lad, aren't you?' He nodded. 'How long will it take for you to bicycle to Sherborne? Twenty minutes? Go to the police station and tell the senior officer there what has happened and ask them to have the coroner visit my house. This scum here,' he nodded towards the corpse, 'has murdered my wife and nearly killed both my chauffeur and Mr Belmore here. Understood?'

'Aye sir. But where shall I say Mrs Granville is, sir?'

'I'm sorry Wilkes. Why should you know? Her body is at the Dower House. And please explain to whoever you see that a doctor won't be necessary.' He stopped and squinted at Julian's face which showed the rake marks of the mortal struggle. 'I think Mr Belmore is going to survive.'

Julian nodded. 'Scratches. Sore – but they don't need any treatment.'

Granville turned to the other man. 'Would you oblige me by staying here until the police arrive. It's important that the body – and anything else – is not touched.' He handed coins to both of them. 'We will be going back to the Dower House now.'

His hooded stare settled on Julian and his driver.

'I owe it to you two to get to the bottom of this. He wasn't working alone: of that I'm certain. I'll have the best of Scotland Yard on the case and you have my word that when we catch his companions, they'll swing for it.'

14

There was a hiatus that day as the police, coroner and doctor arrived to state the obvious – that the wife of the heir to Milborne had been murdered in broad daylight by what appeared to be an Irish assassin. The next day the press turned up in search of heroes and villains, finding the former in Julian, whose Irish background provided just the story that the Unionist newspapers, and more particularly their proprietors, were looking for. As much as he could, he professed an Englishman's modesty and emphasised that the fatal shot had been fired by the chauffeur and that he had been only an observer of events. He was now between the Scylla of his involvement with Daphne's death – and the Charybdis of shooting the Irishman.

But worse than the fear of exposure was his remorse. He had come to love Daphne Granville, a friendship that included elements of sister and mother – and he knew that he was directly responsible for her death. He tried to rationalise it, turning over in his mind the sequence of events, but no matter how he reshaped it, there was no doubt as to his culpability. He hadn't murdered her but, in his own estimation, it was manslaughter at the least. And he knew, at the same time, of what Michael Collins and his assassins were capable; their ruthlessness and reach. Fear, guilt and grief were now his companions and he knew that none of these three would ever entirely disappear, even if he managed to avoid the noose or a vengeful bullet.

The Richmond family insisted that he stayed with them – indefinitely they said. He insisted that it was temporary, but accepted their invitation and moved into an annex attached to the rectory – which was hardly luxury, but no worse than his cottage. Its main advantage was that it sheltered him, to some extent, from the press intrusion that filled the week before Daphne Granville's funeral in Sherborne Abbey. The service was packed, with the churchyard taking the overspill. Julian was asked to be a pall bearer, an honour that he tried to refuse but was obliged to undertake. Only he knew the real burden he was shouldering as he felt the weight of the oak coffin on his shoulder, smelled the wood varnish and imagined the enclosed corpse of his friend with her empty eye socket.

The police had questioned him. However, their deference to him as the hero of the hour and lack of intimation about his prior knowledge of the Irishman began to allay one of his fears. Robert Granville's attitude to him was transformed. The hostility to Ireland and criticism of his hunting evaporated, and instead he found himself the recipient of confidences that he tried to keep at arm's length, without success. He accepted an invitation to lunch at the Dower House on the basis that Granville's company would be diluted by others, to find that he was the only guest – but not the only sufferer from grief and guilt. To his consternation, Granville wept in his presence and professed remorse at how he had treated his wife during their arid marriage. It had taken her death for him to appreciate the qualities beloved by everyone else. With his own burdens, and memories of his first blood-soaked encounter with Granville, Julian could only mouth embarrassed words of comfort and hope that the lunch would end as soon as possible – but wine and port made Granville increasingly maudlin as the meal dragged on.

The police investigation came to an impasse. That the assassin was Irish was not in doubt, but denials of culpability by the Sinn Fein leadership, no apparent criminal past and therefore no fingerprints, left the police with little to go on. They found out where he had stayed in Dorchester when a boardinghouse landlady recognised a photograph of his corpse in the local newspaper; but there the trail went cold – not helped by the stonewalling of the Irish Constabulary whose true loyalty was expressed in their minimum of cooperation. Even when the London CID travelled to Dublin, they found leads blocked, sometimes by hostility, but mainly by obfuscation. They were obeying other masters now. Julian heard all this from Granville whose anger and frustration at the course of the investigation raised yet more weight from Julian's mind. The reporting in the Irish press focused on the role of the chauffeur and made Julian's part appear more akin to self-defence. Reading these, sent by his mother who collected any mention of his name in every Irish newspaper, he felt a lifting of the other sword hanging over his head. Any revenge killing would now be under arc lights – not the sort of publicity needed by a government-in-waiting.

Living within the curtilage of the rectory, he saw the Richmond family every day, sharing at least one meal with them. Rose's hurt and anger on her return from Wales had dissipated with the turn of events and metamorphosed into protectiveness and concern. The whole family had shared his affection for Daphne Granville. Isobel's presence was more difficult. A different person had returned from Paris. The woman that had left in March had been intelligent, with strong shades of a bluestocking in her manner, gauche at times; well educated but inexperienced in the ways of the world. Her clothes had reflected this. Her hair was now shorter and there was a new panache to her dress, helped by gifts from Sophie Aurigny. The bluestocking had developed into something more sophisticated – a better listener and a sharper conversationalist, someone whose horizons had expanded. She had also grown into her looks, less *jolie laide* and more beautiful – but was now constrained by the walls of the rectory, a bird that had outgrown its cage. She was bored. Despite himself, and Daphne Granville's warning words, Julian was drawn to her. He was fascinated by politics and world affairs and, with Isobel's experiences in Paris and letters from her new friends, her views and opinions were the ones he sought – to the irritation of her sister. Her father only exacerbated the fissure between his daughters by doing the same.

As September progressed, the police and newspapers moved on and routine reestablished itself. For Julian it revolved around the early hunting season. Every day of the week, apart from Sunday, he was up before dawn to prepare his hounds. If the meet was within five miles he, Ralph and, on most days, Ariadne would clatter out of the kennels in the dark to hack across country. He loved these early autumn dawns, when the weather was settled, with their slowly lightening skies and the dawn chorus that accompanied them when the strike of their horses' shod hooves was dampened by turf. While his hounds drew the woods, he was left to smoke and eat blackberries while watching the wildlife stirred by their activity: deer, hares with their stop-start flight, blackbirds protesting, and of course foxes. The aim at this time of year was not a pursuit across country, jumping obstacles, where the kill was subsidiary to the chase – but vermin control, containing the fox population to the point where farmers would accept the occasional attrition of their chickens and leave their shotgun unused. Though many of the farmers were tenants of Milborne, it was a subtle exercise in diplomacy that Julian enjoyed. Dairy farmers and huntsmen woke early and theirs was a camaraderie of those who shared this time of stillness and beauty. He found Ariadne changed too. After the murder, she was more silent and self-absorbed. He let this go for a week or two but a moment, when they were both standing in a stubble field on their own listening to the ebb and flow of sound and movement within the covert, gave him his chance.

'You seem a bit withdrawn since... the funeral.'

She looked at him sharply and then back at her horse's mane.

'I'm fine. It's just given us all something to think about, hasn't it? Look at the difference in Uncle Robert. And poor Papa who has taken it so to heart. I don't think he can take any more blows like that. I loved Aunt Daphne.' She paused. 'She was more of a mother to me than my own – but I never told her that.'

She had never admitted to this level of emotion before.

'She was a friend to me too. And I failed to protect her.'

Ariadne did not acknowledge this. Was there an accusation in her silence? Finally she spoke.

'So what are you going to do? Are you going to stay here – or go into business with Evelyn Grumond? I know you've been writing to him – and Aunt Daphne said she thought you needed to do something other than hunting. After what's happened you'll probably want to put some distance between yourself and us.' She drew on her cigarette and looked away from him as she spoke. 'I'll miss you, you know. Having you here, and the war being over, has transformed things for me. Made it bearable.'

'I… I haven't decided anything – yet. And it may get decided for me anyway – as your uncle suggested to me last month, in his inimitable way, that I might get the sack. Mind you, that was then. He's quite different with me now, which is better – but disconcerting.' He cocked his head to listen to his hounds. 'The trouble is that I can't afford to stay. If the rent from the farm in Ireland was more substantial, maybe. Your father's very generous and I'm certainly not complaining – but it's a fact to be faced: I would need a proper private income to carry on here.'

She didn't answer him straightaway but lit a cigarette without offering one to him. 'There is a way round this, you know; that means you don't have to disappear halfway round the world and be a slave to that ghastly man.'

'He's not that bad.'

'He's worse.'

'I don't have many other options.'

'There is one.'

He looked at her quizzically. 'I'd love to know what it is. It's been rather front of mind recently.'

'Me.' She looked him directly in the eye. 'You could marry me.'

He dropped his horn that he had been about to blow. He was thankful as it gave him time, as he dismounted and then remounted, to marshall his thoughts. The conversation on the pier at Stromness now made sense – but it caught him by surprise as he had always assumed that she saw him as something between a brother and servant. It was certainly how she had always treated him. He settled back in his saddle and gained extra time by adjusting the girth that had slipped on the remount. She spoke first.

'Well?'

'Well, I don't know what to say. That came as… something of a surprise.'

'Why?'

'I… I had no idea you felt for me like that.'

'I don't. Well I like you – very much actually – but I don't know about love. Most of the girls I know who've told me they are in love are miserable. Is love and being in love the same thing?'

'I don't know. It's never happened to me.'

'I thought you were in love with Rose. That's what Aunt Daphne said. But I have to say you two don't look like Romeo and Juliet to me.'

At that moment a deer broke cover about thirty yards from where they were standing, stopped, saw them, and bounded off across the newly cut wheat stubble. The sound of the hounds close behind meant it was business as they were close on its trail. One important part of the early season was the training of the new entry, that year's crop of puppies, now fully grown but not yet part of the disciplined pack led by its experienced lead hounds. Deer were not on the menu.

In an instant both Ariadne and Julian applied their spurs and in a few strides they were straddling the route of the deer so that, as the hounds emerged with their heads down on the scent, both of them were waiting with their hunting whips – two-foot long sticks and six-foot tapering leather thongs. With practised skill they cracked their whips over the hounds' heads, catching them occasionally with a flick of the thong. At the same time they shouted and growled at them, driving them off the scent and back into the wood, endeavouring to make it a lesson that would put them off deer for life. For a moment the hounds milled about, seemingly disconcerted; then the sound of other hounds speaking – hopefully this time on the scent of a fox – caught their attention. The deer was forgotten as they streamed towards the mournful sound echoing through the full-leafed wood.

The sun was now up, but at this early hour, tendrils of mist still lay in silver threads under hedge lines, pooling in hollows. The stubble, in the oblique sunlight, was revealed as a sparkling carpet of spiders' webs holding the morning dew. Julian looked down at his boots that were soaked after his dismount and over to

Ariadne who was still focussed on the activity within the wood. He shook his head in anger. How had he allowed himself to get into this mess? He knew the perils of flirtation in this new world they inhabited but could not, in all conscience, say what he had done to elicit this proposal. He realised that he had taken her at face value, had taken her manner as the mirror of her heart and had misunderstood at every turn. Or had he? Apart from on the pier at Stromness she had always treated him with faint scorn, trying to catch him out professionally and teasing with barbed comments that were brushed off rather than laughed off. But then there was Stromness.

That was the warning flag – the moment he should have been aware that there was a softer core under the caustic carapace. But in many ways emotion was not what was being admitted. Love was not what she was offering – indeed she had said as much. It was more practical; financial security. But why him? While she was not a beauty, her looks were interesting and in an any normal world suitors would have beaten a path to her door. Why was she choosing him, impecunious and Irish, when she could have the pick of society? There was hunting, of course – her passion and his. But there was the intellectual in him that she did not – or could not – share. He loved books and retreated into their comfort whenever possible; she cheerfully admitted to having never read a novel for pleasure. He was intrigued by the wider world; she was a provincial and her visits to London a chore. So why him? Was the pool of eligible men really that limited? He looked at her again with fresh eyes as she peered into the wood and tried to imagine her naked and him making love to her. Where Rose's physical presence aroused him and he fantasised about her rounded behind and breasts, there was none of that with Ariadne – almost no bust and thin hipped – wiry and fit, but boyish in flesh and manner. What he found attractive in men was different to his preferences in women and try as he might he could not summon the erotic as he examined her with carnal eyes.

To his relief, Ralph appeared. He could still hear the hounds but could tell it was an intermittent scent. They had been there for half an hour and Ralph was seeking his permission to call them off and move to another draw – a gorse thicket that covered the crown of one of the more prominent hills in the district. Ralph looked at his watch; he never wasted words. Julian nodded in reply and the whipper-in went about his task, calling out in harsh, high-pitched shouts to gather his hounds to him. Julian followed with Ariadne a couple of horse lengths behind. To his relief, she made no more effort to trot alongside him than he made to rein back his horse to walk next to her. He welcomed the time to process the morning's revelations and to work out his response. His heart was heavy as he pondered the implications. How could this end well without causing offence or hurt? The irony struck him that he was hardly behaving like a Lothario, carelessly leaving a string of discarded lovers. It was more a case of tiptoeing around a minefield that was neither of his choosing or making.

*　　*　　*

Isobel knocked on the connecting door to the annex. She has heard Julian's footsteps just before noon – his hunting boots hard on the wooden floor rattling the china on the dresser through the wall. He appeared with his collar undone and britches held up with braces, pink-faced from exercise and sun, his hair plastered down with sweat and still showing the mark of his hunting cap.

'A good morning?' she asked.

'Did we catch anything? No. Was it a beautiful day to be out? What could be lovelier? Would you like to come in?'

'Thank you.' She stepped across the threshold but didn't attempt to go further. 'I'm only here to ask if you can join us for luncheon today. It's just me and Rose. Papa and Davina are organising the harvest festival. Nothing smart.'

'I'd like that very much. Thank you.'

There was a awkward silence. Isobel neither retreated back into the rectory nor advanced into the annex.

'Would you like some coffee?' he asked.

'Aren't you tired? What time were you up?'

'Four. But that's normal – and I'll have a doze in the afternoon.'

'Then I'd love that. Thank you.'

They walked through to the kitchen which was as primitive as that in Julian's cottage. It was summer, so the range was cold and there was only a paraffin ring for cooking. Though the day was beautiful outside, the north-facing yard could have been in deep winter. At Isobel's suggestion, they took their coffee and went into the kitchen garden. The smell of herbs, the bright red of raspberries and the hum of bees surrounded them as they sat opposite each other on a pair of canvas chairs. They chatted idly for some minutes; insubstantial gossip and remarks on the fecundity of the kitchen garden. Isobel picked up where Ariadne had left off.

'I hear you may be off to join Grumond.'

He hesitated before replying. 'How does everyone know this? I've written to him – but that's all. Nothing back from him and certainly no plans. Happy?' There was a tinge of irritation in his voice.

'I didn't mean to interrogate you,' said Isobel. 'If that is what you want then you must do it – but you'll be missed here. I'm interested though. What would you prefer – if all things were equal?'

He sighed. 'But they're not, are they? Here I get pocket money. There I get a salary – and maybe a stake in the business if it goes well. Here I am, and will always be, a higher status servant – and dependent on the whim of your cousin. If I stay long enough I get to work for him – which wouldn't be an unalloyed joy.'

'He's better than you think.'

'Certainly better now than in the past. But to have my life and livelihood dependant on his whim?' He shook his head.

'It sounds like you've made up your mind.'

'About Grumond? No. It's made me focus, that's all: think about the alternatives. Grumond wouldn't be my first choice – but then I don't have many other options at the moment.'

She shrugged. 'I'm in the same boat as you – except that I'm unemployed. But I can't do this for much longer or I'll go mad. Paris was hard work but interesting – and I was being paid. And when I wasn't working I was in the greatest city in the world. Here

I spend all day with Dav and Papa, who are sweet and lovely – but…
and with Rose. We've always rubbed each other up the wrong
way – but it's much worse than before. I know I'm mainly to blame,
but I need to be busy and I don't think I belong in the country.
I want to be in London – but I need a job and somewhere I can
afford to live.'

He considered. 'I might be able to help with somewhere to
live: my cousin has a house in Belgravia with a mews house for
friends and relations. It may not be for long but I'm sure he will
get you going.'

'Would you ask him?'

'Of course.'

She reached forward and squeezed his hand. 'Thank you. I can't
tell you how much I need to get away from here.' She caught his
look. 'Not from you. Not from anyone really. Just to London; where
things happen. I love the countryside but I need the excitement
of the city more. I suppose you're the opposite?'

He didn't answer immediately as he considered what she had
said. 'I know it looks that way – I'm a huntsman after all – and
you don't get more rural than that. But I'm increasingly wondering whether I want to do this forever – even if I could afford it.
Grumond gave me the push I needed; made me widen my horizons
and think about… other things.'

'Paris did that for me.'

'I was perfectly happy before; doing what I thought I do best.
Going with Grumond will be a risk as I've no idea if I'll be any
good at it. Some people love risk. I'm not sure I do, but then I've
never tried, so how do I know?'

They sat in silence amid the hum of late summer. Isobel broke
the silence. 'Can I ask you something?' He nodded. 'It's none of
my business – well, it is a bit – but what are your… intentions…
with Rose. She's unhappy because of you and I'm having to live
with that. She thought you were… that you liked her. More than
that. If you do… like her… why don't you have this conversation
with her? She feels you treat her like a sister. Is that all she is
to you?'

For the second time in a day Julian found himself twisting away from an awkward question about a relationship. He avoided eye contact by staring at the rookery over the garden wall where a squabble had broken out amongst its occupants.

'It's difficult. Everything is uncertain at the moment with Grumond – and what happened last month. And I don't want to hurt her.'

'You're already doing that by leaving her in limbo.'

'I never promised her anything.'

'She's not looking for a promise – just for some indication that you… that you think of her as more than friend.'

There was a testiness in her tone that he couldn't ignore. 'I can see that – and I know I need to make some decisions. Is that alright?'

She nodded. 'It's not for me. It's for her – and you.'

*   *   *

Rose looked surreptitiously at Julian throughout lunch, especially when he was talking to Isobel and she could examine him carefully. Summer suited him; his naturally pale skin was tanned and she loved the crease marks either side of his eyes that crinkled when he smiled. The scar that rose from the bow of his lip to just under his eye also changed colour in the sun – or rather became less prominent as his skin turned darker. That she knew its provenance was a bond between them, one that she had thought about often during the months of separation. It had become a touchstone that had made the coolness he had displayed on his return the more hurtful. Today he was charming – but to both her and Isobel equally – almost worse than distance, rudeness or indifference. An outsider would have seen nothing amiss – but it was a needle in her heart.

Both the servants were with Davina and the vicar, preparing the Harvest Festival. When their simple lunch was over, Isobel announced that she would join them. It was an elegant way of leaving them alone. They washed and dried the dishes in silence. Rose folded the towel, leant against the draining board and watched him as he put away a dish.

'What's happening?' she asked.

He halted his task and looked down at the dish. 'What do you mean.'

'You know. Of course you know. Why have you been avoiding me?'

'I don't think I have.'

'If you haven't been avoiding me, you've certainly not sought me out. You only see me with Isobel – or with my father – or Dav. You didn't do this in Stromness. It's since you came back. I would understand after Cousin Daphne's murder – but it was before that. What changed? Is it something I've said or done?'

He took the dish to the dresser and placed it carefully on the shelf, still not making eye contact. 'I'm sorry. It's been rather unsettling. The murder, of course, but also deciding what I'm going to do with the rest of my life.' He turned and faced her. 'I don't think I can stay here and I don't have any other way of making a living. How can I commit to anything if my position is so insecure? I don't have the money to get married and the only way that I can make some, that I can see, is to take up Grumond's offer and spend the next few years travelling and living in Asia. And even that isn't anywhere near certain. I can't see how a wife or children fit into that.' He stopped and looked at his shoes, shaking his head. 'It's not to do with you.'

Rose felt the irritation evaporating. Without thinking, she stepped forward and linked her fingers behind his neck and pulled him gently towards her so that they were standing ear to ear. She dropped one hand into the small of his back like a dancer. She kissed his earlobe.

'Why wife?' She felt a small start of incomprehension. 'I don't know if I want to be your wife; but I would like to be your lover.' She was close enough to feel his arousal touching her leg. Rather than retreating from it she allowed it to swell and press more urgently against her. She sensed him swallowing. She whispered in his ear. 'There's no one in the house – and no one coming back for at least a couple of hours. We could go into your annex. And you don't have to worry; it's my safe time of the month. Mrs Stopes has a chart.' She squeezed his neck. 'I want to do this – and you do too, don't you?' She dropped her hand and ran it down his leg, feeling the contours of his tumescence. He gave a small gasp. 'Come,' she said.

She took his hand and led him to the door between the rectory and the annex. Once through, she closed it behind her and led him up the stairs into the narrow attic of two rooms. The larger room had a brass bed on the wall opposite the dormer window where the curtains were three quarters closed. A ribbon of sunshine slashed the room. She led him to the bed and they sat together in the part light. Her mouth felt dry and her leg trembled. She faced him and they kissed, deeply with their tongues fencing in a duel of parry and thrust. She felt his hand on her breast and then down her side and hips, his fingers clearly delineated through her light summer dress. She pulled back and looked at him. Her voice was hoarse.

'Should we get undressed?'

He nodded and stood up. Still sitting, she twisted round. 'Will you undo me?' She felt his shaking fingers struggling to the task. 'Here. Let me.' She reached up her back and, with practised fingers, loosened the hooks and eyes until her dress was undone to the waist. She stood, faced him, kissed him again, pulled her arms free of the sleeves – and let the dress fall to the floor. He stood, sweeping her body with his eyes. She had imagined that standing in her underwear in front of a man would leave her shy and uncertain. She was surprised by the power she felt in his reaction to her. Emboldened, she reached forward and released his waist loop and, with unpractised hands, worked her way down his fly buttons, feeling the protrusion of his arousal straining against her efforts. Her own breathing was staccato as the last button was released to reveal his underwear. He took over from her and, in one movement, hooked the waist over his erection. They stood, facing each other, with their clothes and underwear pooled by their feet.

She was fascinated by the shape and angle of his penis: she had seen sculptures and anatomical drawings of men's genitals but had had to rely on imagination for the rest. There was something animal and visceral about the actuality that was both frightening and exciting and it was with both lust and curiosity that she reached out and held him, running her hand gently around the head before grasping the shaft. He almost fell forward with the shaking of his leg and she found herself supporting him. She could hear his breath in her ear, gasping and swallowing. With it came a bolt of arousal and she felt a knot of desire in her stomach. What would happen now? She squeezed again, waiting, she hoped, for him to indicate what she should do. To her consternation he gave a groan and she felt a spasm in her hand and a hot jet of warm liquid on her forearm. She looked down in alarm, still holding this living, spitting thing as another pulse of grey fluid landed on her leg, and another. Nothing had prepared her for this. She had imagined his tongue working around her breasts and fantasied about the moment of penetration and its possible pain. She knew in theory about sperm and eggs, but this was outside anything that Mrs Stopes, her sister or friends had described or discussed. She froze and waited as his breathing slowed and the spasming thing in her hand subsided.

He slowly pushed himself upright so that she could see his face. Distress was all over it. 'I'm sorry. I'm so sorry,' he gasped.

She had no idea what to reply. What did this imply? Was it normal? What should she do with this now softening thing that she still held in her wet hand. She pulled him closer with the other hand around his neck and kissed his ear.

'It's alright. Sit down.'

He did as he was told and both sat on the bed with one hand each round each other's necks and her other hand now on his leg that was shaking uncontrollably.

'I'm sorry,' he repeated. 'How could I do that?' She had no idea what to reply and only squeezed the back of his neck in what she hoped was a gesture of comfort. 'I couldn't help myself. It just happened.'

She found her voice. 'It doesn't matter. It really doesn't. We can try again.' Try what? Did this signify the end? What was supposed to happen now? She had imagined lying together on a bed; coupled;

satiated. 'Lie with me.' She pulled him back on to the bed but had forgotten his trousers, underwear and shoes that he still had around his ankles. Awkwardly he shed both and they lay with the vertical shaft of sunshine slicing across them and a welter of thoughts. She leant over and rested her head on his chest, conscious of the racing of his heart that matched her own.

Neither spoke: there was too much – and too little – to say.

15

In mid-September the weather changed. Summer became premature winter with a dusting of snow on trees that still had, apart from the chestnuts, not even a hint of autumn. A gale that would have been unremarkable in February battered the south of England, catching man and beast in the wrong clothes. Julian returned from hunting to the kennels chilled to the core after an immobile morning swept by snow flurries that turned to sleet and eventually to rain. The normal field of followers, never more than two dozen in the early autumn, had chosen the alternative of a warm bed and a later breakfast. So, at an earlier time than usual, he and Ralph kennelled and fed their hounds and returned, gratefully, to their own breakfasts. The annex to the rectory, unlike his cottage, had the luxury of a bath into which he decanted himself to listen to the sleet and wind rattling the skylight above his head. He dozed until the cooling of the water forced him out and into his bed where he replayed the disastrous scene of two days before. He shuddered at the memory of his incontinent ejaculation – but also found himself aroused again.

They had lain together for some time without speaking, neither knowing how to bridge the gap of mutual embarrassment. They had kissed – but more as a way of filling the awkward silence. As they did, he had hardened again. She did not hold him this time, but sat up and unhooked her bra before running her hand slowly up and down his chest almost as a massage. Her breasts were larger than he had anticipated. Tentatively he had cupped one and then the other and kissed each nipple in turn until they hardened. He felt her relaxing and his own confidence growing as she accepted the pleasure that he was offering. She had trembled as he rolled his tongue around her nipples and stroked the contours of her belly with his fingers brushing the upper reaches of her pubic hair. Their nervousness had receded as each touched the other with building confidence – but then they heard the sound of the front door of the rectory opening.

The moment was gone. They had looked at each other in consternation. He had put his finger to his lips as a gesture of quiet.

'No one will come in here. We could have gone out for a walk – anything.'

'The garden. You stay in the house and I'll go out to pick some raspberries.' She was already out of bed and slipping on her dress. 'Papa won't be looking for anything.'

Julian had watched her dress, still in a state of excitement, keeping his eyes on her back and the shape and slide of her hips. Fully dressed she had turned to face him.

'Are we fated?' He hadn't replied. 'We'll have another chance sometime soon, I hope. But it's a shame; I really thought our stars were in line today.'

All this played in his mind as he lay in bed masturbating, imagining the contours of her body against his and the staccato intakes of breath that he now knew was the sound of her desire. Afterwards he dozed and woke with a start to the sound of knocking on the door into the rear yard that was his front door of sorts. It took him a few seconds to work out that it was more than just the noise of the gale that was still beating the house. A blast of wind and rain hit him as he opened the door to Ariadne who was wrapped in a trench coat and holding a sou'wester on to her head. She entered without a word and leant against the wall as he wrestled the door shut. She shook off the rain, pushed her hair back into some form of order and shed her coat with a shower of drops.

'Snow in September! I can't believe it.' He took her coat and indicated the way to the small sitting room that lay off the hall. She looked at it with a critical eye. 'Why on earth did you move in here when I made the cottage so much nicer for you?'

'You're right – but this was only temporary after the murder. The reporters couldn't get at me here.' She looked unconvinced as she sat on the narrow sofa.

'Tea?' he asked.

'Could you manage a martini?'

'If you give me five minutes.'

He returned with a long glass. 'No ice I'm afraid. But not too long on the vermouth. I learned that from your mother.'

'One of her better lessons.'

They raised their glasses. 'You missed nothing this morning,' he said, 'it was miserable.'

'I thought as much. Ralph said there was no scent.'

'You've been to the kennels?'

'On the way here.'

'And Ralph was still there?'

She looked out at the pulse of rain that was rat-tating on the window. 'Yes, he was.' Julian was suddenly aware of her nervousness; that one thumb was polishing the large sapphire stone on her ring and the other the side of her glass. 'I need to ask you something,' she said. 'Please sit down.' She indicated to the other end of the sofa.

'Is everything alright?' he asked slowly.

She paused. 'I asked you... I suggested... the other morning, that you might think about marrying me.' She looked up at him with rare apprehensiveness. 'Have you thought about it?'

The truth was that after the debacle with Rose, the interchange with Ariadne had not been at the front of his mind. He dissembled.

'I was very flattered.'

'But have you thought about it?'

'Of course.'

'And?'

'I... well the truth is that I don't know why you'd want to marry me. I'm not the best catch around – and you could have the pick of pretty well anyone you wanted. And we haven't exactly been... courting.'

'I need you to marry me.' She gulped her martini. 'More than that. I need you to elope with me. Very soon. To Gretna Green.'

'Why? And why now?'

She looked away at the window again. Her thin mouth was pursed.

'I'm pregnant.' Another pulse of rain spattered the window. She looked at him in challenge. 'And so you don't have to ask, it's Ralph. He's the father.'

'Ralph? That Ralph?' He nodded in the direction of the kennels.

'That Ralph.'

'But…'

'I know. He's a kennel huntsman. Of course I know that. That's why I can't marry him. Impossible. That's why it has to be you. It will only be for form, of course. You can do… do what you have to when we're married; I won't make any fuss.'

'What do you mean?'

'I saw you. You and Ran. In the hotel in Stromness. My room was across the yard from the one you were sharing with him when you stayed the night. You hadn't shut the curtains properly. I saw what you were doing.'

Julian sat blinking for some seconds. 'What about… what about Rose?'

Ariadne shrugged. 'Does she know you're a sodomite?'

He blinked. 'That's blackmail.'

She fixed him with a stare. 'Perhaps. But there's another thing. The Irishman that killed Aunt Daphne. You knew him.'

'I knew him?'

'I was out riding my new horse the week before she was killed – and an Irishman on a bicycle asked me the way to your house. I didn't give it a thought – until afterwards – when I saw the photograph of his body. I kept it to myself because… because I knew then. I knew I might have to do this.' She took another gulp of her drink and Julian could see the emotion on her face. 'I don't want to force you to do this – but I don't have a choice.' She shook her head, looking away from him. When she turned back, the brutality had gone and a sad desperation had replaced it. 'We could try to be happy, couldn't we? More than my parents? We like each other and maybe we could learn to love each other. We have our hunting – and we'll be rich. Is that so bad?'

Julian shook his head. 'Ralph? How?'

He looked at her to see that she was crying; something he had never seen her do before. She put her arm up to her face to wipe away the tears on her sleeve and looked away.

'I've known him since I was sixteen. We've spent pretty well every day together until he went to France in '16. I wasn't his lover until he came back in November. We'd kissed before – that's all. But I can't tell him about this.'

'You could marry him. The world's changed.'

She looked at him with her more customary scorn. 'That much? No.'

He made as if to answer but she spoke before he could. 'I'd be disinherited. Impossible.' She metamorphosed in seconds from frightened girl to imperious aristocrat. He had seen the latter before but the former was new to him. 'I need to know,' she said. 'I need to know your answer.'

'Do I have a choice?'

'No.'

He considered what she had just said. 'Do you think I was responsible for your aunt's death?'

'You knew the Irishman. There must have been something.'

'There was. When I was growing up in Ireland I was involved with… let's call them Irish nationalists. I went to school with them and played hurling with them. But I left to get away from all that after they burned down my mother's house – just because my father was a Protestant.' He laughed mirthlessly. 'The Irishman came to see me for help – but I didn't tell him anything. In fact, he threatened to kill me – and nearly did. Maybe that would have been better in the circumstances.'

She looked at him, imperiousness gone. 'Why didn't you say that at the time?'

'To your uncle? I was trying to work out a way to stop it all – when it happened. And after that, anything I said about contact with the gunman would have had me hanged. And your aunt was a good friend to me. If I didn't kill her, then I'm hardly innocent either.' He paused. 'Why would you want to marry me, now you know this?'

'Want? I have to.' Some of her earlier vulnerability was in her expression again. 'Actually, I would have liked to marry you anyway – and I think we could have been happy. But now it's poisoned, isn't it? No matter what happens, you'll always resent me – and this baby. I've got what I want – but what I want doesn't want me. That's a curse; a punishment.' Tears filled her eyes and for the first time Julian was touched by sympathy rather than anger and fear. What she said was true. He placed his hand on her arm and she looked at it with surprise. 'Maybe everything's cursed,' she continued with filled eyes, 'all of us. Everyone is maimed or lonely, and mourning someone or some thing. And now this. Do you think I want to steal you from Rose? That I want you under these circumstances – especially when I know you prefer men to women?'

He hesitated before replying. 'It's not like that. It's complicated. I prefer women – but it was horrible with prostitutes.'

'So why not normal women?'

'If only that was possible – but you know that it isn't. I loathed it; the money exchange; the smell of antiseptic; the fear of syphilis. It started at school with other boys. There was no alternative then. I enjoyed it. I still do. But I like and love women as much – more.' He looked at her. 'Does that make you feel any better?'

'But you don't want me, do you?' Julian avoided her eye. 'I know. I've seen how you look at my mother. And Rose. And Isobel for that matter. You look at me and talk to me as if I were a…' She shook her head as she grappled for the right word.

Another blast of wind and rain hit the house and the windows ran with sheet water so that the other side of the yard was masked. At either end of the hard sofa they both contemplated the lifetime of unhappiness that they were choosing.

* * *

Half an hour later, Julian was pacing the sitting room. Ariadne had ran out of his annex in tears, leaving Julian looking over the rain-drenched yard through the small window beside the door. He had thought about following her, but a mixture of the sheeting rain and and the cul-de-sac of their exchange kept him where he was. He had a headache.

For the second time in a year he was being blackmailed and all he could see was ruins. He could hear movement in the rectory next door and it brought him back to Rose and the consequences of the decisions in front of him. He cursed Ariadne, Michael Collins, the assassin and Ralph, all of whom, in their different ways, had him in chains. He returned to his sitting room with a glass of whisky and contemplated the half-drunk martini with a lipstick smear on its rim. Ariadne had left behind her sou'wester and the drips from it formed a circle on the sofa fabric. The whisky burned his throat. He paced up and down the length of the room, testing every scenario, knowing that the only option not on the table was to do nothing: the pregnancy was a ticking clock. How serious was her threat? Could he afford to call her bluff? He knew that an insinuation would be enough to ruin him and any connection to the murder would be enough to hang him. And if he married her? The blackmail threat would be gone but so was any hope of an independent life; locked in a golden cage with his jailer, overseen by the malevolent gaze of the man who had turned him into a murderer and in whose wife's killing he was lethally implicated. He tried to think of Ariadne as a partner, as a lover and a wife. Her hard, imperious stare and her lean ranginess failed to fill his imagination with any hint of the erotic. Their friendship, such as it was, had little softness in it. And with a baby that wasn't his. The waters were closing over him and he was out of breath.

*　　*　　*

At the same time as Julian and Ariadne were talking in the annex, Isobel and Rose were standing in the rectory's drawing room watching curtains of hail draw themselves across the park with the force of the wind rattling the decaying window sashes. Both women had shawls around their shoulders against the drafts that eddied around them. Rose held a book at which she glanced between gusts. Isobel bobbed between the window seat and the piano where Davina was tapping out a scale, missing notes. The plans for the day had included a trip to Sherborne Abbey to rub brasses – a hobby of their father's – but the snow, and now the hail and gale, had put paid to that. He had retired to his study for his afternoon nap, leaving his daughters restless and irritable at the enforced confinement. It was Rose who finally snapped when the scales gave way to 'Chopsticks' played at an inconsistent beat.

'Dav! You're driving us mad. Either play something properly or stop.'

She instantly regretted her outburst as tears filled Davina's eyes. She banged the lid on the piano shut and ran out of the room.

'Why did you do that?' said Isobel.

'That awful tune. If it was a tune, I wouldn't mind so much.'

'You've really upset her.'

'She'll get over it.'

Isobel moved towards the door but stopped and turned.

'Rose, what is happening between you and Julian?'

Rose looked up at her sharply. 'What do you mean?'

'You know what I mean. Has he proposed to you?'

Her sister put her book down. 'It's not really any of your business.'

'Not directly. But what you did to poor Dav is. You're like a bear with a sore head and we're all having to live with it.' She could see that her sister was bridling. 'So don't get angry with me. It only makes things worse.'

Rose bit her lip. 'No. He hasn't. But he will. Soon, I'm sure.' She saw a sceptical look on Isobel's face. 'Why are you asking? Do you know something that I don't?'

Isobel shook her head. 'Nothing direct. But I don't think he will.'

'How do you know?' The anger was replaced by hurt.

'From what he said to me. Not about you, but about having to earn a living – with Grumond. You didn't meet him. He came to Ariadne's house party; toad of a man – but rich, and wants to give Julian a job.'

'He told me.'

'About the travelling in Asia? And about how a wife would be too much?'

'Something like that.'

'And that's good enough?'

'What are you saying?'

'I'm not saying anything. Anything will be wrong.'

'Are you saying that I shouldn't marry him?'

'He isn't making you happy.'

Rose deflated and crumpled on the sofa. She was still holding the book as she brushed her sleeve over her eyes. 'No. He's not. But I can't exactly force him.'

'You could give him an ultimatum.'

Rose looked up at her. 'And if he says no?'

'You aren't any worse off than you are now. And at least you'll know.'

'Know that I'm going to be an old maid.'

'There'll be someone else.'

'Will there? I haven't met one. A normal one anyway.' Isobel didn't reply. It was the truth. 'It feels like burning the boats, doesn't it? At least there's some hope at the moment. He might decide to stay here.'

'Where he doesn't have enough money to get married.'

'Is that what he told you?'

'Sort of.'

'Why didn't he tell me?'

'Pride probably. He needs to provide.'

'Why do men think like that?'

'Someone has to.'

'But it's not exactly romantic.'

'Nor is real life. If he stays here he has to live with Cousin Robert's foot on his neck. He's softened a bit since Cousin Daphne died – but would you want that if you were him? I wouldn't.'

'So you told him to go to Asia and leave me here?'

Isobel shook her head. 'I didn't tell him anything. I did say that he was making you unhappy – which is true, isn't it?' Rose nodded. 'So if that was interfering, I'm sorry.'

'It's not. But what I don't understand is why I can't go with him. I would love to go to Indochina – and live there. I can help him with his work. What's wrong with that?'

'Grumond probably. He doesn't want the cost of an expatriate family. A single man is cheaper when you're getting a business off the ground – and that he can work him harder I'm sure has entered his calculations…'

'He sounds a shit.'

'He is. But he's Julian's route out of the life here.'

'Without me?'

Isobel shrugged and shook her head. 'I don't think that he is doing this to avoid you. He needs this job to afford to marry.'

'Me?'

'Yes, I'm sure.'

'I wish I was.'

16

Dorset, two days later

Ariadne was sitting in the bow window of the drawing room that looked over the park. She had just been sick. The nausea hovered as she watched swans on the lake spooning the surface and ducks taking it in turns to dip below water that sparkled in the autumnal sunshine. It was hard to imagine the winter that had descended on the park only days before. She had not left the castle since her ultimatum to Julian. Morning sickness and an unwillingness to see him had kept her away from the kennels and the dawn meets of that time of year. She had heard nothing from him – neither note nor message. The only noise in the house was the metronomes of competing clocks.

The sound of her father's distinctive gait, its limping rhythm the legacy of a hunting fall in early middle age, came from the hall. It was faster than usual, its urgency making Ariadne look up. When he came into the room he was waving a letter.

'How dare he!'

'Who, Papa?' She had only once before seen him this angry.

'Belmore. The bloody man!'

'What's he done?' She tried to keep her voice steady and inconsequential.

'He's gone. The bloody man has disappeared. Left this. How dare he!'

He slammed his stick on the table, shaking his head in fury.

'Show me the letter, Papa. Please. It is from him, I'm assuming.'

He thrust it at her. 'That poor girl. Led her up the garden path. And left us in the lurch when the season's started. He'd better not try for another pack again or even think of asking for a reference.'

She read it quickly. It was only two sides and, apart from an

237

apology, there was no explanation other than that he had to take up an opportunity that required an immediate decision.

'Is there a letter for me?'

Her father was too distracted to notice the catch in her voice.

'From Belmore? Not that I know of. You'll have to ask Goodrich.'

She knew that it would be pointless asking.

'Well? Do you know what's behind this? You seem to have become friendly with him of late. Did he tell you anything that can explain such behaviour?'

She shook her head and despite herself started to cry. Her father looked at her in surprise.

'My dear, are you alright?' Comprehension spread across his face. 'You? As well as poor Rose? The four-letter man!' He sighed. 'And to think I liked him. Never trust the Irish; no morals; no idea how a gentleman should behave. Breaking girls' hearts and moving on without notice or explanation. Opportunity indeed!'

He put his arms around her. She had always been as close to him as she was distant from her mother. He stroked her hair as she continued to sob into the tweed of his jacket.

'You're best off without him. He's the sort of cad that would stand you up at the altar. He wouldn't have made you happy if he behaves like this.' He hugged her tighter. 'You're young and beautiful and…' His sentence died away with her intensified tears. He awkwardly stroked her back, not knowing how to mend a broken heart. She surfaced, red eyed and nosed.

'Thank you, Papa. But it's not him. It really isn't.'

He looked perplexed, relieved, and then angry again.

'That is a relief. Thank God it's not you as well as poor Rose… but it doesn't…'

His voice tailed off as a woman's footsteps rat-tatted on the stone floor of the hall. Her mother's was an equally distinctive gait. Father and daughter glanced at each other. She was rarely up at this hour. When she came in she was wearing a hat, coat and her most insincere smile.

'Ah! There you are.' She air-kissed the space around her daughter's head, ignoring her husband. 'How did you sleep, my dear?

Not hunting today? Good for you to be indoors though. So much better for your complexion.' She failed to notice her red eyes and nose. 'I'm going into Sherborne; to the post office. Do you want anything?'

'Why are you going there, Mama?'

There was coldness in her question.

'Picking up a parcel.'

'Why can't the postman deliver it?'

'I have to collect it personally.'

'Because it's from Nancy?'

'Why do you ask?'

'You know perfectly well. And so does Papa.' There was a snort from her father. 'Of course we know.'

'Well, I don't know what you're talking about.'

'Drugs, Mama. Whatever that powder is that makes you quarrelsome, argumentative and generally bloody. Those drugs.'

'Darling, I haven't had any of those for years. Didn't agree with me. Nancy gets me something now that makes the change of life rather less horrid. You'll appreciate it when it's your turn, I promise you.'

'Hopefully I won't be a drug addict when it's my turn.'

She flinched.

'That is a perfectly horrid thing to say. Darling,' she acknowledged her husband for the first time, 'I won't be spoken to like this. These are lies and calumnies and I won't put up with them.'

'Which bit is a lie, Mama? The drug addict or the bloody-minded bit? Papa? You choose.'

Her father shook his head and changed the subject.

'You haven't seen this, Violet.' He pushed the letter towards her. 'From Belmore. Gone. No explanation – just some twaddle about an opportunity. That's what I gave the man – an opportunity. And what does he do? Leaves a trail of broken hearts behind him and a pack of hounds with neither huntsman nor master.'

'Only one broken heart, Papa. And Ralph is more than capable of hunting the hounds – and Uncle Robert is the fieldmaster anyway. We don't need him.'

'I thought you and he were rather close,' said her mother.

'I liked him. But there was something about him that wasn't quite right.' Both her parents looked at her in anticipation. She hesitated and bit her lip. They saw tears form in her eyes and her hand holding the table with a grip that whitened her fingers. 'No. No. That's just me upset that he didn't come and say goodbye. I'll miss him; that's all. It was nice to have a man here, wasn't it?'

Her mother put her hand on Ariadne's.

'We can find you someone much more suitable, can't we dear?'

'That's what I told her,' he grunted.

'But I'm not looking.'

'Of course you are,' said her mother, 'but you just haven't found anyone yet. And I always thought that scar on his face rather off-putting.' She was now donning her gloves as she stood up. 'Though he was rather charming. Not the usual run of...' She checked herself and glanced at the wall-glass next to the fire. 'Must go. Can't keep Robertson waiting. He's such a dear. Who would have thought we'd be forced to have a chauffeur who doubles as a footman. The war was so tiresome in leaving us so short of men. Will you tell Goodrich that I won't be needing any lunch.'

She blew a kiss over her shoulder. They waited as the steps recessed to silence, to be replaced by the noise of the car starting, then receding down the drive. Neither of them filled the silence for some time. Her father stood, staring out of the window over his park. She sat on the sofa looking at the door, attuned to the clicks of the clocks.

'Don't do what I did; marry for money. I couldn't afford the cost.'

Neither looked at each other, the better to communicate.

'I won't Papa. Luckily I won't have to.'

'Nor other reasons; bad reasons.'

'Like what?'

'Feeling you have to; have to please someone else. Be selfish and only choose someone with whom you can laugh. I think that's it. The rest's detail.'

Out of the corner of her eye, Ariadne saw him dab his eyes. Tears rose in her own; some for him, some for herself.

'What if I had to get married, Papa?'

'I would never ask you to marry anybody, my dear girl.'

'If I was having a baby. And I wasn't married… already.'

Again in her peripheral vision, she saw him twitch. There was another silence.

'In theory?'

'In theory, Papa.'

His shoulders released, but his gaze was still over the park.

'If the… if he wouldn't marry you?'

'Or I didn't want to marry him.'

'And no one else knew?'

'No one. Not even the father.'

'It must have happened before. Probably often. But we wouldn't know about it; for obvious reasons.'

'No, we wouldn't.'

'A baby… a bastard… impossible.'

'I know.'

'Your mother?'

'No. I know what she'd say.'

'Never. I would never allow it. A terrible sin. A crime.'

They both were still looking in different directions but only a foot apart. She reached out and took his hand. He placed his other hand over hers and raised it to his lips. She lent her head against his arm. A wave of nausea swept over her but she felt calm for the first time in weeks.

*   *   *

Morning sickness proved to be just that. There were other manifestations; sore breasts and tiredness that laid her low for hours. But after lunch, as had happened over the last weeks, it cleared and she felt able to leave the castle. She made for the rectory, not knowing whether its denizens knew of Julian's departure. It seemed likely given his physical proximity and his closeness to Rose. Would he have told Rose – or Isobel – anything about her situation? Might her attempt at blackmail end up backfiring? These thoughts were still nagging at her when she rang the front door bell. Isobel opened the door and her distraction was immediately evident.

'You shouldn't come in.'

'Why not?'

'It's Rose. She's not well.'

'It must have been a shock.'

'It might not be safe.'

Ariadne was momentarily stumped. Then she understood.

'She's ill?'

'Yes. Flu. All the symptoms. I think she's looking blue. Thank God Papa isn't here. He's gone to a college dinner in Oxford.'

'Where's Davina?'

'She went with him to stay with her godmother. The doctor's coming later. Please say it's not flu. I don't think Papa would survive another blow.'

'Let me see her.'

'No, it's too dangerous.'

'Not for me. I've had the flu; last year, in the first wave that hardly killed anyone. I read recently that it was a form of inoculation. You stay away from her and let me look after her. It's too dangerous for you. Please.'

Isobel hesitated, then stood aside.

'Where is she?'

'The first door on the right, at the top of the stairs.'

She made to follow.

'No. You stay downstairs. You must stay away. Make some tea. Go. Now.'

Ariadne turned away and mounted the stairs. The sound of coughing, almost choking, emanated from the indicated room. Rose was in a foetal position, half-retching into a towel that was ominously speckled with blood and phlegm. Ariadne sat on the side of the bed and put her hand on Rose's forehead that was radiating heat. She heaved again, unable to speak through a paroxysm of coughing. Was she blue? Red – with the exertions of coughing. Any spots? Ariadne remembered her own scalding lungs and blood-soaked towel. None that she could see. She leant over her and pulled her into an upright position, jamming two pillows either side as support. This seemed to bring respite and the intensity of the retching abated. Fighting the urge to cough, Rose swallowed air in gulps rather than breaths, closing her eyes and slowly shaking her head. Ariadne took a beaker of water and administered small sips that had an instantly calming effect. Her eyes remained closed and her head rocked back and forward: her hair, normally lustrous, was lank with sweat and her complexion, usually flawless, was mottled and sallow.

'Would you like more to drink?'

She shook her head – and was asleep instantly.

Ariadne wiped her face with a flannel and checked her breathing, gurgling and staccato, before making her way downstairs where Isobel was pacing the hall.

'She's asleep,' was her answer to the unspoken question. 'She's very ill – but it doesn't seem to be as bad as I've heard it described. When's the doctor coming?'

Isobel nodded. 'Before lunch, he said.' She sighed, and her shoulders slumped. 'I suppose there's nothing we can do before then, is there? I can make some coffee though. I sent the servants away to the castle when I realised it might be the flu. Come and talk to me in the kitchen.'

Neither spoke as they filled the coffee pot and set out cups on the table. They sat at right angles to each other.

'I came to talk to you about Julian,' said Ariadne. 'Does Rose know?'

Isobel shook her head. 'She was ill already when he came in to tell her. Her or us, I'm not sure which.'

'What did he say?' There was more than a little nervousness in her question that Isobel appeared not to register.

'What I knew already. That Grumond had offered him a job with the promise of a share in the business. I asked him why he had to go now. I don't think he'd even told your father then. He said it was at Grumond's insistence. I can't imagine your father was best pleased.'

'He certainly wasn't.'

There must have been something in her voice that snapped Isobel out of her self-absorption. She looked hard at her cousin across the table.

'Julian? Was there something between you.' The tone was between a question and an accusation.

Ariadne shook her her head. 'No. There was nothing. Really.'

'Are you sure?' It was Ariadne's turn to sigh. She looked away and hooded her eyes with her hand. Two tears splashed on the table.

'Rose is your sister. It's not... straightforward.'

'You can tell me.'

Though she could not see her, she could sense there was good-will in Isobel's words.

'I don't know what to do.'

'About?'

'The baby. I'm pregnant.'

Isobel blinked and swallowed.

'And... Julian is the father?'

'No. No. It's Ralph. At the kennels.'

'Are you sure?'

'That he's the father? Of course I'm sure.'

Isobel shook her head and put her hand on Ariadne's arm. 'That you're pregnant?'

She nodded. 'Two periods missed and I feel so sick in the morning that I can't leave the house. I'm certain. As certain as anyone can be.'

'You've seen a doctor?'

'Around here? Don't be silly.'

Isobel nodded. 'And Julian. He has something to do with this, doesn't he?' The question this time was free of accusation.

'Yes. But he is... innocent. Completely. I tried... to force him to marry me.'

'How?'

'I can't tell you. I'm so ashamed of myself.'

'Is it something to do with why he's not marrying Rose?'

'Maybe. It was unforgivable though. But I was desperate. I am desperate. Isobel, what am I going to do?'

'I… I think I know of… I know someone who knows of a woman in London who might…'

'No. I promised Papa.'

'He knows?' There was alarm in her voice.

'No. And yes – but not about Ralph.'

'How did he take it?'

'He's thinking about it. Darling Papa. He's lost his son and now his daughter has disgraced him.'

'That depends.'

'On what?'

'On what you do about it. No one needs to know.'

'How's that going to happen when I blow up to the size of a brood mare and there's a baby in the nursery with no husband on the floor below.'

'You could go abroad.'

'And then what?'

'You could have the baby adopted.'

'By whom? I've never been abroad. And I'm not sure that Papa has either. Where would I start?'

Isobel stood and walked to the window. She contemplated the garden that was turning autumnal with more deadheads than flowers. She stroked her upper lip in contemplation.

'I might have someone. A good friend of mine. She would know where to go; who to speak to; where a baby could go. You can trust her. I would; with my life.'

Ariadne closed her eyes and breathed deeply. 'Thank you, Isobel. Thank you.'

*　　*　　*

Julian's sudden departure was all but forgotten over the next fortnight. At Ariadne's insistence the inhabitants of the rectory decanted themselves into the castle and she alone stayed with Rose as the illness ran its course. The patient sank and rallied but, a week after the first symptoms, the coughing dissipated, her complexion regained some colour and she was able to walk unaided. Food and letters from the castle were deposited inside the porch. In her isolation Ariadne was even more aware of the manifestations of her pregnancy: a distinct rounding of her belly and a heaviness in her breasts.

As Rose recuperated she asked about Julian. When Ariadne told her of his departure, she softened the blow by telling her that Julian had not been allowed to see her during her illness. Ariadne was surprised at the equanimity with which Rose took the news, as if she was expecting it – or something like it. But though the physical recovery was faster than anticipated, she was withdrawn, often seeming to conduct a debate with herself, her eyes closed and her lips moving. Occasionally tears would pour down her face that she would make no effort to staunch – as if she were unaware of them. When Rose's father and sisters returned to the rectory, and Ariadne to the castle, they were all struck by the change. It was as if she had taken a blow that left no mark on the outside but which had resulted in internal bleeding. Isobel was sitting with her at the breakfast table alone the following day.

'Did Julian leave anything for me? A letter? Something?' asked Rose.

Isobel shook her head. 'He came round to see you.'

'Us.'

'No; you,' she lied.

Rose pondered this.

'But why no letter?'

'Maybe there's one on the way. He was off to Singapore on a ship so he may not have had a chance.'

'If he'd wanted to write a letter, it would be here by now.' Her sister looked down and didn't reply. 'He never wanted to marry me, did he? I know he needs to leave here and work for Grumond. But just to disappear with no word and no letter. No hope. How could he do that, Isobel? How?' She blinked away some tears. 'Was it something to do with Ariadne?' She looked sharply at her sister. 'Was it? Why was she so sweet to me when I was ill?' She hesitated. 'But if he wanted to marry her and her money, why has he gone off with Grumond?' She shook her head. 'That was horrid of me. She didn't have to look after me, did she?'

'You're lucky to be alive.'

'I know. But where is Ariadne? I haven't seen her since she went back to the castle two days ago.'

'She's gone… travelling.'

'Ariadne? For how long? She never mentioned anything to me.'

Isobel shrugged. 'You know Ariadne. She does what she wants.'

A cloud passed over Rose's face. 'She's gone east hasn't she? With Julian?'

'No. She's gone to France to learn to speak French.'

'Ariadne? French?'

'Apparently. She was getting restless and maybe the party this summer made her want to do something other than hunt. I can understand that.'

'Ariadne too. Only us left. What are we going to do?' asked Rose. 'It's all very well for you. You're going to London. Away from here and you know what you want to do. I've got Davina to think about. And Papa.'

'So do I.'

'If you're in London, it's not going to be you looking after them.'

'But it would have been me if you'd gone east with Julian.' Rose nodded her acknowledgement. 'But I'm not going for a bit as I've been given a commission to make the Sherborne war memorial. Cousin Robert recommended me and they liked my portfolio. I begin next month.' She saw that this news only emphasised the black dog that was hanging over Rose's head. She reached over and took her hand. 'You've been ill. You aren't yourself – and Julian isn't the only pebble on the beach. Ran Godwin has written to you and Dav – you met him in the Orkneys apparently – asking to call in on his way to Exeter. Dav said he really liked you. He's coming to stay for two or three days next week.'

Rose nodded and smiled weakly. 'Yes, he is nice. He's the one that Julian lived with in the Orkneys. He was with us when the German fleet scuttled itself.'

'I remember now. Dav's delighted – particularly that he wrote to her.'

They both sat in companionable silence, united in their quasi-parental pleasure at Davina's anticipation. They heard a car draw up outside and the engine idling as footsteps approached the house, the front door opening with no ring. It was their father – distressed as they had never seen him before, in tears and shaking his head as if he hoped to shed some unbearable burden.

'Terrible! I can't believe it...'

'What, Papa? What?'

'James.'

'Lord Milborne?'

He nodded. 'It's not possible. It can't be.'

'Tell us Papa. Slowly.' Isobel held his arm as he rocked in shock.

'The kennels. Ralph the huntsman. He's dead. James shot him. The police are there and have taken him to Sherborne.' He covered his eyes as if this might wipe away the deed. 'Why? Why would he do such a thing?'